# The Black Path

ANTONY CURTIS

Further information and contact details can be found at the following website –

www.antony-curtis.com

and

www.anisianpublishing.com

ISBN:978-1-7397962-2-8

# DEDICATION

Dedicated to the unsung heroes of the everyday. The people who get up, work hard and take care of their families and friends. You are the heart of the community and the glue that binds the past to the present. To my fellow Knowle Westers.

**Other books include:**

Souk Daddy

The Exchange – Book 1

# ACKNOWLEDGMENTS

Thank you to everyone who helped with the creation of this book. The people I trusted to read the early work and those that helped shape it into what it became, Kim, Jane, Peter, Sam, Jill and Brandon. Your help was invaluable.

Thanks to George and Lou who helped with the cover photograph, my wonderful family and a special thanks to Sadie, my muse, who had to work hard to inspire me to complete it.

And thanks to my dad, who has always been there for me and been my biggest cheerleader. I love you.

# 1. THE TRIKE

## 1977 – AGE 4

No one noticed the paint peeled trike slowly edge down the enclosed driveway before it disappeared. The four-year-old in the seat had been riding around the back, side and front of the semi-detached council house all morning and was looking for something more, something that pushed the boundaries of his miniscule world.

His mum had been hanging out the washing on the rotary dryer that sprung up from the middle of the garden like a strange skeletal flower; its petals the drooping and dripping folds of cloth pinned to its branches. Now, however, she was nowhere to be seen. His dad and older brother were also not around that morning, but that wasn't unusual. He lived in his own world for the most part, a nice bubble of ignorance that at this moment involved just him and his trike.

The driveway arched down from the side of the house towards the road, getting steeper as it went. He slid slowly, feet skimming over the concrete until he reached the bottom and stopped. He checked behind and carefully lifted the latch on the flimsy metal gates and slipped out onto the cracked pavement beyond. He didn't hesitate and turned right instinctively and pedalled along the uneven slabs that lined the floor. Although the direction he took was slightly uphill, he didn't dare go left. That way led toward the big road and roundabout which frightened him. While he had been riding around the garden, he hadn't seen a car on his road at all, so turning right felt safer somehow.

He continued past his neighbours' houses, quiet and peaceful, until he reached the corner and almost without thinking turned right again. That Sunday morning was particularly bright; the blue sky overhead held no barriers for the sun's transit as it began to make its journey above the horizon. As the oversized front wheel turned in time with his feet, he felt no danger or awareness of distance, taking pleasure in gliding down the dropped driveway's edge and then almost jumping up the return to pavement level. He felt free and at peace, an unusual sensation.

Although the sun was just poking its nose over the rooftops it was still bright enough to make him squint as bright flashes of sunlight reflected from the windows all around. Each flash came with it a warming glow that seemed to spread from his face into the rest of his body.

When he reached the next corner he stopped suddenly, his feet braking hard on the ground. He was caught in a dilemma. If he turned right again, he would be heading towards the big road, toward danger. He could keep going straight, but he knew that he wasn't allowed to crossroads and although she was nowhere to be seen, the presence of his mother's voice made itself very clear, *'You don't cross the road on your own!'* He swivelled in his seat to look at the way he had come. Going back was an option of course, but he favoured this less than turning right. He was out and having too much fun to think about going back to semi-circling the house so soon.

He looked right again towards the main road. He could see the end at a distance and could almost hear the traffic going by, the people walking along, the feeling of danger. No, definitely not that way. He looked around at the relative safety of this corner to try and spot any cars that might have crept up on him, but he saw none. He stared across at the distant bank, across the tarmac ocean that never moved itself, but flowed with unnatural metallic creatures that were so fast and deadly they could take you at any moment. So, delicately at first, he edged forward until his front wheel bumped off the edge of the kerb, then, when the rear wheels fell, he instantly began pushing his legs hard, speeding across the distance before anything could come out of hiding to get him. He didn't dare look around for fear of seeing something far too late to do anything about.

When he reached the other side, he realised that he couldn't simply ride up over the pavement's edge, so he jumped out of his seat whilst it was still in motion and dragged the trike over the lip and up onto the bank of this distant shore.

His little heart raced as he returned to his seat again; surveying these foreign lands that didn't look that much different to his own, but somehow felt a world away.

The council houses he passed were of the same size and shape as his own he noticed. Semi-detached, they stood side-by-side with their neighbour. One could almost imagine the buildings with an arm around each other's shoulders in friendly union, holding each other up. He knew, however, that friendliness with your neighbour was not something that was common. His own 'attached' neighbour consisted of a large round woman whose voice could be heard anywhere in the local vicinity. Her husband, he guessed, was the tall thin man who seemed hunched over with the weight of the words that flew out of her. There were several children who played in and around the garden at various times who used the same interesting language that the woman had often shouted at them. He was not allowed to play with them. His 'open' side neighbours were a different story. They were an elderly couple who often allowed him to sneak through the gap in the hedge and eat slices of apple pie and raw carrots they kept in the fridge. They had an apple tree in their garden, so the smell of fresh pie was a common aroma that drew him near. He would peer through the gap in the hope that he would be noticed and invited in. He called them Nan and Granddad even though he knew they were not.

Riding past the small squares of gardens at the front of these houses, he tried to imagine what each one looked like inside. They would typically have a living room just through the front door taking up half of the ground floor with a kitchen/dining room filling the other half. Above would be three bedrooms of decreasing size from double to single to box and a bathroom somewhere in between. Not big in size, but manageable and certainly bigger than the high-rise flat he had been born in. He could tell from the curtains alone if they contained old people or not, but if that was combined with a garden that was neat and tidy, then that was a sure sign of elderly residents. There were more on this side of the world than his own he saw with a sudden taste of apple pie returned to his lips.

He reached the next corner in what seemed like no time at all and prepared to have the same dilemma as before, but this was different. Staring ahead he realised that there was no going forward again. In front of him, at the T-junction, there now stood a long row of houses blocking his way. He strained his neck left, but all he could see was the road and houses snaking off into the distance and as he followed them back to the right, he saw the road abruptly stop dead a little distance down and instead of it continuing to the main road, there lay a small green field in the way. The houses down there were very different to the ones he had passed. These were bright white in colour and looked brand new. He had never seen anything like it before.

Enthralled at what he had found, he felt like an adventurer encountering a new and undiscovered land that had similar features but was altogether different from his own. Without thinking he turned right and began rolling towards it as if being drawn by some unseen force. The cracked and scared pavement under his wheels transformed into large grey slabs that were so smooth it felt like his trike had suddenly taken flight. He looked at the path that stretched before him and a song came to mind about following a yellow brick road. He wondered what people lived in such a place.

The road ended with a wide sweeping circle that allowed cars to turn around if they had wandered down here by mistake. He followed it until he reached the furthest point and stopped, his wheel hovered on the verge of the grassy border. It wasn't a large expanse of openness but was unquestionably larger than his own back garden. Beyond the far end of the field, he could see another road start just as this one had ended. The main road in the distance didn't feel as dangerous as before; seeing it across this bright green filter somehow removed some of its associated fear.

He was just about to ride onto the grass, still glistening with the morning's dew, when all of a sudden, he noticed something to his left; a young boy about the same age as him, staring from behind a small white bollard almost as tall as he was.

As he sat there staring at this native, the boy started walking towards him until he was directly in line with the front wheel.

"Hello," the boy said.

"Hello," he replied. "I'm Tom."

"My name's L L L Lee," the boy stuttered. "Can I have a g go on your b bike?"

"Okay," said Tom, only too happy to share with this person who could become his new best friend.

They spent a while taking turns going up and down the enclosed pathway that led to Lee's house while the other one stood on the platform between the back wheels. The hard rubber tyres clunked between the gaps in the slabs, the extra weight making the noise echo off the faces of the long narrow strip of houses that made it feel more like a cave than a path.

Lee then took Tom around to the field and showed him where his back garden was, behind a tall half-poled fence that stretched the entire length of everyone else's back garden here. As with most children, they didn't need to speak very much, they just followed each other's lead; running here, climbing there, jumping over that. Tom had never known such enjoyment could be had playing with someone else; he had spent the majority of his life so far on his own. He was enjoying it so much that he completely lost track of time. He looked up at the sun that had risen much higher than before when a sudden realisation exploded into his mind.

Panic erupted from his stomach like an explosion, filling his small frame with fear.

"I have to go," he blurted out as he jumped into the seat of the trike and began speeding away without a look back at his new bewildered friend.

The trike raced much faster than before. Houses flashed by in his periphery as visions of his mum calling his name and searching around the garden and streets engulfed his mind.

He looked up and stared at the sun high in the sky and tried to figure out how long it would have taken to climb so high, but he had no idea. What he did know, however, was what the consequence would be when he was discovered.

He crossed the road with hardly a glance and leapt from his seat to drag the wheels over the edge once more before continuing at a pace. He was just approaching the last corner when he started to strain his ears over the rumble of the wheels to try and catch his mum's voice calling his name. Nothing. That must be bad. She's probably calling the police or his father to come and search for him. He turned the last corner and could see his garden wall in the distance and the partially opened driveway gate. Had he left it open or was it where his mum had run out looking for him?

His heart pounded like a hummingbirds in its tiny chest and was only matched in pace by his breathing from the fervent effort of pumping his legs. He skidded to a halt next to the gate; the deafening sound of silence swept past him and drowned out the thumping blood in his ears. His eyes swept across the front of the building and peered into each window in search of clues as to what was happening inside; what frantic activity was taking place because of him.

He stood and pulled the trike in through the gate, quietly closing it behind him. He dragged it around the back of the house, but all was still, quiet. He reached out his hand to touch the cold metal handle of the back door, afraid that it would unleash a torrent of shouting and anger as soon as he it opened. He took a deep breath, turned it and crept inside. As he toddled through the kitchen and into the living room, he saw his mum sitting on the sofa watching TV. She looked up and smiled briefly before returning her gaze to the box; the obvious fear on the boy's face lost on her.

'*Didn't anyone know I was gone?*' thought Tom as he walked back out to the garden breathing a sigh of relief. The washing on the line formed a kind of makeshift tent now, its folds flapping like fish tails in the breeze. He sat inside and contemplated if anyone would have cared if he had come back at all.

## 2. SUNDAY

The orange-peel sun began to roll itself over the rooftops just enough to throw a warm glow of potential over the houses below. The breadth of light available was filtered down to a single shaft between the slightest gap in curtains, and as if by coincidence, or perhaps provenance, an eye lay exactly in its path. Just the one eye however, as the other was buried deep in the soft fresh folds of the bedding he lay upon; safe and secure in the dark recess while its counterpart started to become aware of the contrast.

Despite the protestations from the dark, the eye opened to examine the cause of this incongruence and instantly regretted it. The piercing shard of light was thrust into the iris and made the face behind it wince and roll over, showing a back to the day that was dawning into consciousness.

The light now behind him, its daggers removed, yet another of his senses began to take note of its surroundings having landed on a cushion cover of soft brown hair that smelled of a familiar combination of conditioner, red wine and home. This contrast however, produced a satisfied smile on the face as the body beneath shuffled closer to the root; to coil itself around the delicate frame that seemed to fit so precisely, like the contours of a perfectly placed puzzle piece.

The combination of the smell, the body and the warmth began to betray the growth of his desires. He was not the only one to become aware of its size. A gentle hand reached behind and slowly snaked its way between their bodies to wrap itself around his shaft, pulling it lower with a gentle toothless grip. A gasp of pleasure escaped. He loved the way that they didn't have to say a word, they just knew, just felt each other completely. Her soft hand moved in long, smooth, deliberate strokes that drove him wild. He began to slide his hand from her waist to her breast, following the well-known contours of her skin, the map of which he knew better than his own.

From a distance came a noise. At first, he couldn't get the sense of whether it was real or not or where it might be coming from. Then the familiar patter of tiny feet raced along the corridor and brought the answer. His wife's hand froze at the sound. Then as slowly as it arrived it withdrew, patting it on the head like you would a dog that was panting and wanting more as if to say, *later*.

The body before him slid out of place, leaving him alone with his desires. His ears replaced his eyes as he sensed her position in the room, the exact drawer that she pulled open, the jumper that would be yanked out and rolled over her head. He could hear a silent pause as she looked back at him; thinking what he wondered? The bed lowered as she climbed on for one last kiss before following the small steps that had clambered down the stairs.

As he lay there, holding onto the slowly decreasing warmth of his wife's body and his gradually deflating excitement, he tried to understand just how he had managed to be here. After everything that had happened, how had he found a woman he had no right in holding each night, with a son that made him glow inside, in a house that was safe and secure; a million miles away from where he had escaped?

Once his desire had abated to a manageable level he sat up and finally allowed both eyes to open together, to synchronise. He pulled the curtain to the side and gazed out over the silhouetted rooftops of the neighbourhood, their windows glistening like sunglasses on their cool façade and a familiar lazy Sunday morning feeling flowed over him.

Throwing on some clothes and his newly purchased Mahabis slippers, he followed a trail of toys and books that led through the house and all the way to the kitchen. A picture-perfect scene lay before him as he reached the doorway. His son sat at the table slurping an orange juice in a cup that took two hands to manoeuvre, looking hungrily and expectant at his mother who was standing at the cooker whisking up a batch of her delicious scrambled eggs in an old, stretched jumper that stopped just above her knees. *Morning Song* by Jewel was flowing from a Bluetooth speaker nearby with its lyrical desire shared by all. Music had always had the uncontrollable effect of making his wife sway and dance no matter where she was or what she was doing. He had even known her to start to move during an argument which ended up completely defusing the issue and them making love on the floor where they'd stood. He felt an almost overwhelming sense of love for these two people.

He scraped back a chair opposite his son and contorted a goofy looking face that made him snort his juice out through his nose. They both burst out laughing as his wife brought over two plates of breakfast with a despairing look. She wiped the explosion from her son's face and grabbed her own plate to join them.

"What time are we heading to your mother's?" Ali asked as everyone tucked in.

Tom glanced up from the fork that was already in his mouth with a look of *'oh shit I forgot'*. His reply crawled out through the mouthful of golden mush, "How about we go this morning and get it over and done with?"

A pregnant pause echoed around the walls before he was answered with another question, "Will your brother be there?"

Tom's brother had been at his mother's house increasingly so over the past few months, the reason for which Tom didn't ask or want to know. It felt to Tom that they were always huddled together making plans, scheming schemes that, although he had no interest in, made him feel like an outsider.

Tom just shrugged.

"Okay, that's as good a plan as any," she replied. "Shall we get you ready to see your Granny?" Ali sang to William who was currently trying to magically scrape more egg from his empty plate.

She knew that his mother hated to be called *Granny*. That she still thought she was a much younger version of herself which tended to cause some amusement to Ali. Tom groaned inside hoping that it wasn't going to be one of those visits. He would plan on calling his father later too, to get them both out of the way.

It didn't take long to get everyone dressed, ready and in the car. After Tom's usual routine of checking every window, he closed and locked the front door, headed for the vehicle and slumped behind the wheel. He didn't know how Ali managed to do it, to remain positive and restrained doing the things she hated. He wondered if he would be able to do the same if it were her parents he didn't get on with. One more reason he loved the bones of her.

The journey took around thirty minutes but seemed to go by all too quickly; relativity had much to answer for. The mandatory singing in the car did little to raise the front occupants' spirits. As they approached the house, there appeared to be a collective glance of anticipation at the cars parked outside, followed by an almost audible groan as his brother's van came into view, parked in the same space as always. A creature of habit!

Tom purposely drove around the corner to park in a different spot, making a point to himself that he was not the same. His motivation wasn't lost on Ali though who silently obliged with the extra sixty seconds of walking without complaint.

Moving past well-known houses on this cracked familiar pavement created an unusual sensation of anxiety in Tom's stomach every time he returned. He opened the gate that used to be his perch as a child, its musical creak the accompaniment for many an hour watching people pass by. As they gathered at the door, Tom knew that it would be unlocked, that he would be expected to just walk in, that it was his family home after all, but he could never remove that barrier from his mind. He knocked.

"It's open!" yelled a voice from the bowels as they obligingly crossed the threshold and entered.

Stepping through felt like being transported back in time, every step forward taking years off Tom's life until the child that he kept buried deep inside was standing in the kitchen doorway.

Tom's mother looked up from the table where it appeared that a serious conference was taking place with her other son. Her glance didn't linger long on him though but slid lower to her grandson.

"Billy!" She called out with her arms outstretched inviting him to dutifully run over for an obligatory hug.

"It's William," Tom corrected under his breath.

His mother had always insisted on calling him Billy, despite the numerous conversations and heated exchanges between them. She would always argue that Billy was a much naughtier name and suited him better. *'A boy needs to get into trouble sometimes just to find out who he is'*, she would say.

Tom let it go this time; he was keen to get the visit over and done with so that he could return to his own life, the one that he had built.

Ali, as always, remained quiet.

"What you been up to kiddo?" asked Charlie, his brother. Another 'naughtier' name than the Charles he was christened, but this time it did actually suit him for that very reason.

"Nothing much, just work as usual! What about you?" he dared ask.

"Yeah, work's a bit quiet at the moment. Been doing some plastering for Dave over the road last week and I've got some plumbing to do for Mr Hedges in number 32," he replied, but there was something more, something unsaid that caused a break in his words and a look as if he was sizing up the situation as to whether to continue.

Tom saw it and waited for what he knew couldn't be kept in if it wanted out.

"Can I talk to you outside for a moment? Have a catch up?" Charlie asked, already standing as if the answer was irrelevant.

Tom and Ali exchanged a look that he hoped was read as somewhere between *'here we go'* and *'help me'*. Ali could do nothing but raise an eyebrow that was a mixture of *'this should be good'* and *'what the hell do you expect me to do'*!

Ali sat down at the table and began with the usual conversation starters as Tom opened the rear door and headed out. He leaned against the back of the house while his brother followed, closing the door and fumbling in his work trouser pocket for his cigarette tin.

The faded gold and green Golden Virginia tin was rusted around the edges and had been the keeper of Charlie's tobacco and cigarettes for as long as Tom could remember. Charlie leant back on the building, mirroring Tom. He lit up and exhaled into the sky in a long continuous stream as if it were his first breath.

Looking down now while he formulated his words, Charlie took another puff.

"I'm glad things are going well for you little brother," he began. "You've got yourself a nice little home and family there."

Tom kept still and quiet. His brother had no idea what it had taken to get to where he was.

"Your niece is doing well. She starts college in September. How the time flies!"

"What's she studying?" Tom asked, trying to keep it light.

"Hair and Beauty. Not as academic as you, but that's what she wants! She can't wait to get out of that school. I told her that she ought to have gone to our school if she wanted to know a shithole!"

Both Tom and Charlie had gone to the local secondary school. It was an all-boys' school, with the girls' version over a mile away. It had been closed down a while now following successively bad inspections and a natural inclination of the people who lived here to get out whenever possible.

Tom made an amused noise and nodded.

"With the lack of work lately it's been tough to keep it all together; you know how Suzie can be!"

13

Charlie had met Suzie in a field one night at one of those random raves that were so popular back then. As the half-remembered drunken story goes, there was a large group watching and cheering on an old guy stoned off his face while he tried to fly to the moon using some form of existential dance routine. While everyone was cheering, from across the expanse, their eyes met. They walked around the crowd to find each other and just started snogging. The rest was history. Suzie had just started working in sales back then, but as soon as Charlie got a job she quit and became a stay-at-home girlfriend, mother and then wife.

"Yeah," replied Tom, knowing exactly what Suzie was like.

"I've been doing some jobs for Stan-The-Man," said Charlie.

Silence.

The words sank into Tom's head for a second bouncing around like a tennis ball in a ping-pong tournament. He turned, still leaning on the wall, "Are you out of your mind?"

"He's okay, just a guy trying to get by," but before he could follow it up with any evidence of the fact, Tom replied.

"Okay? Are you fucking kidding? He's into all sorts of dodgy dealings." Tom's Bristolian accent tended to return slightly when he got angry, or drunk. "Christ, he nearly had me at Filwood Broadway. You know he used to drag kids in who were walking past and shave their hair off just for shits and giggles! If I hadn't said I was your brother, I would have been scalped!"

Charlie tried to subdue a chuckle unsuccessfully.

"I know he doesn't have as many scruples as you, but he's a good guy. You can't believe all you hear!"

Many years ago, there had been a young man murdered in the area and Stan was the prime suspect. The murder was particularly brutal, all blunt force trauma to the head and neck. So much so that it wasn't until his girlfriend reported him as missing that he could be identified.

"So, what are you doing for him?" Tom asked, knowing that a specific answer wouldn't be forthcoming.

"Just stuff. Moving things from his warehouse, picking up packages, driving some of his guys around. Nothing dodgy at all."

Tom could only raise his eyebrows as if to say *'yeah, because that doesn't sound dodgy at all'!* He was still waiting for the bombshell that had dragged him outside.

"So, how's work going?" Charlie asked again, as if deliberately repeating himself to begin a train of thought or a rehearsed speech.

"Work is fine," replied Tom, not going into detail as he wouldn't really understand it anyway.

"Any big holidays planned this year?"

"Nope, nothing planned."

"You not going down to see Dad?"

"No plans to."

A pause; a change of tact. "How's the car running?"

"The car's good. MOT coming up but should be fine." To Tom it felt like Charlie was pushing all the usual soft buttons of life to see if he could get a finger hold in one of them.

"A house like yours must be costing you a fortune with the mortgages the way they are."

Tom was sure that Charlie had no way of knowing what mortgages were like, but he decided to throw him a bone and actually get to find out what the hell this conversation was all about.

"No, it's not cheap," he replied.

Seizing the opening he began, "No, it's not! So, a little bit of extra money might come in handy?"

And there it was. He needed something doing, something dodgy.

"Not really, work is good, and Ali has started to pick up a little consultation work part-time now that William's started nursery." He tried to close the hole he'd made before it opened up any larger.

It was too late. "Yeah, but a little extra is always good. Maybe even look at that holiday you haven't planned yet!"

Tom took a deep breath and looked at his brother.

"Look Charlie," he began as calmly as possible. "I don't need any extra money; I'm not looking for quick cash or to get involved in anything other than what I'm doing. And I especially don't want anything to do with Stan-The-Fucking-Man!"

Charlie looked as if he was about to begin a response, but then thought better of it. They have had many such conversations over the years and this one was going to be no different.

"Alright Tommy boy! Your loss. I just needed a second pair of hands for an easy pick up and drop off in a few days and thought someone with your skills might come in handy. No sweat! If you change your mind though..."

"I won't," Tom replied before he could finish.

Charlie took one last draw on his cigarette before tossing it into the garden to join its dead comrades who were in various states of decay. Before he turned to head back in though, he stopped. Tom saw a shift in his face, a worry that washed over it like there was something else, something deeper to say, to consider, but before it came out, Charlie's confident mask of bullshit reappeared and kept hidden whatever was behind it.

Back inside, Tom's mother had come to the end of her usual banter with William and was telling him to go up to his dad's old bedroom to play. It seemed like the limit of her motherliness was around five minutes, a fact that Tom knew only too well. He offered to take William up to his old room which was met by Ali with a look of *'don't you fucking leave me here on my own any longer'* that he knew he should heed.

"I'll be back down in a second," he said to anyone who was listening as he opened the door to the living room and disappeared.

Heading towards the front door Tom glanced around at the living room that had hardly changed in all the years that he had known it. It was a throwback to the 80s with everything from a donkey pulling barrels, a wind-up windmill and a lamp of Venus surrounded by oil dripping wire that was supposed to resemble rain, he presumed. Turning left at the front door they made their way up the stairs that were fairly steep and narrow. There was a round, slippery handrail that had grown thicker every year from new coats of gloss white paint, so much so that Tom wondered if there was even any wood in the centre anymore! The stairs had always been a source of fear for Tom. Not because of the climb or the less than useful handrail, no, it was because as a child, he had always thought that he was being watched or followed when coming up or down them. He would walk the steps sideways so that he could see the top and bottom at the same time. Ridiculous he thought now as he started to climb, his son holding his hand. He was an adult now, the protector, so why couldn't he overcome the urge to check below when he was halfway up?

At the summit, they both stood in the narrow hallway. Looking anti-clockwise from his mother's room to their right was the bathroom in front, his brother's old room at the end of the hall and his room directly to their left. William knew the way and shook off his father's hand and ran in. As Tom followed, he was struck with how small everything looked. As a child he took up much less room and had a considerably shorter vantage point, but still, he found it hard to reconcile the difference, as if this was a model of the life he knew before rather than the real thing.

William was already in the cupboard, pulling out toys and games from a forgotten age. Tom stepped forward and looked out of the window. Beyond the back of the houses opposite was his old junior school, the playground visible between the houses. To the right was his old infant school just out of sight. Tom had a flashback of hearing the screams of laughter and play whilst being held up with chicken pox one year; straining to see his friends, to pick out their voices as they echoed across the street.

"We're just downstairs," he said to William who was too busy playing to hear.

Tom turned and hurried down the stairs sideways without a second thought to save his wife from the awkward silence and stilted conversations that tended to happen when he left her alone for too long with his family. She was from a different world as far as they were concerned. No issues with money, drugs or the police; a happy childhood far from this side of town. Her parents were still together after thirty-seven years of happy marriage. The difference between her family and his was about as stark as you could get and all too apparent when a conversation tried to move past the pleasantries.

As Tom entered the kitchen, the persuasive tones of his brother suddenly ceased, and his guilty eyes switched from Ali to Tom to the floor in quick succession. Tom knew exactly what he had been talking about, laying the seeds for a later conversation with Ali regarding some extra money no doubt.

In an attempt to release some of the tension that had entered with Tom like an evil spirit blowing through the doorway, his mother got up and put the kettle on again. Nothing that can't be fixed with a cup of tea!

The kettle was old and loud which made conversation impossible while it was boiling away to itself. Everyone just shuffled around where they sat or stood pretending to be perfectly content with doing nothing while they waited. After what seemed like an age, the kettle finally flipped its switch and silence descended in the room.

"So," Tom's mother began. "Ali tells me you don't have a holiday booked this year?"

Tom glanced at Charlie who suddenly became engrossed in a piece of dust on the table.

"Nothing yet," he replied, returning his gaze to his mother. "We may just go to the coast for a few days or see what last minute deals come up."

"To see your father?"

"Maybe."

The tea was being rattled from side to side with the teaspoon. He never understood why his mother stirred tea that way, it wasn't even stirring. It was more of a shake that rang out like an old-time dinner bell, calling all the workers in for food. A throw back to her own upbringing no doubt. She was Irish by birth, both parents hailing from a small village near Cork. Seven siblings were born before her father decided that he had had enough and legged it, but not before transporting his wife and children across the Irish Sea and depositing them all alone in England. His mother was the eldest, so he imagined that a lot of responsibility fell to her to look after the other children while her own mother went out to work. Tom didn't know what his grandmother did or how she got by as she had died when he was young, and he didn't really get a chance to know her. There were plenty of other, more forthcoming grandchildren that sought her attention. Tom always felt a little guilty about this, about not knowing a lot of the history of his family.

"Do you remember that caravan we stayed in on the Norfolk Broads with Auntie Nicky and Uncle Alan? You were always off on your own looking for crabs and girls!" His mother laughed at the memory and the comical connection.

"Mum, I was ten."

"You started young!"

"You should come to Turkey with me," Charlie began, taking his tea and a half-eaten packet of biscuits from the tray his mother offered like a waitress. "I've got the usual booked in for September."

"I don't know how you can go back to the same place every year," Tom replied. "Don't you get bored? Don't you want to explore new places, go somewhere you've never been?"

Both his brother and mother looked at him with a bewildered expression. "Why would I want to go somewhere I don't know, full of people I don't like and not know what I'm doing? I know Yusef and his family who own the hotel. I get special rates and meals. I know everyone there and they know me and what I like. Plus, he speaks English which is a lot more than most places! I don't get why these other countries don't learn English! How are they going to expect us to go there if they can't talk proper?"

His mother was nodding throughout this drivel with a distinct smell of bigotry floating in the air. He contemplated trying to explain that he would be visiting their country so should show them respect by learning their language, or that they probably had tourists from all over the world with different languages of their own, or more likely (especially if they knew him) they probably didn't want you to go there in the first place. The idea of a small town or local village having to put up with Charlie and his family brought an unconscious smile to Tom's face and he thought that they were better off without him.

He eventually settled for saying, "Yes, but Yusef didn't always know you. You had to go there for the first time once!"

Another look of complete bewilderment washed across his face. *Forget it'* Tom thought as he picked up his tea and took a mouthful. He coughed and choked and barely kept the liquid in his mouth.

"What's up Tommy boy? Forgot how to drink?" Laughed Charlie.

Regaining his breath, Tom wheezed, "How many sugars are in this?"

"Just the usual three," she replied.

"Mum, I haven't had sugar in my tea for twenty years!"

"Oh, I keep forgetting. Maybe it's because I don't make you tea very often these days!"

Tom felt the dig at his apparent removal from the family and the undutiful visits he rarely made. He felt Ali's hand rub the small of his back that began to ease some of the tension. She had a way of grounding him with the slightest touch, like an earth wire in an electrical circuit. She could bypass the overload.

The rest of the visit went according to script. They talked about William, about work, about the state of the neighbourhood, the old people dying and the new people moving in. Although his mother would call the visit fleeting, it always felt to Tom like the end of an arduous climb. When it was over it wasn't followed by a euphoric sense of achievement at the summit, but more like the struggle for breath and a clinging to life.

The drive back from these visits were always quieter than the journey out. It was like they all needed the silence in order to empty the noise that they had just endured and equalise the pressure and return to normal; their normal. As they drew nearer to their sanctuary, Ali asked about his conversation with his brother outside. He explained that he just wanted a smoke and a catch up. He didn't say anything about his offer of some dodgy work or the fact that it was for Stan-The-Man. That would have caused unnecessary annoyance on both of their parts. Ali had a way of knowing when he was holding back though, but after a short pause, he was grateful that she didn't press. Tom didn't ask what his brother had been talking to her about before he entered the kitchen either, he was sure he already knew.

Back in the safety of home and the continuation of their own lives Tom tried to put the morning behind him and cleanse his mind of the memory. What he was finding difficult to erase though, was the fleeting look on his brother's face. He could only remember two other times when he had seen it and both times had not ended well.

# 3. BROADWALK

## 1978 – AGE 5

On several occasions each month, Tom's mum would need to visit the local shopping centre. It was at the end of a long stretch of wide tree-lined boulevard where you could imagine the Victorian gentry happily strolling next to horses and carriages from days gone by. Even its name, 'Broad Walk' gave the air of civility.

Outside the entrance was a main junction that led in one direction towards the city centre and in the other, out to the southern outskirts. The area around the front had shops and services from fast food restaurants to hairdressers to dentists. Opposite stood the cricket club that always seemed to Tom to be a strange place to put it and he often wondered how many balls went flying into the road each game. The manicured lawn and grounds were juxtaposed with the roaring traffic just outside its walls. Perhaps it was a leftover from an early time of muddy roads and bushy moustachioed gentlemen.

The rear of the shopping centre opened onto a small car park and public toilets, neither of which were used all that much. Tom didn't know many of the shops there were in or around the area, but he loved to be taken inside. The other shopping district he knew was in Bedminster, which was on a long stretch of road that was much busier and smellier. Broadwalk in comparison was new and exciting.

Tom's mum parked in the near-empty parking lot, and they walked over to the rear entrance almost side by side; Tom a little behind like a duckling trying to keep up. Looking around, he was always struck by how plain the back was compared to the front; as if the front was for show, to draw the customer in and it didn't matter what the back looked like. If you were here, then you were already committed to going in. Or perhaps it looked more like a service entrance for staff rather than customers? This made Tom a little nervous; he didn't want to be in a place where he wasn't supposed to be, to be caught being naughty.

He dutifully trotted behind his mother up the ramp and stairs turning left and right without much knowledge of where they were going. They stopped at several shops on the bottom floor first. They bought a birthday card for someone and some wrapping paper. Tom remained quiet, not making a sound; he knew better than to ask for any of the sweets or chocolates displayed right in front of his eyes at the counter. That would only annoy his mother and she might shout at him. He didn't have many memories that he could draw on for reference and couldn't recall ever asking for such things to be sure, but he got the impression that she would, so never risked it. He seemed to just live in the here and now despite the ever-present fear of doing the wrong thing. It felt like living in a bubble that could burst at any moment if he wasn't careful, so he was careful.

That's how he felt now as he followed her around the aisles, noticing the wobbly wheel on the trolley and his mother's attempts at keeping it straight. He could feel her annoyance growing and he kept himself out of sight and invisible enough to not tip the balance.

He stood at the checkout while his mum arranged the goods on the conveyor so that all the price tags were on top and facing the checkout lady. He didn't know why she did this, but it made some kind of logical sense. Having picked up the full carrier bags, his mother headed for the escalator. The dull strip lighting of the bottom floor opened out into sparkling daylight as the magical stairs elevated them upwards. This was his favourite part, where all of the exciting shops were located. There were toy shops, clothes shops and book shops. He felt a sense of excitement as they all came into view. They headed towards the glistening window of the jewellery store, its sparkling displays of silver and gold glinting in Tom's eyes. He didn't know why, but he loved watches, loved looking at them, imagining the workings inside. Even at this age he could appreciate the watch face and design and stare at them for ages.

His mum walked into the shop, but Tom stayed outside, looking at the display in the window. One watch stood out more than the rest. It was large, with a complicated pattern of dials and numbers around the edge that looked like it was used in the army. He was so mesmerised, staring at the different hands going around its face that he didn't notice a man coming up behind him, standing close. All of a sudden, the man spoke and jolted Tom out of his trance. He looked around at him, having not heard what he had said, wondering if he was in trouble for something. The man looked at Tom and repeated his question, "Do you know the way to the toilets?"

His voice was deep and rough, and his eyes darted around as if he was looking for someone rather than focusing on Tom. He knew where the toilets were; outside in the car park, but he didn't know exactly how to get there. He thought about his journey up from the car park and tried to retrace his steps but couldn't. Disappointed in himself he replied, "I'm sorry, I don't."

"Okay," said the man with a warm, friendly smile, his eyes falling back on Tom. "Could you come and help me find them?"

Thinking only of failing to help this person and wanting to be a good boy, Tom replied, "Okay."

The man started leading him towards the exit at the front of the shops as Tom tried to figure out the right way to go. The man held his hand out for Tom to take and as he reached up and took hold, he realised that he didn't even do this with his mother; she rarely took his hand in hers. They were almost at the large row of glass doors when a bellowing voice echoed around the hall.

"Oi!"

Tom turned around to see his mum drop her bags and come running after them. He was just about to explain to her that he was helping this man find the toilets, that he was being a good boy, but the man had disappeared out of the door, leaving it swinging in its frame behind him. Tom's mum ran past him and followed without even a glance. It looked like she was chasing him! He stood at the entrance alone, wondering what had happened and if he had done something wrong. People around him were whispering and looking at him. He felt small, embarrassed, his bubble shattering around him. His mum swept back in through the door out of breath and grabbed his arm, dragging him back to her dropped bags and their spilled contents, shouting at him all the way. She repacked the bags and ushered him back towards the escalator to go down. He wanted to explain that he was only trying to help, but the words got caught in his throat, they couldn't get past the sobs and tears that flowed so easily.

# 4. MONDAY

However much he protested, the snooze button could only do so much, and after the third attempt at making it reset the day back to the weekend he gave up. Ali was still sleeping next to him which made leaving the bed that much harder. With a sigh of resignation Tom swung his legs over the side, his toes blindly groping for his slippers that were somewhere beneath. They were a fairly new addition to his bedroom attire, but after stepping on a discarded piece of Lego that William had strategically scattered across the hallway like a minefield, was enough to make the purchase an easy choice.

Stumbling into their en-suite, Tom ran the cold water and splashed his face. He had seen it in a movie once when he was a young adult trying to figure out how to be a grown up and had adopted it into his morning routine. He wasn't convinced it did anything but annoy his face, but he was stuck with it. The things he did at certain points, like in the morning, when leaving the house or going to bed, were all put together carefully into a routine that flowed and was both efficient and was sure to cover everything. The military had taught him many things and setting good routines was one of them.

With the cold tap still running, the plug was lowered, and the hot water switched on at the right point to reach a perfect temperature for shaving. Foam was spread across his face just as the water was ready. He reached for his razor and began; first with careful downward strokes and then back across in the opposite direction for a smooth finish. As the soapy water drained, he turned back and switched on the shower to allow it to warm up to temperature while he cleaned the sink of stubble residue. Foam and razor put away he stepped into the shower and began his routine. Hair washed and conditioner massaged in to give it the maximum time to do its thing. Then shower gel, working in sequence from his face down to his toes. Then the rinse; headfirst, allowing the water to wash all the soap away as it cascaded down to leave a fresh, clean body behind. Shower off he stood there, hands up like a boxer, allowing the water to drip and drain from his elbows that sped up the drying process; swiping off any excess water that still clung to him. This made him as dry as possible before towelling. Another trick from military life; a dry towel is a life saver.

Antiperspirant, after shave and hair product was applied before finally his teeth. This part he always had a doubt over. In his mind he knew that he should eat his breakfast first and then brush his teeth to have them perfect before leaving the house, but the lack of efficiency in leaving the bathroom and then having to come back again was too much. He did them now and would have a quick inspection in the mirror before walking out the front door.

After a check of his nails, nose and ears he put his slippers back on and left the room. Ali hadn't moved from where he had left her, and he had to subdue the urge to crawl back into bed and wake her up with his love. He dressed in order, pants first, then socks (left then right), trousers, watch, shirt then tie. He had designed this sequence with one sane thought, *'if there was an emergency at any point when getting dressed and I had to move, what are the essentials'?* And also, one irrational thought, *'if I suddenly disappeared at any point when dressing into an alternative reality or back in time, what would I be glad I put on first'.* Both thoughts led to the same routine, but he liked the thrill of the second one more, his love of sci-fi playing a large role in its creation.

He moved over and crouched down beside Ali and kissed her forehead. She frowned, rolled her head over and puckered her lips for a sleepy kiss. Tom willingly obliged and whispered, "Have a good day. I'll see you later. I love you."

A girlish smile spread over Ali's face as she mumbled something like, "I love you more."

Leaving her all snuggled up there was hard, it felt like she had a hold of his heart and the further he moved away from her, the more it hurt, which of course she did, completely. She knew everything that was inside of him, all of his quirks, his joys and his darkness and still loved him anyway. He would never understand how, but was grateful and would happily thank any of the gods there may be for making it so.

As he passed William's door, he gently opened it to check on him. He was lying diagonally across his bed, half in, half out of the duvet that he had obviously been in a fight with for most of the night. Tom couldn't see his face but knew what it would look like. He was a good mix of the both of them, mostly Ali he thought gratefully. He had her smile, her lips, her chin and face shape, but there was no denying that Tom had given him his eyes. That cool blue/green mix that changed shade depending on what colour he wore. He knew that it was natural to feel a protective urge over his son, but somehow, he felt it deeper than he thought others might. The need to show him that he was safe and loved and that nothing or no one would ever threaten that ran deep. Tom had worried about the strength of this feeling as William approached the age for nursery school. The fear of him being in an environment other than home loomed large and the thought of him being bullied caused dark feelings to bubble inside that had to be kept in check. They were only kids and things were a lot different since he was young, especially over this side of town. He closed the door quietly and froze as he heard a shuffle; he stayed quiet for a second and then carefully raised the handle back in place.

He made his way downstairs for a simple breakfast of two soft boiled eggs (cooked in the air fryer to save on washing pans and boiling water). The air fryer had been Ali's idea, a simple way to be healthier yet still maintain that delicious fried taste. He checked the windows and back door and headed for the hallway.

Shoes on, a quick check of teeth and hair in the mirror and he was ready. He removed his car keys from an RFID blocked box under the mirror, picked up his leather satchel and he was out the door, closing it just as quietly as he did William's door. If he woke him, he would undoubtedly run and jump on his mother and Tom would certainly know about it later!

Tom's drive into work was fairly short, the distance from his house to the university was barely a few of miles and he had often considered cycling it, but the annoyance of having to change when in work had proved too much of a barrier to his ordered approach. Plus, it didn't seem to be the best idea given the constant probability of rain. He had become accustomed to being warm and dry in the car and wanted to keep it that way.

Pulling into the car park he saw Professor Gainsborough heading for the door. The old man was practically retired but still insisted on being there early every day. Tom loved the Professor's office and considered it to be exactly how a professor's office should be. Full of books and research papers scattered around the room, odd curiosities picked up from his travels and a deep, worn desk that was almost as old as the university itself. The Professor's wife had died recently and Tom had noticed that he had practically moved into his office and that there were now tea making facilities and a fridge in the corner. He couldn't blame him; it must be terrible to have to return home to a place that held so many memories and yet caused so much pain.

Tom jogged over just as he was entering. "Good morning, Professor."

"Ah, good morning my boy. How are you on this fine day?"

"I'm well thank you. And thank you for moving the research review to next week."

"No problem my boy, you're the one with the funding from the difficult client! How are the military finding the collaboration between muscle and musing?"

Tom chuckled, "they are surprisingly accommodating. As long as the research provides a tactical advantage that they can brag about to the rest of the world, they're happy."

"Well, that's all thanks to you. You are a rare breed Tom, a hybrid, someone who has come from the arena of the body to the universe of the mind. Knowing both worlds gives you somewhat of a unique perspective on the matter wouldn't you say?"

"Well, it certainly helps," he replied as they walked down the corridor.

"Well, this is me," the Professor said as they reached his door. "Come on down later for some tea and we'll talk some more. I read an interesting article over the weekend from Yale about the top-down, bottom-up process and how the brain learns what to ignore. I thought of you instantly."

"That sounds interesting. I'll pop down later to hear more."

Tom headed for the stairs. He had read the research the professor had mentioned and had even spoken to professor Avilo who ran the project. But it was always good to hear the professors take on it and it never hurt to bat ideas back and forth with a giant like him.

Opening up his own office Tom noticed the difference between his space and the Professors. Although Tom loved the idea and romance of the Professor's, he couldn't bring himself to have a room so disorganised. His books were all neat on the shelves that lined the small space; there was a tidy pile of papers that needed marking from his undergrad students on the corner of his desk and the usual writing implements on the surface. Not set at ninety-degree angles or perfectly separated like some OCD obsession, but simply in an ordered and easily accessible position.

Tom moved to the tall window behind his desk and stared out over the back part of the campus grounds. He could hear the calling of the little Goldcrest that had made its nest in the drain just above his window. It wasn't considered the most beautiful bird with its dull greyish/green body and pale belly, but he liked the yellow stripe on its head that reminded him of Mr T from his childhood.

Tom turned and sat in his chair and with a deep breath he picked up the top paper from the pile on his desk and the red pen that was close to hand and began marking.

*\*\*\**

The rest of the day was spent reading and collating relevant research from around the globe, considering their impact on his own work and setting out some ideas for further development. He had an academic research review the following week which saw the professors and senior lecturers come together to discuss, analyse and basically see if they could pull apart the work that Tom had done. They took turns to present each month and it was a great way of making sure your findings were up to standard. This month was Tom's turn and it was one that was particularly important as it was the first time that an outside collaborator was going to attend. Major Simons was his liaison within the military and he had asked to attend the meeting and possibly input into the discussion. It was unusual for this to be allowed, but the level funding the university received from them made it difficult to refuse.

Checking his window was locked and his desk was neat, Tom left his office and locked the door. He started walking down towards the Professor's room when he felt a buzzing coming from the leather satchel slung across his shoulder. He tried to open it and search for his phone, but it was buried deep within its dark recesses. By the time his hands felt the cold metal frame it had stopped. The screen showed a missed call from his brother. That was a bit weird, but Tom was at the Professor's door now so put the phone back in his bag and forgot about it as he knocked and entered.

"Hello, Professor," Tom offered as his eyes scanned the room for the old man. He was sitting on his couch at the other end of the room; a couch that he had recently been turned around so instead of it facing into the room, it now faced the window so he could watch the world go by outside.

It took a second for the Professor to register the words and turn his head slowly towards the door. "Ah, Tom," he finally said and patted the empty space on the couch next to him.

Tom began to move towards it when suddenly, like Archimedes himself raising a finger, the Professor yelled "Tea!"

Tom detoured off and went over to the other window at the side of the Professor's desk and flipped the switch of the kettle. As he was preparing the Earl Grey for the Professor and green tea for himself, he glanced at the old man. He seemed particularly melancholic today.

The kettle was a new purchase and was both quiet and quick so in no time Tom went over with two steaming cups and placed them on the windowsill and sat down next to the Professor.

"It's all wrong, isn't it?" the Professor began enigmatically. Tom sat in silence waiting for him to elaborate.

"The natural entropy of life is all backwards. Just look," he said motioning to the students walking around the campus. "They have no idea what life is all about and what potential they really have. And by the time they figure it out they'll be old men sitting and staring at the youth around them too, unable to fulfil their dreams and unable to do anything about it."

Tom remained silent, unwilling to pop the pensive bubble that seemed to have formed around them. Then, coming back around, the Professor slapped the space on the couch between them and concluded, "Well, that's enough of that! Tell me, have you come up with a better name for your research title yet? *The decreased cognitive perception and illusory elements in both static and propelled forces through mixed environmental arenas'* is a bit of a mouthful. How about *'Camouflage and how not to get shot'?"* The professor began chuckling to himself.

Tom blushed and smiled along with the old man.

"I'm only joking with you, my boy. It's a fascinating field of experimental psychology, biology and real-world application; and your work on pattern depth perception is a real breakthrough!"

The blushing deepened. To have any praise, especially from this giant in the field, felt amazing and unusual; he didn't always know what to do with it.

"Thank you, Professor, it's been an interesting project and

one that I can see will lead on to much wider applications and research proposals."

"I'm sure it will, I'm sure it will." The professor's eyes were being drawn back towards the window as his gaze became less focused.

"Are you doing ok, Professor?"

"It's my wedding anniversary today, or would have been I suppose and I can't help but think back over my life during that time. The things I've done, the many things I haven't and wonder at the meaning of it all. Sure, there will be an academic legacy of sorts, but how long will it really take for my name to be just a footnote in some dusty old reference book that's left discarded in the back of the library? Untouched. Unneeded. I wish I had more experience of life under my skin, some danger, you know?"

The Professor let out a deep sigh that seemed to reverberate around the entire room.

"Life is a strange thing," offered Tom. "They say that life is short, but really it's quite long, made up of short moments strung together. We so often find it hard to see the moment we're in because we are still reminiscing over the moment we have just left and trying to predict the moments that will come. We seldom have the understanding or awareness of the moment right here, right now, and so that too passes into memory. Einstein would attribute this to our own perceptual position that affects our relative sense of time passing, but I like to think of it more like this: when you have your hands on a beautiful woman, an hour can feel like a second, yet when you have your hands on a hot stove, a second can feel like an hour."

The Professor laughed out loud and slapped Tom's shoulder. "What is that, Kierkegaard?" He chuckled.

"LL Cool J," Tom blushed and laughed as well.

They settled, more relaxed by the change of air and took up their tea. The conversation would have naturally shifted to family and life outside of the University, but those questions rarely came up with the Professor and Tom didn't want to mention them with his recent loss. He liked him a lot and felt a close bond that was akin to something like a father and son. He wasn't sure if the Professor felt the same way, but they always enjoyed each other's company and were open and relaxed together. Tom often tried to imagine what it might have been like if he really was his father, to have that stable, kind and intelligent figure in his life. What difference that would have made to his childhood, to the person that could have been sitting here today. To what extent does nurture override nature? He tried to picture the Professor with his mother and in his neighbourhood, in his old house, but the fantasy shattered around him instantly. There's no way the Professor would be in either position! Who would be by choice? So what does that make someone who grew up in it? Was he truly a hybrid, able to live and grow in both worlds; the one he had grown from and the one he had grown into, or was he a fraud in both, an imposter that didn't belong to any?

They finished their tea and talked about the project some more, expanding on the research the Professor had read and also how Tom's developments could move into other fields. This was the bit that he liked the most, discussing and dreaming with the old man, creating new worlds and futures from a single idea. It always took him aback how an idea can form and turn into an action that influenced decisions, shaped choices until a future existed where once lay only an idea.

\*\*\*

Pulling up into the drive was one of Tom's favourite parts of the day. The anticipation of the excited greeting he'd get from his son and the warm, welcoming kiss from his wife made his heart sing. He sometimes spent a little longer in the car to build up this feeling, making the joy of it that little bit deeper by withholding it for a while.

As he stepped through the door the familiar run of tiny feet came from the depths of the house and crashed into his leg. He bent down and lifted William up for a squeezy hug and a kiss that smelled like fresh soap. "How was your day?" Tom asked.

"Great!" William barked back with a huge smile.

"Great!" returned Tom with the same childish look of excitement.

Ali came behind looking amazing in just leggings and a strappy top, her bare feet silent on the wooden floor. They had a moment of just staring at each other while William climbed down and ran off to carry on whatever he was doing which then left plenty of room for Ali to slide up and kiss him. This is heaven he thought as they held each other for a while.

"Work ok?" She asked.

"Yep, all good," he replied. "How's your day?"

"It's all go here! We had an art class after breakfast thanks to CBBC. Learned some sign language with Justin and then took a trip to the park where William proceeded to run around like a wild thing and then go sliding in a pile of dog shit! Back for a quick bath, some food then nursery in the afternoon."

"Wow! It is all go!"

"I'm making a lasagne for tea if that's ok?" Ali offered as she skipped up the hallway leaving Tom to take his shoes off and place his keys in the box. She didn't wait for an answer and Tom just sent a smile to follow her on her way.

He went upstairs and took off his work clothes and replaced them with jeans and a T-Shirt. It helped him move from academic mode to home mode. Changing clothes was like a change in load-out to Tom, a switch of gear and equipment for a different environment that helped shift behaviour styles too. It was an effective way of changing mindsets and mannerisms that could help you blend in unconsciously. Although his days of combat and stealth were far behind him, there were still some useful tools he kept.

Returning downstairs, he followed the aroma of food and joined Ali in the kitchen for another hug. She was cutting up some salad for the meal when he grabbed her from behind and pulled her close.

"Careful!" she joked, waving the knife around. "I could take your eye out with this thing!"

"It wouldn't be the first time someone has tried!" Tom joked. It made Ali wince at the thought and she quickly put the knife down, turned around and kissed him.

It started to get a little passionate until she pulled away with a gasp, "Whoa there tiger. We'll never have dinner at that rate!"

"I don't mind."

"You might not, but the little man in there certainly would!" Ali retorted, picking up her knife again and waving it in the direction of the living room.

With a large sigh Tom acquiesced and walked away, but not before slapping her bum and stealing a piece of lettuce.

"Cheeky!"

He went into the living room to find his son building a city of bricks for his small toy cars to move around in. He got the dimensions pretty spot on for the car to just have enough room to turn the corners as he drove it through the gate and around the streets inside.

"That looks amazing buddy."

"Thanks! This is the gate and the car has to go around without touching the walls to make it into the centre to win the race!"

Tom looked again and instead of seeing a building with walls inside he could now see a maze, a series of roads, dead ends, loops and junctions that was pretty complex.

"Did mummy help you with this?"

"Uh huh," he replied, racing the car around.

Tom smiled and nodded. Ali had been a civil engineer before they had William, leading projects on train lines, bridges and tunnels all over the country. She loved it and it was never far from her mind. William had definitely picked up his interest in buildings and structures from his mother which she encouraged wholeheartedly. She would set out challenges for him to complete and things for him to build and construct to meet certain goals. Tom loved watching her set him off on a new challenge, explaining the scope and purpose, outlining the rules and boundaries for the building and what the success criteria would be. She could pretend to be a project manager all over again with a willing work force of one.

Tom sat back into the single leather chair and watched his son try to make it all the way around. He noticed the book he had been reading sat on the side cabinet so reached over to pick it up; *Perception and Representation – current issues*, but as he began to open the pages and flick through the numerous tabs he had marked along the edge a call came from the kitchen.

"Dinner's ready!"

William was up and gone before the end of the second word and Tom wasn't far behind. As they all sat around the table, he had a weird urge to say grace or something. He was in no way religious or spiritual, but he couldn't help wanting to give thanks to someone, something, for the two people sitting with him now. He laughed to himself internally and blamed it on his diet of American sit-coms growing up.

After they had eaten and cleared away the dishes, he told Ali that he was just popping out to the shed.

She rolled her eyes, "your man-cave! You ok baby?"

"I'm okay, just taking a breath."

She nodded as he closed the patio door and walked across the grass to the large shed that was tucked in the far corner of the garden. Ali had called it his *Man-Cave*, but it was more of a space where he could be alone. She knew that he felt at peace when in isolation and that a sense of enclosure made him feel at ease.

Entering the code on the keypad he stepped inside. It had all the usual things found in a shed like the lawn mower and garden tools, but these were either hung up or stored near front corner, out of the way. There was a two-panel window on the main wall overlooking the garden which Tom had covered with a film that allowed him to look out, but no one to look in. It helped to allow the light to enter whilst also maintaining that secluded feeling. Below the window sat an old, heavy wooden work bench with a vice and cupboards underneath for storing tools. Tom had found the table searching for business auctions and closures and had managed to take it off the hands of a local company upgrading their equipment for next to nothing.

The back end of the shed had another of Tom's finds. An old, beat-up leather chair that wouldn't look out of place in a therapist's office. It was so old and worn that Ali wouldn't allow it in the house, so the shed was its home. He loved it being here so had no complaints. There was a small thin bookshelf that contained volumes of gardening, plant care, woodwork guides and an eclectic mix of manuals. Tom hadn't most of the things these manuals referred to, but he liked examining them anyway, to find out how they worked.

Almost obscured by the chair, in the far corner, was a large chest. Not the type with a curved top for pirates to hold their treasure in, this one was more like a footlocker that could have been found at the end of the bed in any American army movie. In it Tom had placed everything from his days in the Marines. His uniforms, his equipment and every single picture of him had been safely packed and stowed away. It wasn't that he was ashamed of his service, but more like a clear acknowledgment that that part of his life was over, with a clear permanent black line drawn underneath it.

He walked over and slumped in the chair; leaning back into the leather with a comforting creak as he slid his bum down to stretch his feet up and onto the edge of the table. He closed his eyes and with a deep breath let the walls close in on him, feeling the space shrink to an almost suffocating size. To anyone else, this would have caused a sense of fear or panic, an eruption of heart rate and breathing that signalled an emergency, but to Tom it had the opposite effect. His breathing calmed, his heart rate slowed and his mind relaxed. He was in his protective coffin-like bubble with no space for anyone or anything else but him.

An hour or so every few days was often all it took to maintain calmness and clarity, but sometimes, when he had been busy, it could be almost a week before he got the chance to go in. Then he started to feel it, an emotion building, an urge to relieve the pressure so that no matter what he was doing, he had to go in. It was strange, but whenever they went away on holiday, even the three week vacation for their honeymoon, he never felt the need for this space. Perhaps he was too distracted and enjoyed his time away too much to even think about it. Perhaps it was the day-to-day aspects of life that drew this feeling from him or maybe some dark memory from his past. Whatever it was, sitting here now with his mind emptied, any care or worry had no room to get a hold.

# 5. NOVERS HILL

## 1979 – AGE 6

Three months after his sixth birthday, Tom was allowed and finally felt able to be alone outside again. He went to school of course, Novers Hill Infants, but this was as easy as crossing the road outside his house and walking up the street. The junior school he would eventually attend was 100 yards in the other direction, so he never had far to go. He could see part of the playground from his bedroom window and found it fascinating to see and hear the fun and games they all seemed to be having.

The most exciting thing about Tom's school was the large metal climbing frame shaped like a ship to the left of the playground as you entered. He had grown in confidence since his first attempts at climbing it and could now stand on what would be the deck. He hadn't dared venture higher to the cabin or crow's nest yet. His favourite though, was swinging upside down by his knees on the bars. There was something thrilling about being the wrong way up and trusting your head to the strength of your legs curled over. The concrete below didn't seem to bother him or his parents and teachers so there seemed nothing to worry about.

Past the school entrance was Novers Hill, a steep long road that quickly lost its houses and pavements at it falls so that only cars and lorries could safely descend. There stood, on the last plot on the left, a run down and derelict cottage that, as far Tom could remember, had never been lived in. It's peeled green paint, dust covered windows and slightly slanted stance deterred most daring adventurers from entering. There were of course urban legends of people daring each other to stay overnight with ghostly goings on, but you never knew how much was real and how much was just bragging. Tom always passed on the other side of the road to avoid walking too close just in case. Just over the brow of the hill there was a corner shop that sold all of the essentials and was one of the main places his mum went to get her weekly shopping. It was a weird place, it looked like someone had converted their house into a store and Tom had the impression that he was going into someone's home whenever he entered. Behind the counter was a door that looked like it went into a living room or some other part of the house where the owners lived. He didn't know; it was just a feeling.

On Sundays, Tom's father would send his brother to the shop for the papers, and he would often tag along to get a piece of the reward they were given as an incentive. Ten pence of the change would be given over to spend on chocolate or crisps, but was typically spent on getting a small bag of sweets that was filled with random penny and half penny treats from a selection behind the counter. If you were brave enough, you could select the sweets you wanted, but when Tom was in the shop he just asked for a ten-pence-mix-up and left it up to the clerk to choose. This was dangerous as they may select things that you didn't like, such as blackjacks or fruit salads that then had to be eaten in disgust.

It was a Sunday in late July when Tom was asked to go to the shops for some milk and the papers with the obligatory sweet incentive. He hadn't been to the shops on his own before, but his brother wasn't around much lately so it was up to him to go today.

He felt excited about having the sweets all to himself for a change (his brother often took his unfair share when they went together), but he was also filled with fear at the thought of what might happen. This was the first time he was alone out of the garden for quite a while. He knew the rules well enough, having had them drummed into him; *don't talk to strangers, go straight there and back and do not get into any cars!* He knew them, but there were always doubts about what might happen and how he would react. There were so many variables that it blurred the crisp clear edges of the rules. He wondered if he was taken, how long it might be before they would realise he was missing. A long time, he feared.

The worry on his face didn't translate as his mum gave him the money and shoved him out the door. As he neared the boundary between the safety of his garden and the street beyond he scouted around to try and spot any potential danger that may have been lurking. He couldn't see any cars or people, so gently he lifted the latch on the gate, hearing its melancholy squawk as it opened. He turned right and began walking up the street. As he reached the first corner, he looked around before crossing. He knew these streets well, but didn't feel as confident in straying as far as he once had into the unknown.

He crossed over and continued walking. He passed the entrance to his school on the other side and saw the climbing frame come into view. The sight brought a relaxed and confident feeling with it as he remembered his ability at climbing all over it. Just past the gates to the school the abandoned cottage came into view and he quickly whipped his eyes back to the front to avoid looking at its dead sagging face as he went by.

He continued on to the next junction that led into a cul-de-sac. He looked around again and found himself alone. Crossing the road, he looked left and right as he was told and from the corner of his eye he noticed someone coming up behind him. When he reached the other side, he glanced back again and saw a lone man not far behind, closing the gap quickly.

Tom's heart leapt as he increased his pace. He fought to maintain a good speed with his small legs without breaking into a run which would surely alert the person following that he was onto him. From the fleeting glance, he tried to piece together what this person looked like. They were male, adult, they were looking at him, but he couldn't make out the detail of the face. He quickly reached the last crossing before the shop and was too scared to turn his head and look for cars; instead, he relied on his ears to help provide the clues as to what was around him and where this person might be. He could hear a noise, a scrapping of a shoe perhaps, that sounded close. He turned his eyes and looked at the houses to his right, making a plan to run and knock on one of the doors if he needed to get help quickly. He could see the shop in the distance and increased his speed to almost a jog. The doorway was coming closer and closer as he felt at any minute he would be swept away from its safety and without slowing he grabbed the handle and burst through the shop door and into the sanctuary beyond.

He looked back through the doorway breathing hard but saw no one there. He waited to see if the man walked past or followed him in. A car drove by and then silence. A brief sense of relief washed over him as he started to regain control over his lungs. He closed the door, still looking out as he did, but still seeing no one until a realisation began to occur to him. The man could simply be waiting for him to come out and that he had the long walk back home again. The sense of safety the shop provided fell away and left him feeling trapped, as if he was stranded on a desert island with a perfectly working raft, but knowing that just off shore a deadly shark was circling.

He scanned the shop and saw the large owner standing behind the counter staring at him. The thought crossed his mind to tell him about the man who had followed him, but he wasn't entirely convinced that he did. It could easily be all in his head. What could he tell the shopkeeper that wouldn't make him sound crazy? He decided against it ... for now.

Tom began moving around the store, grabbing the milk from the fridge, in no rush to leave. He picked up the thick Sunday paper and approached the counter.

"That all?" Asked the shopkeeper, knowing that sweets were always a wanted option for the kids in his shop.

Tom's eyes moved past the robust figure to the sweets beyond, scanning the myriad of brightly coloured cartons, their labels stuck to the fronts. His eyes moved higher and noticed the items hanging from cardboard backing above; YoYos for twenty pence, toot-sweet whistles for ten pence and above them all, sparkling in the sunlight, were dangling bright silver penknives. The blade couldn't have been more than a few centimetres, but the thought occurred to him that it might be enough to scare someone off.

His eyes were then drawn to the star shaped circle where the price was drawn in thick marker, fifty pence. Damn it! He was only allowed ten pence to spend. He weighed up his need for the knife against the likely backlash of spending more than he was allowed. If he actually needed it to defend himself then surely it would be seen as a good thing that he had the foresight to buy it. But if he wasn't attacked, he would somehow need to explain the purchase and unauthorised use of the change. He could lie and say he dropped it on the way back perhaps.

"Well?" The shopkeeper pressed.

He made the decision that his life was worth the risk, "I'll have one of those please," Tom replied, his tiny finger pointing to the knives.

The shopkeeper looked up and then back at Tom. He appeared to be weighing something in his mind. Eventually, he reached over and plucked a silver case from the cardboard and placed it on the counter. Tom handed over the money and waited for what little change was due before scooping it all up into a plastic bag and turning for the door.

When he reached it, he took a deep breath and stepped outside, over the threshold of relative safety, pushing the raft from the shoreline. No one was there so far. He closed the door behind him, reached inside the bag and took hold of the knife tightly in his hand and ran.

The houses and streets seemed to streak by as Tom's eyes darted around in search of any sign of danger, any breach of dorsal fin. He sprinted across the roads without slowing and passed his school with barely a glance. He got to his gate in no time and ran into his garden and straight around the back of his house. His chest was burning; his little lungs were trying to suck in more oxygen than they could hold. He slumped against the wall and slid down to the floor. He had made it back.

He was slowly returning to normal when he looked at the back door, knowing that another danger now lay beyond as soon as he handed over the money. That, however, was a more common threat and one that he was used to dealing with.

He stood up and went into the house. He put the bag and the change on the kitchen table and walked into the living room. "It's on the table," he said to his dad as he headed for the stairs and his room. His dad didn't know how much money his mum had given him so he may just get away with it.

Closing the door to his bedroom, Tom sat down on the floor and opened up his hand. Lying on his red, moist palm, its edges glinting from his sweaty grasp, lay an object that could save his life. He suddenly sensed a feeling of power emanating from this object that made him feel stronger, as if it contained some mystical force, like it was a magic bean or powerful sword. He felt protected.

# 6. TUESDAY

Evelyn Cooke was a ferocious administrator that unfortunately belonged to the School of Psychology at the University. She was a throwback to the 80s where it appeared she learned not only her dress sense, but also her demeanour from watching too much Dallas or Dynasty at an impressionable age. Always immaculately dressed in a skirt suit or power dress she stalked the corridors of the building with purpose, like a shark swimming down the halls; the only warning of approaching danger was the loud clack of her heels on the hard floors beneath. This echo rippled ahead of her and was easily picked up by the staff and students who usually darted into the nearest door to avoid contact. She must have thought the building half empty most of the time for the lack of people she came across.

This morning, however, there was no escape for Tom as his office was the predetermined destination of her attack. His ears pricked up as he sat behind his desk scanning over research summaries for the meeting next week. He rarely heard her this far north, yet despite his initial reaction to run and hide, he had to resign himself to being cornered.

Three firm, officious knocks rattled his door frame and without waiting she entered.

"Tom," she stated, walking directly in front of his desk, stopping within an inch of actually making contact. "I need the master report for the academic research review next Wednesday. It needs to be checked, duplicated and bound in time and my team are already busy with late requests for teaching material from staff and even later submission deadlines from students."

She took a breath and stared, waiting.

Tom gently tapped the ends of the papers he was holding on the desk and placed them down. He slowly sat back in his seat and looked at her. He didn't know why, but whenever he found himself in a threatening situation his heartbeat slowed, his mind calmed and he felt much more in control of the usual anxiety he felt leading up to an event.

He smiled, "Good morning, Evelyn, it's nice to see you. As you can see, I am in the process of finalising the information required into a coherent and logical sequence for the participants of the meeting. I do believe I've already completed the request form for your team to do this work on Monday. Did you not get it?"

Evelyn stood there and bristled, she detested people who weren't afraid of her and especially hated being questioned.

"Yes, I received the completed form, thank you. But as I have mentioned, my team are extremely busy at the moment and the earlier these documents are ready then the better prepared we will be to complete the request."

Tom's smile broadened as he picked up on her clear signs of annoyance.

"I'm sure you and your team have everything in order and are more than capable of efficiently completing the task. I will have the master file ready for Monday morning as expected."

Her eyes shot daggers at his stoic impudence that splattered like flies on a car windscreen. He had faced much harder and meaner faces than this in his time.

"Very well, Monday morning." She turned on her heel and strode out the door, closing it somewhere short of a bang.

Tom waited a few seconds until the sound of her stomps had faded, then he let out a deep breath as his heart returned to beating a little faster than normal. Smiling and shaking his head he returned to the papers on his desk.

From below a buzzing began to draw his attention away from his work once again. He rolled his eyes at yet another distraction

47

and slid his chair back to retrieve his satchel. His brother's name illuminated the screen and he contemplated whether or not to answer. He did have a deadline to get this work done, one that had just become increasingly important to reach, but he knew that his brother would keep pestering him until they spoke. He remembered the missed call yesterday which tipped the balance.

"Hi Charlie, what's up?"

"Tommy boy," came the reply that was hard to make out. The background noise of traffic and wind made it difficult to catch all the vowels. "Did I catch you at a bad time?"

"No, it's alright. What's the problem?"

"No problem, I just wondered if you had a chance to think about the thing we spoke about the other day?"

Tom thought back and tried to recall anything that he was supposed to be thinking about. Then it hit him. "You mean the job?"

"Yeah, just a few hours of helping me out and a few quid thrown your way."

"Look Charlie, I thought I made it clear. I am not now, nor will I ever be, interested in doing anything for Stan-The-Man."

A pause, a sigh perhaps. "Look Tommy," he began, much slower and serious. "It's not doing it for him, it's doing it for me. I need a second guy and don't trust anyone apart from you; my blood, my brother."

"Charlie, I am not putting myself or my family at risk by doing something as stupid as a job associated with that guy. I appreciate that you're in a bind, but it's not going to happen."

Nothing.

"Charlie, you there?"

"Yeah, I'm here little bro."

Silence.

The emptiness that accompanied the silence filled Tom with a worse dread than the words that had preceded it. He could hear cars passing close by and the occasional whip of wind across the microphone.

"Charlie?"

"Okay Bro. Listen, do me a favour will you? Have lunch with me tomorrow and let me explain a little more. Then if you don't want any part of it, so be it."

"Charlie..."

"Just lunch and a chat. Surely you can give your brother that?"

He knew that he would never hear the end of it if he didn't see him at least. He had little choice. "Okay, meet me here at one tomorrow, and don't be late. I've got work to get done."

"I'll be there...where is it again?"

Tom gave him the address and hung up. What the hell had his brother gotten into now and why was he trying to drag him into it with him? He picked up the papers again and tried to concentrate, but the words just seemed to float in and out of focus; his mind found it impossible to think about anything other than that call and the look on his brother's face on Sunday. Throwing the papers on his desk he leaned back and swivelled his chair to stare out the window, contemplating what his brother had said and what he was going to say tomorrow; what buttons he may try to push and what history he may invoke to get his way.

*** 

The first Tuesday of every month was Date Night, an evening dedicated to just Tom and Ali having some alone time together that was established once William was born. Mrs Fitzsimmons was a neighbour and a widower who was only too happy to have William stay over in her son's old bedroom. The two of them had quickly become as thick as thieves to the point where William would often ask to go and see her during the week. Ali really enjoyed spending an afternoon with her and William, watching her dote and play with him with as much affection as a real grandparent. Ali's own parents didn't live close, so Mrs Fitzsimmons was an excellent substitute.

Tom was in the shower while Ali took William over which gave him time to try and break out of the headspace he had remained in since his brother's call. His focus on work had vanished and even his welcome home did little to break the fog. Luckily his shower routine didn't take any thinking space as he robotically went through the motions while his mind debated whether or not to tell Ali about the call.

If he told her then she would be worried. She would never tell him what to do, but the concern on her face would be enough for him. He had never lied to Ali before and didn't want to start now. But surely then, if he wasn't going to help his brother it didn't need mentioning.

The shower door opened behind him and he turned with a jump. Ali had returned and silently slid out of her clothes to join him.

"I thought we could start tonight's date night with a bang!" she whispered. Her hand wrapped itself around his manhood, the soap running down Tom's body made the movements smooth as her fingers slid easily up and over, teasing the head then returning to the base.

Tom's mind instantly went blank and focused on nothing but the hands of his wife, moving his hips in rhythm. He pulled her close and kissed her deeply, the water from the shower head falling between their lips, tickling their tongues. Breaking for air Ali turned around and placed her hands on the wall, arching her back and looking over her shoulder as an invitation for Tom.

He didn't need any encouragement as he moved towards her, his fingers slid between her cheeks to find a very wet opening. He slid two fingers inside and felt her gasp as they went deep. Moving them back and forth in a rocking motion his thumb slid up to her other hole and began circling around it, teasing its edges. The conditioner in Tom's hair ran down her back that made entry easy for his thumb to slip inside.

A deeper gasp as Ali's hand reached back and groped for Tom's penis, pulling it in time with the motions in and out of her. He released his thumb and turned his fingers around, curling them inside and felt the rough mound that housed her sensitive spot. He began beckoning with his finger and heard moans of pleasure echo around the cubicle, increasing in volume as he increased in speed until he felt the warm silky liquid running past his fingers and into his hand. He pulled them out and moved closer, Ali guiding him inside her. He held her waist with both hands as he thrust himself deeper, Ali pushed hard against the wall to take as much of him as she could.

He began to speed up as Ali raised her head back, allowing her hair to fall lower on her back. Tom scooped it into his hand and pulled it back as if taking the reins of a wild horse that was bucking wildly beneath him. One hand on her waist, the other in her hair Tom felt the sensation building up within him, spurring him on quicker, deeper as he let out a long moan of satisfaction and became frozen deep inside, not wanting to move or the feeling to abate.

He slowly came back into the room and released his grip. Ali turned around with a sly smile and kissed him hard.

"Right, hadn't you better get ready? You've been in this shower long enough," she said with a slap on his arse.

Tom smiled, rinsed off and exited the shower, closing the door as she began cleaning herself up whilst humming a tune. *'Oh my god'*, he thought. *'She is simply amazing'*. With a sharp stab, the fear of lying to her brought his brother back to mind again. He always had a way of getting to him, but isn't that what brother's do? They give you dead arms, Chinese burns and poke you until you react. Well, Tom was determined not to play ball this time.

\*\*\*

The drive to Tortworth Court was quiet, but no more than usual. Tom had tried to keep himself calm and natural and empty his mind of all thoughts that didn't belong on their date night which included his brother, Evelyn Cooke and the review meeting next week. As they drove slowly down the narrow road to this Victorian gothic mansion Ali reached over and placed her hand on top of his with a smile. This had been the location of their first date all those years ago and it still brought a smile to both their faces every time they came back.

They had messaged each other for a couple of weeks after meeting before Tom actually found the courage to ask her out and the initial spark that was struck was quickly fanned into a flame. He chose this location to impress her; it was a lot better than the bar they had met in and after she had told him that one of her favourite books was Dracula, it was a done deal. It wasn't quite the Carpathians, but it was as close as he could get for now. He remembered sitting outside in the gardens waiting for her to arrive. There was a wedding reception taking place inside, so he had stayed out of the way; he wasn't entirely sure he was allowed to be in this part of the building.

When she finally came through the gap in the hedge wearing a blue summer dress and small black boots she took his breath away. He got up to walk to her, but she simply ran towards him, threw her bag on the floor and wrapped her arms around his neck, not wanting anything to get in the way. They stayed in their embrace for a long time before releasing their hold and sitting down. They talked lots, well, Ali talked lots about anything and everything and when Tom had asked her if she had been thinking about him, she paused, and as if unable to verbalise her response, she simply leaned across and kissed him. It was a pleasant surprise and they spent the rest of the evening talking and kissing; the wedding party looked on through the windows full of smiles at the sight of another pair of lovers.

Parking up now, their heels crunched towards the large open entrance; they both looked across at the gardens and pulled each other close. They walked the well-known corridors until they came to the restaurant, a large mahogany panelled room with intricate carvings and candles that enclosed beautifully white and sparkling table tops. They were shown to their table with a familiar smile.

"So," began Ali. "How's work going? Almost ready for the review meeting next week?"

"I will be," he sighed. "Especially if Evelyn Cooke has anything to do with it!" He chuckled.

"Good, you need someone to give you a kick up the arse sometimes!"

They ordered a starter, posh prawn cocktail for him and cured beef bresaola for her.

"Any news about the consultancy work for British Rail."

"Yeah, I spoke to Alan yesterday about the bridge project in Filton and he wants me to check over the plans and do some on-site visits when they start. It's going to be a big one with manufacturing and fabricating done on site!"

"It needs it. That bloody tunnel is so narrow. It's about time they sorted it out."

"Don't worry, I'll make sure it's all fixed, just for you."

They laughed as their plates were taken away.

Tom's brother found a gap in his defences and started trying to poke through. He quickly continued with the conversation to return his focus.

"The bridge is on Gypsy Patch Lane, right?" Tom said.

"Yep. What a strange name. I don't get how these people come up with names for places. It's like they just put random words together sometimes. Take Fishponds for example. I know fish live in ponds but to call a whole area that is ridiculous. And they don't even have any ponds or fish for that matter!"

She laughed and Tom chuckled. He had grown up with these names so had never thought them as odd. It takes an outsider to notice these things.

"That's nothing," he added. "I once lived opposite King Dicks Lane!"

Laughter erupted from them both and people began to stare.

They settled down a little by the time their main courses arrived. If it was a special occasion they would have the steak, but seeing as it was just a regular date night, they both had the sea bass, but not without making the obligatory *'frickin' laser beam'* quote from Austin Powers.

They only drank water with their meal as they usually headed to the bar afterwards for a drink and a snuggle on one of the sofas. It was a beautiful bar surrounded by bookcases filled with old volumes of encyclopaedias, novels and poetry. Whenever they could they grabbed the second blue sofa on the far wall. Behind it were piled a number of books that looked like they were just placed there at random, but over the years they had gone there, they had played a game of 'finding a book you like and moving it over here'.

They had tried a variety of tactics for this game such as nonchalantly perusing a book whilst edging back to the sofa, or just slyly sliding a book out without even looking at it. They even went as far as the other one running interference by causing a small scene like dropping some cutlery or sneezing loudly to draw attention away. That was especially good when moving the larger books! It was like they were spies playing their own version of the movie *True Lies*.

They were always surprised when they returned to find the books remained where they had been placed and that the other people in there were more interested in the alcohol than the library of words that surrounded them. It was places like this that made Tom feel safe; bookshops were his 'Tiffany's', nothing bad could ever happen in them.

Their sofa was free tonight, and they instantly made a bee-line for it even though the place was practically empty. Tom headed to the bar to get the drinks while Ali slumped in the seat and picked up a book from their pile.

While he was waiting, he glanced back to watch her. His heart leapt whenever he caught sight of her, but watching from a distance, the rest of the room noticing her as well, made his heart hurt. She looked up from the book she held and smiled at him, and he could have easily died right then and there a happy man. A frown creased its way across his forehead, at a niggle that stopped him from enjoying the moment fully.

Charlie, of course, came bounding into his mind having finally pushed through the defences Tom had been putting up all night; his own traitorous conscience helped bulldoze him through at the thought of keeping a secret from her. He may as well have been sitting on the sofa next to Ali for all the good it did him now.

There was only one thing he could do about it and that was to tell her about his phone call.

Returning with the drinks he sat down.

"Cheers," she said, clinking glasses. She took a sip but continued staring at him, knowing that something wasn't quite right.

"What's up?"

"I had a phone call from Charlie today. He wants to have lunch together tomorrow."

Her eyebrows raised in a look of curiosity and scepticism. She waited for him to expand.

"When we were outside on Sunday, he asked me to lend him a hand for a few hours for something."

Silence still.

"I told him no, that I wasn't interested, but when he called today he seemed pretty desperate."

The eyebrows strained higher.

"So, I'll have lunch with him tomorrow and tell him again that I'm not interested and that will be that."

She allowed the pause to linger before she answered. "Look honey, I know he's your family and that relationship for you is complicated. I can't tell you what to do, but I trust you." She held his hands in hers, delicate and cool to his hot and clammy.

He wished she would just tell him not to go, to tell his brother to fuck off. But she left it up to him to decide what he should do. Looking down at their fingers unconsciously playing with each other, the matching gold rings, he knew why; because she loved him and knew that he would never do anything to hurt her or William. But she didn't know his old world like he did; didn't know his brother and all the chaos that he could cause with all the best intentions. He was less sure of what to do now and felt the wheels of his life caught on the tracks of his past life, unable to switch them back across.

# 7. WILL'S

## 1980 – AGE 7

Holding it close like a lover or a friend, Tom had begun carrying his secret pen knife everywhere he went. It was small enough to fit into his pocket and disappeared easily amongst a handful of change. He would often find himself with his hand in his pocket, just moving it in his fingers, stroking it with his thumb like a safety blanket or lucky charm. No-one had tried to grab or attack him since he had bought it. It kept him safe and allowed his confidence to grow to a point where he found he could explore further beyond his immediate neighbourhood.

He met up with friends from school and often went to their houses to play. The closest, and so most popular friend, was a kid named Justin who lived just past the Junior School entrance. Over the past few months, Justin had been showing Tom around his area. It was only 200 yards from his own house, but up until then, it had been unexplored territory. Although the houses here were probably built around the same time as his, everything seemed newer and more exciting.

He would often meet Justin's other friends too who lived nearby and play hide and seek with them, climbing atop garages or jumping into people's gardens to find new places to escape. He had never felt so free, although he had to be strict on time. He would be given a set hour to be home by his father and he wouldn't dare be a second over. He had seen what befell his older brother when that happened, and he didn't want to be on the other end of that.

He learned a lot about what not to do from his older brother. He seemed to do the complete opposite of what was allowed that led him to greater and greater punishments, even for minor offences.

Tom knew how many seconds it took to run home at full speed, so he always made sure that his little plastic watch was in time with the main clock in the kitchen before he left.

On this particular day, Justin had decided to take Tom to Wills's to explore. Wills's was a large tobacco factory that was at the end of the main road past Justin's. The road was so big that it had a dedicated crossing to get over. The factory had what seemed like an expanse of forest and grass to one side and a river that ran through it.

Justin didn't have to convince Tom very hard to come with him. Walking towards the main road Justin was telling him all about Wills's while Tom smiled nervously and fingered the knife in his pocket for courage. They got to the road and pressed the button to cross. Cars sped by, the wind buffeted Tom a little too close to the edge of his comfort zone.

Once they had crossed, he could see the start of the adventure, but instead of walking up the path into Wills's, Justin stayed on the pavement and led him further along the road.

"Where are we going?" asked Tom.

"If you've never been here before," replied Justin, "then you've never seen The Cage!"

*The Cage! What the hell was that?*

As they walked along a side path came into view and there it was.

The Cage was shaped like a small house that was sunken in the ground, but instead of bricks and mortar it was made from thick metal bars. When they got there, Justin pushed his head between them, his cheeks squeezed thin, hocked his throat to let a big green glob of spit drip from his mouth. Tom got to the edge and looked down in time to see its little splash in the water below.

The Cage seemed to be a meeting point for around half a dozen pipes coming from all sides. They were big pipes too, at least as high as Tom's shoulders that could easy be crawled through.

Justin looked over at Tom and said, "Do want to know the legend of The Cage?"

Tom nodded his head.

"There was a murderer that lived in this forest years ago. He was an old homeless man that used to live in there, but no one could ever find where he slept. He would come out every few weeks when he was hungry and be tormented by the kids in the area. One day he just snapped and started snatching any kid he came across who was walking through Wills's on their own. Several kids went missing before they realised what was happening. Apparently, a skeleton washed up through one of those pipes; someone saw it and called the police."

Tom's heart started racing as he looked down. He could well imagine a skeleton coming through them.

Justin saw Tom's eyes widen as he spoke and his voice took on a spooky tone. "They didn't catch him, you know. They couldn't find where he disappeared to when he went back into the woods. It's like he just vanished into thin air!"

"How long ago was this," asked Tom?

"I don't know, a few years ago, I think. Everyone who comes over here knows about it."

Tom thought about how likely it was that what Justin had said was true, but he couldn't be sure. He knew that there were bad people out there.

"Come on then," said Justin, slapping his shoulder and walking in.

The path going in led to a bridge that crossed a large pond. Where the water went under the bridge there was a wide metal grate that filtered it as it flowed through to the other side where it trickled down a steep moss-green slope that looked like a waterslide. Either side of the slope was a slightly raised section that didn't get wet. It funnelled the water into a small round pond at the bottom that Tom figured fed into The Cage.

As they looked over the bridge they saw kids in shorts on either side of the slope, splashing water and trying to jump over as others slid down it.

"We'll have a go later if you want," said Justin. "The slide is so slippery you fly down!"

Tom smiled and nodded but was sure that he wouldn't be allowed to get wet.

They continued to walk up the path that followed the river. Every now and then there would be a pile of stones that made small crossings across the water. At these places there were kids with fishing nets on long poles trying to catch fish or tadpoles as they floated down.

The noise of water and laughter filled Tom with a deep sense of happiness. He had never been to a place where kids could do what they wanted before, without adult supervision. Justin pointed to a place a bit further up. This crossing was a bit larger and had a huge tree leaning over the river. Hanging from one of its branches was a rope.

There were kids already there, standing in line at the top of the slope as they took turns leaning back and swinging out over the river.

"How cool is that!" Asked Justin?

It was very cool. Tom and Justin joined the back of the queue to take their turn. It was remarkably civilised considering it was just kids. Each one had a swing until it came to a relative stop, then they would slide off the stick, and walk it back up, handing it to the next one waiting.

Tom was behind Justin, and he paid close attention to his technique as he flew away with a whoop, swinging back and forth with glee until he slid off and walked the rope back up to Tom. Tom had been watching the others intently to learn how to both jump off and get your legs around the stick at the same time. He held the blue nylon rope high in his hands, leapt up and wrapped his legs over the make-shift seat perfectly. As he swung through the air, he closed his eyes. Gravity tugged at his stomach in all directions as the wind flew through his hair. This was living.

He got off and passed the rope to the next person and immediately joined the back of the line again. There wasn't much conversation going on apart from some of the boys who were arriving or leaving. Tom just wanted that feeling of flying through the air again and again. The tree and rope, although creaking under the strain, seemed sturdy enough and as the hours passed the people in the queue changed but the number remained steady.

On the next swing Tom was feeling more daring and started to lean back and raise his legs to really get a good swing, but as he did, he felt something slip from his pocket. He immediately snapped back to reality and looked down at the dirt slope. As the rope reached the furthest point, and without thinking, he let go and leapt out towards the edge of the river in one parabolic gymnastic move. He landed three quarters of the way onto the river with a splash and quickly raced back up the slope. He scanned frantically and saw a tiny silver object tumbling down towards him. He reached out and snatched it up.

He wasn't even aware of the noise from the other kids until he put his knife back in his pocket. Then he looked up and all of them were laughing and screaming at him, at what he had done. No-one had ever jumped from the swing like that before! Tom grabbed the rope and passed it onto the next who was being dared to do the same.

Justin looked at him in amazement, "what the hell was that?"

"I thought I had dropped something, so I just got off," Tom replied.

"Just got off? That was awesome!" Justin slapped Tom on the shoulder approvingly.

They swung some more before it was time to go. Everyone said goodbye and waved at them as they carried on launching themselves off the swing and into the river. Tom and Justin were laughing at the act that had made him famous, if only for an afternoon. As they walked towards the bridge, they could hear shouts and screams that seemed different from those of the fun they had been having. As they got closer, they could see a large crowd gathering around the bridge and the sides of the slope. Justin saw someone he knew and asked what had happened.

"Oh my god! This kid went down the slope and got cut by a piece of glass that was sticking up! His big toe is hanging off!" His friend exclaimed. He seemed so excited at having been here when this had happened. It was obviously going to be a new legend added to the place that he could claim to be the keeper of.

As they moved through the crowd to get a better look an ambulance began reversing up the path towards the bridge. When they reached the edge, they could see a wet kid being wrapped in a towel, bent over and holding his foot. Red streams of blood were flowing over the rocks and turning the green water a darker shade of black.

The ambulance crew got to the boy and began examining him. Justin and Tom still didn't have a good view, so they walked towards the back of the ambulance to try and see some of the action. Tom noticed that some people were starting to look at him strangely. Maybe his exploits from the swing had reached further than he realised. Then he heard a word whispered and spread through the crowd. He couldn't make it out until he saw someone's lips form the word 'Brother'.

Tom felt his stomach lurch as he realised what it meant. He pushed through the crowd to the edge of the slope in time to see Charlie being lifted up and carried towards the ambulance. He saw the blood-soaked bandage around his foot growing a crimson colour as a wave of nausea washed over him, the thought of the toe dangling underneath being held on by the tiniest slither of skin.

As the gurney was bumped and loaded into the back of the ambulance, he caught his brother's eye. They stared at each other for the longest second, a look of worry Tom had never seen before washed across Charlie's face as he faded into the depths of the ambulance. The doors closed and it began picking its way slowly through the crowd to the road.

Tom's initial thoughts of disgust and concern were instantly overshadowed by a new thought that emerged. His brother could tell their parents that Tom was there, at Wills's, to divert some of the shouting he would get from them. That would be an easy thing for him to do. Tom hadn't told them where he was going and was sure as hell that they wouldn't have let him go if he did. He was going to be punished if they found out.

Instinctively, he put his hand in his pocket and grabbed his knife. He clenched it tight as he turned on the spot and began running home as fast as he could. If he was there before they got the call from the hospital, he might just be able to create an alibi.

# 8. WEDNESDAY

Black clouds, dark and menacing, circled over the University like a scene from a horror movie; bleak and oppressive. Tom walked in and to his office alone, not wanting to see or speak to anyone; his mind wrapped up in his lunchtime appointment and straining against a lack of sleep. As he slumped behind his desk, he picked through the papers he had abandoned the day before and began to feel himself circling the dark well of catastrophising the day to come. He sat back in his seat and told himself *to 'snap the fuck out of it and get back to work'.*

He had this little voice in his head sometimes, whenever he was in a situation where he felt stuck. Being stuck in the field meant being dead and the ability to make a decision, any decision, was often the difference between life or death. He was thankful for it this morning as it helped him get started on yesterday's backlog.

He focused on several papers he had used in his research that would make excellent additions to the report, the clear synopsis and conclusions led well into his own findings. He read them through again and pulled out the relevant sections for what seemed like hours. After he had finished, he leant back and looked at the clock; forty minutes had passed.

*'What! How can that be'?* He thought to himself. Albert Einstein had a lot to answer for with his bloody relativity. His mind was on the hot plate and minutes passed like hours, yet he knew he had to keep it there all morning, sizzling away.

He got up and started pacing the floor in front of his desk

with a few more papers in his hands, but could neither read them with his movement nor concentrate on the subjects. He tossed them on his desk with a, "Fuck."

He had a lecture scheduled for the first year undergrads at eleven that would take him up to lunch and he knew that would help lubricate the passage of time, so he only had to make it until then. He needed to make a plan. Stopping dead, he could feel the presence of his inner voice looming and although it didn't shout any commands, he knew what it wanted...it wanted a decision.

*'Right, I need to clear my head and focus, so I am going for a walk, followed by lecture prep, then the lecture itself, lunch, then I can finish what I need to do today this afternoon'.*

Satisfied with the plan and ignoring the lack of detail around his lunchtime appointment, he grabbed his jacket and headed out.

The ominous sky continued to press down on him as he left the building, the warm humid temperature did nothing to ease the tension. As he walked across the car park towards the cycle path close by he noticed that the Professor's car wasn't in its usual spot. He walked a few more steps trying to remember the last day that the Professor had taken off and failed. He recalled the times when he had been ill with the flu and dragged himself in, and even after the funeral for his wife, he was in his office bright and early the next day. In fact, the only day he could recall not seeing the Professor was the day that she had died. It would take something that serious to keep him away. The thought made him come to an abrupt halt. He turned one-eighty degrees and headed back into the building.

Evelyn's office was close to the entrance and Tom was knocking on its solid wooden door in no time. The door felt firm in its frame like a portcullis except the wood was clean and smooth as if no one had ever knocked on it before. From inside a familiar voice rang out.

"Enter!"

Tom pushed the wooden sentinel and went in.

Evelyn was sat behind her small desk banging away at the keyboard. She typed as she did most things, with severe effort.

She looked up and was surprised to see Tom standing there, and then a look of expectancy crossed her face. It took a second for Tom to realise that she was hoping for the master file for duplicating early.

"The Professor's car is not in the car park. Is he in today?"

Disappointment swept over her face as she continued making the keyboard suffer. "That is correct; there was a message on my machine this morning saying he was taking the day."

"Did he say why?"

"He did not, and even if he did, I would not be able to share that information with you."

Tom's patience was not in the best shape that morning. "Don't you think it odd that he took the day?"

"The Professor can take any day he wishes"

"Yes, but when was the last time he did?"

"Personal information such as that is not privy to colleagues unless..."

"Damn it Evelyn," Tom snapped. "Don't you have any emotions at all, or do you keep them stuck up your arse?"

He turned and left the room, leaving the door open and a startled Evelyn staring at his exit, mouth agape. He knew that he would pay dearly for that outburst, but he had bigger things on his mind at the moment than an officious prude. He headed back to his office where he kept an old-fashioned phone diary in one of his desk drawers. After a few seconds of rummaging, he found it and opened the page to the Professor's home number. He lifted the receiver on his desk and paused as his finger hovered over the first digit. Was he being oversensitive? Maybe. Is the issue with his brother and the lack of sleep influencing his emotional state and decisions? Definitely. Would he still have been worried and called on any other day? Absolutely. He started calling.

The phone rang for what felt like an age until it was lifted.

"Hello," came the Professor's, croaky voice.

"Hello, Professor," Tom replied, feeling more than a little stupid at disturbing him now.

"Oh, hello my boy. Are you okay?" He coughed, clearing his throat.

"Well, I was calling to ask the same thing of you. I noticed your car wasn't in the car park and thought I'd check to see how you were." He tried to make his voice and intentions calm and collected.

"That's kind of you and very observant. I woke up this morning and had the overwhelming urge to do something different today, something other than the university. It's a terribly strange sensation and one in my years, I thought I would never get. So I decided to embrace it and head to the beach with a good book and a thirst for an adventure."

Tom felt both relieved and ridiculous. "That sounds like an amazing day. I won't disturb you any longer from getting started."

"No problem at all my boy. I'm here anytime you need me."

He hung up and took a deep breath. The Professor was finally doing something different, finding a life for himself beyond these walls of academia, beyond the all-encompassing sensation of grief and solitude. Tom felt proud of him and an even greater level of respect.

What a mess he had created in his own mind; from a relatively small influence he had blown everything out of proportion. Guilt now began to raise a hand, wanting to remind him that he had something he needed to fix. He stood and headed back down towards Evelyn's door. It was closed again. He knocked, softer this time, and the same voice repeated itself.

"Enter!"

Tom gingerly pushed open the door and found her standing behind her desk and staring out of the tiny window at the world beyond. She turned around and was surprised to see him there. Her face showed concern that another barrage of abuse was to follow.

Tom stepped forward like a naughty schoolboy, "I'm sorry Evelyn, for what I said just now. I've been under pressure and haven't slept much and became overly concerned with the

Professor's wellbeing and I just snapped. I respect you and what you do very much, and I really didn't mean to upset you in any way. I hope you can forgive me."

He could see used tissue paper on her desk and he felt a sting of pain at what he had done to her.

"Well, I have to say that I was very surprised and upset by your outburst."

Tom stared at his feet.

"I am under a lot of pressure myself, you know. This department doesn't run itself, and with the Professor taking more of a back seat, it leaves me to pick up the slack so we don't all fail."

Tom let his eyes wander around her room again, this time actually taking in what he saw. There were several wipeable calendars on the walls with dates, deadlines, holidays, teaching timetables, research requests, filing dates and reporting activities all marked fastidiously over them and colour coded. He could see for the first time that she had been labouring under the enormous pressure of keeping the department going while the rest of them just carried on with their own things. That as the Professor became increasingly absent, mentally if not physically, she had felt the need to step up. He felt the pain of her burden and how he had added to it.

"Look Evelyn, I really didn't understand what you were going through, but I can see now just what a job you're doing." He motioned to her walls.

"I want you to know that I respect everything you do for this department, and I know that we would all fall apart without you."

She smiled and blushed.

"But I don't want you to feel that you have to do this alone. There are plenty of people here that can take some of the slack, especially if they knew."

The smile quickly faded. "I have been trying to get people to do their part, but that's easier said than done! And besides, it's my responsibility to ensure the smooth running so there's nothing for them to know."

She moved back to her seat and shuffled forward. She swept the tissues into the bin and coughed to regain composure. Looking straight at Tom again her eyes became serious, "So if that's all, I have plenty to get on with as I'm sure do you."

Tom paused for a second and nodded. He walked to the door and turned to offer a smile and thought he saw the slightest hint of one returned as he closed it.

The last ten minutes had taken its toll and he no longer felt the urge or need to continue his walk. He returned to his office and sat behind his desk with a somewhat clearer mind. He picked up the papers and began to work.

\*\*\*

The rest of the morning didn't go much quicker, but he managed to keep himself on track with regular admonishments of the morning's scene. Lecture prep was straight forward; it was just a rehash of the same module as last year with a few tweaks here and there.

As he walked up to stand at the lectern his mind was purely focused on his delivery, and he even managed to find some excitement. It was one of his favourite topics and always drew even the most party-weary students from their slumber. *'Why the sensory information that falls into your eye is meaningless'*. It was concerned with how the brain is an isolated organ, trapped in its bony cage with no real experience of the world around it other than sensory signals in the form of electrical pulses. It has to learn to make sense of the world outside through the intensity of the shocks that were sent through elongated nerve fibres without having direct access to what was on the other end. It did this in order to find behavioural meaning from the patterns that were delivered to it so that it could keep itself alive. It often blew their minds that the eye does not send an actual image to the brain but a constant stream of signals from each individual rod and cone receptor being stimulated. The brain then has to try and collate all of this data in real-time to create a representation of the world in the simplest and most effective way to allow you to function and remain alive.

What really got them though was telling them that this representation of the world is not reality at all; that the things they saw were representations of the objects in front of them. If we saw reality as it was, we would quickly die out as a species due to the energy cost of processing such huge quantities of information. This was the *'Interface Theory of Perception'*. Telling them that their minds create icons of these images as best it could as representations of the things and their usefulness. We don't see a bundle of molecules vibrating with electrons whirring around. No, we see a representation of what those molecules represent, like the email icon on our computer screen. Our emails are not really inside that small red envelope on our screens. They are contained in zeros and ones, electrical fluctuations and temperature variances; a series of computer chip gates being opened and closed. If we had to decode all of that information every time, we would never get to read our messages. Instead, we create icons and an interface, a screen of consciousness, where these things can be easily represented for our understanding that is both quick and energy efficient. We do not see reality as it is, but only a representation of it, an oversimplified cartoon version for our understanding. We are the Simpsons!

The *Fitness Beats Truth* theorem is another example of this. The analogy he most enjoyed sharing was that of the lowly dung beetle. To us, a big pile of steaming hot shit is pretty unattractive. We don't want to smell it and certainly wouldn't want to eat it, yet the dung beetle can't think of anything better than munching its way through this delicious mound of gooey brown goodness. Is our perception of shit wrong and the beetles' right or the other way around? Neither of course. Our perceptions are derived from what is *'fit'* for each species. We cannot use this waste product so perceive it as disgusting yet to the beetle it's a veritable gastronomic mountain of deliciousness, so it perceives it as extremely desirable.

He always left a good portion of time at the end of this lecture for the inevitable series of questions and debates and for their minds to simply sit there and try to maintain a grasp on their ideas of reality that had just been blown apart.

Standing there at the end he checked his watch with a sigh. He thanked them all and made his way out of the lecture hall and towards the entrance. Before he even made it through the doors, he could see his brother pacing back and forth through the window, looking as out of place as it was possible to be. Crossing the threshold and into the open air he made his way over. Charlie saw him and threw his cigarette on the floor as if he had been caught by the teacher.

"Tommy boy!"

"Hi Charlie, I can't be long. There's a coffee shop around the corner we can go to."

They headed off, Tom leading at a pace, wanting to get this over and done with.

"How's your morning been?" asked Charlie.

"It's been fine." Tom didn't want to offer any more information than was necessary.

They entered the coffee shop, ordered their drinks and picked up a couple of sandwiches. Tom grabbed a slice of apple pie for good measure, he needed some comfort. The sofa in the corner had just become free so Charlie grabbed it while Tom paid.

He sat down, laid out the lunch on the table and sat back to wait for it.

Charlie was straight in the food and had devoured half the sandwich before stopping for air.

"Thanks Tommy boy, I was starving!"

"No problem."

Charlie could feel the tension, so after taking a sip of boiling coffee, he sat back and faced Tom.

"Thanks for meeting today, I really appreciate it."

"It's okay."

"Look, I know you've already said no to helping me out and I understand that, but I wanted to explain what's going on and why I need you."

Tom waited.

"You're right in that it is for Stan-The-Man and that it involves a little more than a collection and drop off, but I'm in trouble, Tommy."

Tom's eyes rolled, so far this wasn't a surprise.

"In a couple of days I have to go and pick up a large package and take it somewhere."

Tom waited for the details.

Charlie hesitated and went quiet.

"And...? What's the story Charlie? Tell me everything or I'm walking out of here right now."

"Okay, keep your hair on! The package I have to pick up is a quarter ton of cocaine that's being stored in a warehouse in Avonmouth. It's in a building by the port. We have to pick it up and take it to Stan at Filwood."

"Come on Charlie, and the rest. You don't need me to help with a pickup and delivery"

"Well, the package is not Stan's exactly, but belongs to a rival who's been stepping on his toes lately. We have to go in and take it without getting caught."

"What the fuck Charlie!" Tom lowered his voice as heads turned.

"What the fuck Charlie. Are you insane? You want me to help you sneak into a warehouse of an up-and-coming drug dealer and steal a quarter of a ton of cocaine without getting caught and then deliver it to Stan-The-Fucking-Man?"

Charlie looked sheepish. "Yeah, that's about it."

"No way! No fucking way!" Tom leaned back to breathe. "How can you ask me this? You need to walk away."

"Yeah, well I sort of can't this time."

Tom turned his eyes to look at Charlie without moving his head.

"I did something a little stupid a few weeks ago and this is my way of making up for it; so I have no choice."

"What the hell did you do where the only thing that would fix it is to get killed stealing coke?"

Charlie leant forward and took another few sips of coffee, delaying the explanation.

"I've been moving a lot of goods for Stan lately, more than usual. And, well, some of the merchandise sort of went missing."

Tom let that play out in his head for a while.

"You mean you stole drugs from him?"

"It wasn't a lot, just a little bit here and there. How was I to know they weighed it so accurately?"

"You're a fucking moron," replied Tom. "They sell this stuff by the ounce. How accurately did you think they weighed it?"

"Alright! I thought, you know, that there would be some wiggle room with transport and all."

Tom just shook his head.

"So, you see, if I don't do this, I'm done for."

"Just offer to pay for the drugs you stole and be done with it."

"I tried that, but you know Stan. '*It's the principal*' he said. So it's either this or I'll be fertiliser for the daisies; a warning to anyone else who might try."

Tom couldn't believe what he was hearing yet he had no trouble in accepting it. The ridiculousness of the situation and yet expecting nothing less from his brother and the old area. He considered his choices. He could walk away and leave Charlie to do this alone or with some other half-brained idiot where he would undoubtedly get caught. His mind showcased for him all the things that the movies had happily demonstrated befall people who get captured in that situation. It wasn't pretty.

Or he could help and at least have some way of pulling it off and then live with the outcome, no one else the wiser. Images of Ali and William burst forth to show him just what was at stake if he was caught up in this. They wouldn't survive the pain caused from his going to prison or being killed doing something as stupid as this. Yet he also couldn't allow the death of his brother.

Tom must have been shaking his head subconsciously as Charlie placed his hand on his knee and made Tom jump.

"Look little brother. I know it's a lot to ask and I wouldn't if I had any other way. But I'm up shit's creek and you're my only paddle."

"Fucking hell, Charlie. I can't. Do you know what you're asking? What about Ali and William? What the hell am I supposed to tell them if it all goes wrong?"

"You don't have to tell them anything. We'll just get it done and no one needs to know."

"I can't lie to her."

"I know it's hard. We all make hard decisions to protect family." He gave Tom's leg a squeeze.

They both stared at each other with a knowing look.

"Charlie, that was a very long time ago. I..."

"I know it was Tommy, but I was there and did what needed to be done, for you. Now I'm asking for the same."

"You can't use that against me."

"I'm not using it, I'm just reminding you of what families, brothers, do for each other."

Tom just sat there in a daze contemplating the many varied paths of life. It appears so complicated looking back over your shoulder, like forking branches in a tree. Each opportunity throws out numerous directions for you to pick from. Every choice took you further forward; solidifying the road beneath your feet, making it thicker, deeper until you become entrenched in the straightforward and the choices become ever more limited. Looking back now he had difficulty in believing there was really any choice in the paths you choose; that they weren't all multi-coloured and varied at all, but were singular, in outcome and in colour; that all the potential paths were mere illusions that really took you to the same places via different scenic routes and that the key events happen no matter which direction you took, like the lines in a magnetic field, they wrap around but ultimately end up in one place. It's this that gives the impression of free will and he guessed that this decision, whether it was offered in a coffee shop, a pub or street corner, was bound to happen sooner or later.

"Charlie, I'm a senior lecturer in a university now."

"Yes, but you still have the skills."

"I'm not that person anymore."

"You're always that person."

Tom thought for a moment.

He just couldn't seem to escape the past. It kept dragging him back no matter how far he tried to run. He had an impossible choice and yet a choice had to be made. This had to be it; there could be no more of his old life returning to haunt him ever again. This was the thing that would break all ties to his past, to his family, his city, hell maybe even the country. Simply take his new family and escape to truly start somewhere new, where no one knew his name or his history. He cursed himself for not having done this in the first place.

"If I do this Charlie then we're done. I don't want anything else to do with you, the family, anyone or anything from the old days ever again. I won't be in your life and you all won't be in mine. I don't want the past ever to be brought up again and as far as we are concerned, it makes us even."

Charlie thought he may have been over exaggerating. "Tommy, really?"

"Yes, really. You know what you're asking me to do, so if you want me to do it, then that's what it's going to cost."

Charlie weighed this up; not for as long as Tom would have liked.

"Okay, sure. If that's what you want."

Fuck, now there was no going back. Without even realising it Tom slid forward, loosened his watch strap and rotated it so the bezel was facing in.

"Right, tell me everything, EVERYTHING, about this job."

\*\*\*

The lunch extended well beyond the hour, but by the time it was over and several more coffees had been consumed, Tom knew all the information and details that Charlie did and even managed to pry out more that he didn't know he had.

After leaving Charlie, he returned to his office to continue his research and planning. The package was being stored in a building on the Northwest corner in the Westland area of Avonmouth Docks. There were only a few other buildings there. A large fertiliser warehouse in the opposite corner; probably a front or at least a side hustle for nefarious imports and exports. Fertiliser hid the scent of munitions incredibly well. Along the lower side of the docks was a large manufacturing company working on the tunnels for the next nuclear power station. That meant security would be tight.

The actual building was difficult to make out and as Tom zoomed in all the way on his computer, he could see the relatively small rectangle behind a maze of storage containers and products being housed across a wide yard. There was just a single road in and out and when he hit the 'directions' button the route came up with a yellow flag warning of private and restricted roads. Simply driving there was not an option.

Another way in would be via the water. A small boat silently slipping up the Bristol Channel wouldn't be seen and if no engines were used it would be as silent as the waves brushing the shore, but on closer inspection, the internal waterway had two enormous sluice gates that would be impossible to get through or open without obvious detection. The two easiest ways in were ruled out. He couldn't call on a helicopter drop off or extraction like the old days so decided to let that problem sit in the back of his mind for a while so it could chew over the details.

He turned his attention to the people they were stealing from. The main guy was known as Ry-Man. Tom chuckled and thought it sounded like the stationary company. His real name was Ryan Mannings, a thug who had grown up in the tough streets of London before being forced out to the sticks to set up shop in Bristol. There were a few articles about arrests and links to him, but nothing concrete, nothing on who he was or how many people he had. Information like that would undoubtedly be held by MI5 or even Special Branch, but he no longer had access to either and trying to re-establish those links would cause red flags to go off. He was in the dark and getting nowhere fast. He was coming up with more questions than answers. That's okay he thought and began listing the questions in order of importance, linking some together that should naturally follow. Memories of insertion techniques, close combat manoeuvres around buildings and exfil strategies flowed out and he wished he still had the same network on tap to help fill in the gaps.

Having completed as much as he could he locked the paper away in his drawer, picked up his satchel and headed home. He had no idea what he was going to tell Ali. The truth was out of the question, but a version of the truth was the next best thing. He was trained to know that a lie scattered among truths is as hard to find as breadcrumbs amongst the birdfeed.

*\*\**

Pulling up in the drive, Tom sat there for a while as usual, this time trying to quell the anticipation rather than let it build. He checked the top of his wrist to find the time and was surprised to see the strap instead of its face. He twisted his wrist over and saw the complicated pattern of dials and numbers pointing to read five fifty-seven. He undid the clasp and returned the face to its upright position and pondered on the automatic action elicited by such a switch in focus. He hadn't worn his watch that way for over eight years and yet it had been the most natural thing in the world to do. Is it always that easy to slide back into long forgotten behaviours?

Entering the house, the familiar run of tiny feet came from the hallway as William clamped himself to his leg.

"Hey there buddy," Tom smiled.

Ali followed behind. "We watched a program about octopuses today and now he just loves to use his *suckers* to stick to everything!"

"Wow, that's so cool!"

"Uh huh!" Ali rolled her eyes and leaned in for a kiss. "So how was your day?"

"Interesting," he began, dragging his leg after Ali towards the kitchen with William still clinging on.

"Really?"

"Yep, the Professor wasn't in today. I admit that I did panic a little thinking he might have fallen down and cracked a hip or something, but it turns out that he just wanted to head to the beach for the day."

"Wow, that's unheard of, but good for him!"

"Yeah, I think he may even consider retirement if he carries on!"

"Ummm, how did you know what he was doing if he wasn't in?"

"Well, I sort of called him."

Ali gave a look.

"I know!"

"The poor man can't be left alone for a moment without you badgering him."

"I was hardly badgering!"

"Uh huh! And how was your brother?"

Tom's heart skipped and stomach fell.

"He's fine. He's ordered some bloody piping and tools from China to save money and they come in the night after next. He wants me to help him pick them up and drive them to his lockup. His license only lets him drive up to seven-and-a-half-ton lorry, but I have a HGV that's still valid from the military."

Tom didn't know where this lie came from and was just as surprised at the words leaving his mouth as anyone.

"Where do you have to get them from?"

"Southampton."

"That's a bit of a journey!"

"Tell me about it!"

"So, not really as bad as you thought then?"

"No, but you never can tell with him!"

"That's good. Do you think you'll remember how to handle something that big?" She giggled.

Tom tried to match her mood. "Well, if I can't, it's big enough to not come out on the wrong side of an accident!"

Tom spent the rest of the evening playing with William on the floor and reading him an extra bedtime story. Tucking him up and kissing his cheek he was asleep before he'd even left the room. Tom stood in the doorway for a while trying to believe the lie that he told so convincingly, seeking to comfort himself that it would all be alright.

When he returned back down to Ali, she had poured him a glass of wine.

"A drink on a school night?"

"I thought you could use one after your interesting day!"

He took a sip and then leaned over to kiss her. The kiss became heated quickly and Tom pulled her close to him.

"Hello tiger!" she mouthed.

Tom kissed her again with passion and began unbuttoning her blouse, his lips unwilling to be parted from hers, maybe to stop any further questions from coming out. Their clothes quickly fell or were rapidly pulled off as he scooped her up and laid her back on the sofa. Climbing between her legs he found her wet and wanting and entered easily. He began moving deep inside, filling her up as she arched her back for a better angle. He started pushing harder, his feet pressed against the arm of the chair. Ali raised her hands behind her head, pushing the sofa's other arm to steady herself. He increased his speed and power, driving her into the sofa, watching the shock waves ripple through her breasts. She was breathing hard, the barrier between pleasure and pain so close. Tom could feel the tingling start to build inside as he continued pounding until an explosion suddenly erupted from him.

Both gasping for air, Tom dropped to her neck, a filter of hair in his face. She could feel his gasps and heart racing. She held him tight and slowly, with one finger began to trace out a meandering path across the skin of his back. He shuddered and began kissing her neck.

"You okay Baby?" She whispered in his ear.

"I'm okay."

They held each other like that for a long time, Tom hoping that she wouldn't guess something was wrong and if she did, prayed she wouldn't ask.

"I'm sure it'll be okay," she finally said.

Tom froze, unsure of what to reply.

"He's finally coming to terms with being alone and allowing himself to feel some kind of happiness again. That should be a good thing."

The Professor. "Yes, I know."

"I know you two are close and I'm sure he won't do anything drastic like retire without you knowing about it first."

"You're right. He's fine, I know." He allowed his mind to be filled with a false worry about his mentor rather than the real issue, which somehow allowed him to rest a little easier. The real issue was not going anywhere, but it was nice to focus on the acorn rather than the oak tree behind it for a while.

# 9. THE CAR

## 1981 – AGE 8

In the home, Tom and his brother hadn't spoken much since his return from hospital. The doctors had managed to save his toe although most of the movement and had gone from it. A part of Tom felt that his brother now resented him in some way. He had never told on Tom for being there which meant that his brother took the full force of his parents' anger with Tom simply being left out of it.

He wished that he could thank his brother somehow for keeping his mouth shut, especially when they started saying that they wished he was more like him. That must have burned. The shouting and arguments made his brother become more outspoken and he would openly begin to do his own thing in opposition to their wishes, unconcerned at the consequences. They had thrown their best punishments at him and he had survived, so anything that followed had little effect.

His newfound fame from the accident increased his popularity outside of the house and exacerbated his defiance inside. He was taken in by new friends, older friends with cars that only brought more worry for his parents. He started to have money that seemingly came from nowhere and when questioned on its origin he would say that a friend had gotten him a part-time job, although the details were a little vague.

Tom looked at his brother and tried to remember how old he actually was. He never really bothered with things like that, the details, so he couldn't work out if the issue had stemmed from his age or from the type of job itself. His brother was still at school, so he knew he wasn't old enough for a proper job yet. He did remember the first time his mother started to find things that he was buying with his money though. Tom walked into the kitchen while his mother held up a pair of socks from the wash.

"And where did you get these?" She said to Charlie.

"I bought them myself."

"And how much did they cost?"

"Six pounds."

His mother went crazy. Six pounds on one pair of socks was the most expensive pair of socks Tom had ever seen. And all because of a little crocodile that was sewn onto the side of them. His brother told her that it was his money, and he could spend it on anything he wanted. She couldn't disagree, although he felt some kind of jealousy from her that he was able to do just that.

Over the next few months, he began wearing more and more expensive clothes; all designer and all worth more than he could legally earn. There were no more outright arguments, and everyone kept to themselves, but the tension was palpable. Tom's brother became more reclusive, and his physical appearance started to change as well. Not just because of his clothes, but he started to become more gaunt, spotty and was often disorientated coming in through the door.

His parents talked less and less to him, and Tom could feel a real shift in the family dynamic. This became apparent one day when a stain was found on one of his expensive jumpers. It was a small patch of glue near the collar that Tom's dad was holding and pointing to. Tom couldn't understand why a bit of glue would cause such shouting. He had plenty of stains on his clothes and didn't get told off for them.

His dad was also pointing to his brother's mouth and when Tom took a closer look, could see that it was red and spotty all around his lips.

There were a couple of words that were shouted that Tom picked up on but didn't quite understand. Glue-sniffing kept

81

coming up in the argument and Tom tried to picture what that meant. Every time he smelled glue it was disgusting, especially the stuff in the pots at school, so he couldn't figure out why anyone would do that intentionally.

During the shouting a car horn beeped that seemed to be a signal to his brother. He snatched his jumper, walked out of the house and jumped in, disappearing up the road.

Tom had seen the car a few times before driving around the streets, dropping his brother back late at night. He saw it later that evening too. He often heard it pulling up outside and sprang out of bed to peek through the window to watch. A lot of Tom's life was spent watching life through the window, from the shadows. As he peered out tonight though, after hearing the engine and tyres come to a sudden halt, he saw the car door flung open and his brother unceremoniously dumped on the pavement like a sack of potatoes.

His heart raced as he watched his brother try to stand, but fail, holding onto his side as the car door closed and sped off up the street. Tom didn't know what to do. His parents were in their room, but he was afraid of waking them. He just froze and kept staring. His brother's face looked weird and there was blood on his clothes, his nice new clothes.

The light came on in the hallway and Tom's stomach dropped. He silently leapt back into his bed and under the covers with a single deft movement. Although he could no longer see, his ears took over, straining to pick up clues as to what was happening. He could hear voices and his mother crying. He expected to hear his father shouting, but didn't. After a few moments of silence, he heard them all shuffle inside and up the stairs.

Tom's door was always left open to let the light from the hallway spill into his room and he had placed his black and white TV on his chest of drawers to act like a mirror, reflecting anything that passed by straight to his eyes while he lay in bed. From this he could now see his brother being helped along into his own room next door. What was most surprising was that it was his father who took most of the weight.

He heard shuffling and moans of pain, whispered voices. Tom could imagine his clothes being taken off gently and his broken body delicately placed into bed. His parents left and went back into their own room, his mum stifling sobs. They looked in on Tom as they passed, but he was an expert at feigning sleep. He eventually drifted off that night to the sound of his mother crying and the image of his brother, bloody and broken, being pushed from that car.

The bruising went down after a week or so, but the pure hatred of that car grew more and more inside Tom's stomach, knotting it up every time he thought of it and the image of his brother lying next to it. Each time he glanced at his brother's face and a bruise shone he felt it rise.

One morning, Tom was on his way to Justin's house to play. As he crossed the road outside his junior school a car came around the roundabout with a familiar guttural tone and passed him. He knew it was that car before he saw it.

It turned into Justin's road and stopped a few doors up. He saw the driver, fat and bald, get out and knock on the door.

The evil feeling of hatred started to rise in Tom's stomach along with his temperature and instinctively, his hand reached inside his pocket to find his faithful knife. Tom watched the exchange of words on the doorstep and the man entered. As Tom approached Justin's house, he walked straight past, casually trying to glance inside the window of the house the man had gone in. He couldn't see anything; the curtains were drawn tight.

He continued to walk up the street and around the corner, stopping when he was out of sight. He stood there, playing with the cold metal in his pocket, hatred welling up inside of him. He could feel his cheeks flushing. An idea came to him. He took out his knife and opened the blade. Its small silver edge coming to a point a short way past his knuckles; it seemed to be willing him on, giving him courage.

83

Tom held his arm by his side keeping the knife out of sight and started to head back towards Justin's. As he walked his heart began pounding like he had never felt before. Scared for sure, but determined also. As he got closer to the car, he was focused on keeping to a regular speed and not looking out of place; his eyes moved between the car and the windows of the house without twisting his head. A few steps from the car and Tom moved a fraction toward the edge of the pavement so subtly that no one looking would have noticed. As he reached the front end of the car his hand turned out and brought the tip of the knife into contact with the paintwork. As he continued to walk along, he could hear the satisfying sound of scraping next to him. He didn't look, but could just imagine the cavernous line he was carving; could almost see the long trail of paint being peeled off like an orange rind. He came to the end of the car, folded the knife on the side of his leg and put it back into his pocket with hardly any noticeable movement.

He strolled up to Justin's door and knocked, his heart pounding hard. Moments passed and no answer came. The pounding inside began to intensify as if to break free from its ribbed enclosure and run away. He knocked again, a little more desperate. It took what felt like an hour for the door to open and relief to wash over Tom as he was welcomed inside carrying a smile that was unusually large.

# 10. THURSDAY

Light from the dawn found Tom already up and out. If he was going to formulate the plan in time for tomorrow night, he didn't have hours to lose. He had wanted to see how close he could actually get to the building before security started to be an issue and going this early meant that he would be caught in rush hour and wouldn't stand out amongst the other cars, lorries and trucks bustling around.

Driving along McLaren Road towards the roundabout just outside the docks, he felt the change from a residential to commercial area. As he turned left onto King Road towards the dock entrance, he noticed the Bristol Port Company to his left and a line of trucks that were queued up outside, awaiting entry. There were three trucks ahead of him as he joined the back of the line, a miniature amongst giants. He could see that as they ducked under the long white enclosed platform ahead, they stopped. From an almost invisible booth, a man leaned out and raised his hand. He was offered some documents to inspect that were returned after a cursory glance. There was no barrier to prevent onward movement, but this was clearly the first line of security and one that Tom shouldn't get close to. He could see the road turning back on itself, so he pulled out of line and followed it around. As he turned, he strained to see past the entrance to the buildings beyond, but a gigantic mountain of rubbish blocked any view and as the next truck in line rumbled over the railway line before the entrance Tom was driving away.

He turned left at the roundabout and hugged the coast to find the next opening that would afford him a view. There were buildings and warehouses along the whole stretch and at times he had to move further away in order to continue. A sign for Severn Beach began to appear and he decided to follow. Ten minutes later he was led into a fairly new residential area and towards the water. As he stopped on Riverside Park, the Bristol Channel was just 50 yards ahead of him, the old Severn Bridge in the distance.

A cold blast of wind shook him as he got out of the car, autumn was on its way. He walked up a short slope and onto the Severn Way footpath that ran alongside the waterfront. There were several joggers and early morning dog walkers already there heading up the Channel, but the path left, the one that led closer to the building, was blocked off by a large, grated fence. Last year's storms that raged along the coast had eroded away some of the support for the path and repair to stop the whole lot slipping into the drink was being carried out. This was as close as he could get. He walked to the barrier and strained to see anything in the distance. Nothing of use.

He sat down on the edge of the defence wall and looked out over the water. It was brown and murky and although you could probably find a way of staying close enough to the shoreline to not sink into its unforgiving depths, it would be pretty impossible to traverse. Neither he nor Charlie would have the energy for that, especially carrying a quarter ton of coke. A fresh breeze found the gaps in his clothing and wrapped its icy fingers around his skin. His mind was on other matters, however. What was he missing?

There was a small cafe along the road, 'Shirley's' and Tom walked towards it feeling the need for sustenance. The queue was filled with big burly guys in luminous vests with logos from transport companies, builders or railway networks. The guys in front of him were giving their buddy a hard time. He had ordered a large breakfast, but then asked for his eggs to be hard boiled which drew groans, then he asked for a glass for his can of coke, and then for ice to go in it. His mates called him a fussy bastard. "The can is warm!" he insisted, but they were having none of it. Their accents were a mix of broad Bristolian and Welsh which made Tom smile and although he certainly wasn't dressed like it, he could easily find himself at home with these lads. That sense of camaraderie he missed so much.

He ordered breakfast as well and found a table outside. Next to him a group of guys were talking about a missing trailer that had been stolen from one of their yards. Tom couldn't see the face of the man talking, just his mountainous back. He felt sorry for the Network Rail jacket he wore that strained against his bulk.

Tom had noticed a very small train station just along the road and the memory of the truck bumping over the lines at the port entrance came back to him. There would be no checkpoints on the railway lines. Maybe that was the opening he needed?

He pulled out his phone and opened up the map. Severn Beach station was literally a few doors along and was a termination stop; the end of the line. He followed it as it snaked its way towards the docks. It split into two, one moving away from the water while the other continued in the right direction. That one then opened up to five lines, like the head of the Hydra, that spread and swerved across the floor. He followed them and found the line that branched off towards Westland. The size of the screen and the sun made it difficult to see specifics, so he decided to put a pin in it to come back to.

His order number echoed across the garden and he raised his hand for the waitress to bring it over. He tucked in as soon as it was delivered, his mind racing with possibilities.

It wasn't long before his plate was emptied and his legs were carrying him towards the station. Sixty seconds later he was on the open platform. It was curious to see the tracks lift up from the ground to form a barrier, a full stop. There were no turnstiles or ticket offices; no guards or passengers for that matter. As he walked along, analysing the line and the gardens behind, a train came into view. It moved slowly towards the station and came to a steady halt a few feet from the end barrier. The doors opened and six people disembarked from the three dark green carriages that made up the service.

Tom stepped aboard. The carriages were quiet and empty with the majority of the passengers having exited long before it reached here. He contemplated staying on its return trip to the next station, but he wasn't sure when the next train back would be and the likelihood of having to walk made it undesirable. He stepped out onto the platform again and noticed a station worker come out of the last carriage, heading towards the exit and approached him.

"Excuse me. Can you tell me what the next station along is please?"

"Yeah, it's St Andrew's"

"Thanks."

Tom drew open his phone again and typed 'St Andrew's Station' into the map search. It was tiny, even smaller than this one and was exactly opposite Westland. He hit 'directions' as he moved with purpose back to the car. The station was only eight minutes away. He drove quickly and turned off the main road to follow an almost invisible sign towards the station. He pulled up alongside a metal pedestrian bridge that took you over the five-track split and onto the platform on the other side.

In the shade of the car, the map was a little easier to see. He traced the railway line from where he was until it broke off a little way up the track and did indeed snake its way towards Westland, stopping about nine hundred metres away from the building. That would equate to a ten-minute walk, twelve carrying a load.

He got out of the car and walked towards the bridge, scanning for security and cameras. There were none. At the top he could see across the wide landscape of the docks, but his view was hampered somewhat by a large sea freighter unloading in the nearest mooring. Directly in front of him were two large silos and a pale green building nestled in between. Several cylindrical truck trailers were parked outside with the word 'Hanson' clearly printed on them. There was no movement from the building and the trailers looked like they had been there a while.

There were bright red cranes along the water's edge, and although Tom couldn't see the building itself, he could just make out the top of the large white fertilizer plant that was located in the same area. He continued across and down to the platform. Again, there were no cameras, no ticket office and no people. There was just an old, decrepit shelter for passengers to wait under that looked as if its last inhabitant had used it before Tom was born. He sat inside and studied the map again. Getting from the train line to the building was simple enough, but to then to run back up the line to Severn Beach station was going to be a nightmare. Not only the distance, but the gravel, sleepers and quarter ton carried between them would be too much of a challenge. He closed his eyes and tried to imagine bumping that weight along the tracks and shook his head. He would find it difficult, let alone Charlie. Even if they could do it, the time it would take was unacceptable.

Fuck it! The train line is out as well. Now what?

He walked outside the hut and looked through the fence across to the docks beyond the ship and the silos. His focus drew nearer and nearer until he was looking at the fence itself. It was faded red, around eight feet tall and topped with razor wire. Three-inch wide metal slats ran down between two crossbars: one at the top and one at the bottom. Heavier posts were set in the ground every two metres, and it ran almost the length of the track. Towards the end it turned inward ninety degrees and buffeted up to a taller concrete wall that was part of a containment section inside the compound.

Tom walked along the platform to where the fence turned in. There was an overgrowth of bushes behind a non-existent barrier that was supposed to continue to the end of the track. He looked again at the fence and saw that the slats were held in place by two rivets at the top and bottom. If both bottom rivets were removed and only one from the top, the slats would swing sideways freely, opening up whilst giving the appearance of being in place. If that was done within the undergrowth here, then no one would even see.

A plan started to form. Here is the ingress and egress point, hidden from pedestrians, no security or cameras and no trains to worry about. He walked back up to the bridge and looked across to where they would have to run. He stood there judging the distances, calculating the pace and times. It was probably just over a thousand metres from here to the building; twelve to fourteen minutes under load, over a flat surface, then through the fence, over the bridge and clear to the road. That was more like it.

There was only one main road in or out of that area which meant that they would be easily spotted by anyone racing along looking for a van. Tom sat back in his car again and studied the map. There was no way of getting out of this area cleanly apart from this one road. If the alarm was raised then they would be caught on it, no doubt.

He sighed and lifted his head, just letting his mind and eyes wander. On the opposite side of the road there was a sign, 'Avonmouth Space Program' with a picture of a cartoon spaceship alongside. He chuckled, it was nothing more than a self-storage lot filled with large blue shipping containers, but the thought of folks blasting off from here amused him.

Then an alarm bell sounded, or maybe it was an overexcited ping of inspiration. Why escape during the heat when you can evade and hide? He got out of the car and made his way over to the gate. There was a small blue hut on the far side with a sign that read, *Mission Control. Please Come In'* so he made his way towards it. As he got close, he noticed a man in black suit trousers and light blue shirt contorting himself, looking like he was stretching his shoulders. He was facing away but as soon as he heard Tom approach he turned with a jump.

"Hello, sir."

"Hi," replied Tom casually.

"Overdone it a bit last night at training," he said, motioning to his shoulder.

Tom nodded in acknowledgment.

"What can I do for you?"

"I'm interested in renting out a container for storage. I work at the university and our lab could use a little more space so we're looking for somewhere to store some old equipment."

The man's eyes lit up. "Of course! Nothing explosive I hope," he chuckled.

Tom grinned. "No, nothing like that; just some old tables and chairs and things."

"Well, I can certainly help with that! Our containers have been fully reconditioned and are completely waterproof. We have small units between twenty-five to forty square foot, all the way up to one hundred and sixty; it all depends on how much you need!"

"We don't need a lot to start. Perhaps something on the modest size to begin with?"

"Absolutely. You can always upgrade as you go! May I recommend our five by eight by eight? It's probably our most popular size."

Tom was led around the corner to a row of half sized containers.

"Each one comes with a personalised heavy-duty padlock and key." He pulled back the bolt on the third container along that was unlocked.

"You have complete access to your container and hold all the keys. Unless you want to sign up for our 'Secure & Sign' package, where we can sign for and put away deliveries for you; then we'd need a key."

"That won't be necessary. What about coming in late at night? You know how students can often have unusual hours."

"That's not a problem!" We are open and manned from eight in the morning 'til eight at night. After that there's a keypad to allow entry to the site twenty-four hours a day."

As Tom walked into the container, the size was obviously larger than needed, but would be perfect.

The man was waiting in anticipation of the next question, eager to land a sale.

"Looks great, I'll take this one for now and see how we go."

The man beamed, "Great choice, great choice."

"I'll need to sign it up under the university if that's okay?" Tom asked.

"That's not a problem. Most businesses have it under their names, makes it easier for the tax."

Tom followed the man back to mission control and filled out the forms. He bought a new padlock for cash and locked up his container.

"Here's the access code for the main gate and I look forward to seeing you soon!"

Tom walked over to his car as the man began to twist himself into different positions again.

The plan was finally taking shape.

***

The drive back to his office was a blur, his mind racing as it mentally took notes and created lists of tools and equipment that would be needed. As he moved through the university building, he felt like he was in an out of place dream, as if he was walking into work naked, exposed for all to see; all of his intentions and plans laid bare, an imposter. He quickly made his way up and opened his office, grateful to close the door behind him, pleased of the solitude. Unlocking his desk drawer, he retrieved the list from the day before he began crossing off those questions that his morning recce had answered.

He took stock now; entry and exit into the area had been sorted, a delayed exfil with a secure safehouse had been secured. The next thing that needed attention was the movement of the package itself. A ton is roughly one thousand kilos, so they had a package of around two hundred and fifty kilos to move over a kilometre of fairly flat terrain.

Tom fired up his computer to try and get an idea of what 250kg looked and felt like and found a website called '*The measure of things*'. Some comparisons were interesting, but not particularly useful, such as it being about 1.3 times the weight of the heart of a blue whale, or about 0.56 times the weight of a grand piano. But some were useful enough to get an idea about what they would have to carry. It equated to 1.1 times the weight of a cubic metre of snow; that gave him some idea regarding dimensions. That it was 85 times the weight of a brick allowed some sort of reference to the load itself.

He opened up a new tab and typed 'lifting 250kg' into the search bar. Up popped a video that showed a large guy building up to a deadlift of that weight which instantly answered one question, they would not be able to carry that weight over any distance by hand. Another search brought up a range of trolleys and sack-trucks within that weight range. Another thing to add to the equipment list.

Now to the hard part, how to get into the building without being seen, or at least reducing casualties to a minimum in both volume and intensity. No deaths, on either side.

That was difficult to answer as there was no information on the number of guards around the building; no idea of what CCTV was being used, if any. No way of knowing the internal status of people, rooms or exact location of the package. If this were a military operation, then it wouldn't go ahead without at least a preliminary scout or inside intelligence gleaned from an agent or captive. No chance of that here, so they would have to go in blind. Never a good idea.

He sat back and tried to pull from memory all the non-lethal weaponry that he had used or knew existed. A quick cross reference online with what was actually available to a civilian left a dismal display of bats, sprays and knives. Useful, but not ideal. Where were the rubber bullets, the tear gas and cattle prods? Then it popped into his mind, a stun gun; popular in the states but not exactly legal here. Well, that's something for Charlie to worry about. Thick cable ties would also be essential, and not the cheap kind either.

Collating the equipment list together he called Charlie and ensured he had the full details including to make sure that the drill and stun guns were fully charged, that he knew the right sizes and type of drill bits, and to double check the trolley's maximum weight limit; basically, anything he could easily fuck up. He also told him the type of dark clothing that he needed to wear and informed him of the distances that would need to be covered so there were no surprises.

"Leave it to me, Tommy boy. I've got it."

Those words scared him more than anything else he had seen that morning.

"Are you sure there's no more intel on the location? The number of people likely to be there? Security around the port area? Hell, even what shape and size the package actually is would be useful. Is it in one lump or in blocks?"

"I'll try and find out what I can from Stan, but this new guy has his shit pretty locked down so I wouldn't expect much. Nothing we can't handle though, right bruv?"

Charlie's cocky optimism ran over raw nerves.

"Charlie, this isn't a game. Serious consequences are either side of a thin line of success and the more of a prick you are, the thinner that line becomes."

Tom heard a change in attitude coming down the line. "Okay Tommy, I get it, I know. It's just nerves you know."

"I know," Tom breathed, forgetting that not everyone had his past experience to draw from.

When the call ended, he looked up and saw the time was long past four in the afternoon. He stared at the clock and a wave of guilt flowed over him as he realised that he had actually been enjoying himself. He had been in a flow that had overtaken him and now he felt terrible for it. How could he be enjoying something that had the potential to blow his world apart?

He closed down the internet and brought up the research summary he had been writing feeling like a naughty child caught pulling wings off flies. He knew he shouldn't like it, but it seemed to be in his nature, a part of himself that was difficult to shake off. It somehow made him feel free, adventurous, able to do things that no one else could, using the skills he knew he was good at. He had the ability to see things, to find ways of solving problems that drew in many disciplines and much experience and knowledge. He wasn't showing off to anyone but himself, but he enjoyed it. It made him feel special, unique.

He forced himself to focus on his actual work for a couple of hours so that he somewhat caught up. He eventually closed his computer down and left the office. He seemed to float along the corridor like a ghostly spectre while the staff and students that were still around passed by at a greater speed. His mind was playing games with time that he no more liked than the list of all the unknowns that lay beyond the fence to the docks. He would have to do something about that. He couldn't walk into a completely unknown situation with so much at stake. That meant his evening was going to be a long one.

*\*\**

While Ali was loading up the dishwasher after dinner, Tom headed out to the man-cave. If he was going to do a recce of the building tonight, then he would need some tools. He emptied out an old rucksack and placed his cordless drill and bits inside. He then walked over to his chair and slid it to one side revealing the chest that had been waiting so patiently behind. He felt like it knew this day would come, the day when it would finally be opened again and all the old things from memory would come tumbling out.

Hesitantly, Tom took the keys from his pocket and unbolted the padlock. The keyring felt a little heavier, unfamiliar with the new addition from the lockup earlier. When he lifted the lid, he had expected an old, mouldy smell to escape that often went hand in hand with rummaging in old boxes, but instead it was as fresh as a daisy. Then he remembered that he had placed silica gel bags throughout the box to prevent moisture build up and a few sheets of freshener from the tumble dryer. *There's nothing like forward planning'* he thought.

On the top level of the chest were several neatly folded pieces of uniform, medals and chest ribbons and small bags of varying sizes that held old equipment. He knew the bag he was looking for and after moving a few bits from the top he found it nestled in the corner. He took it out and pulled the drawstring open to uncover his Swarovski STR spotter scope. It was a newer purchase and one that hadn't seen much action, but the dimmable illuminated reticle made it ideal for calling shots and for general surveillance. He brought it to his eye and checked the battery by clicking on the illumination and flicking through the brightness settings. All good. He always kept a head torch in the front pocket of the rucksack so did a quick check on batteries and he was done.

He took out a pair of tactical gloves from the box as well as a black beanie. He wasn't getting close tonight so wouldn't need anything else. Locking the chest, he placed the rest of the items he needed in the almost empty rucksack and propped it up by the door that would make it easier to grab for a quick and quiet departure.

He stood there for a while, leaning forward on the workbench, looking out across the garden to watch Ali in the kitchen, following her movements as she went into the living room. What the hell was he doing? He looked down at the chest, then across to the rucksack and felt as though he were in an alternate reality; that he was just going through the motions of a disjointed dream, that any moment now he would wake up and find himself lying next to his wife in a warm comfortable bed and smile to himself at his wild imagination.

With a sigh he left the man-cave and went back into the house. He played with William until it was time for bed and then carried him up to his room for the usual bedtime routine, plus an extra story again. When he came down this time Ali was sprawled out across the sofa with a book instead of some wine; opera delicately playing from the speakers. Tom leant over and kissed her.

"How was he?" She asked.

"He's fine. He seemed pretty tired tonight."

"The half days at nursery are really taking it out of him. He's due to start full time next week so I'm expecting him to be a zombie by the end."

Tom smiled and sat in his chair. He picked up the book next to him and opened it. His eyes were staring at the pages, but he wasn't really focused on the words at all. His mind was visualising the movements needed for the task ahead. Parking up, moving over the bridge to the station, walking to where the fence turns, stepping into the overgrowth, drilling the holes and moving the fence panels aside, running across the open field, climbing the external ladder to the silo, sliding on top and getting comfy.

He would have to lay there and wait for hours to get the information he needed, but that wouldn't be a problem. Waiting and observing in the dark was second nature to him; it was almost like he was born for it. His ears pricked at the song now playing, 'Nessun Dorma' from Turandot. Tom felt the irony of it; nessun dorma – none shall sleep.

His mind went through the route and routine many times before he finally came back into the room. Looking over he saw Ali staring at him. He had been focused on the same page since he had picked up the book, so she looked concerned.

"You okay baby?" She asked.

"I'm okay; just running through some work stuff."

She didn't look convinced. "You've been in the man-cave a lot this week."

"Just been sorting some things out in there."

"Like getting around to mowing the lawn stuff or other stuff?"

"A bit of both."

Other thoughts started to float from his subconscious into his awareness that brought their own questions. "Do you ever think about moving away?" He asked.

"I did move away; I live here now"

"No, I mean away away. To another country perhaps?"

Her forehead wrinkled. "What's going on? You've been so tense these last few days and now you're talking about fleeing the country?

"Not fleeing the country, just thinking that there is so much more to see of the world; more things to do."

"Isn't that what holidays are for? To be able to experience different places but still have a stable base to come home to?" She was staring at him now intently, a little worried. When something new was on his mind like this he found it hard to drop, and before you knew it, he would be off doing it.

Tom didn't know how to respond. He knew she was right, but that didn't stop him from pushing a little more.

"I know, but to really know a place you have to live there, be a local, live and breathe the place. I was just thinking about it, that's all."

"It's a great thought and one we shall definitely do one day. But William has just started nursery, we have the house, you have your work which is going really well and I'm just getting back into mine." She paused. "Where is this coming from, Tom?"

She used his name, she hardly ever did that. He had worried her, he could see that now; he needed to calm things down before any suspicions took over.

"Nowhere; I was just thinking out loud. Maybe we could see if we could fit in another holiday later in the year instead of just having the one over the summer?"

"Now that's a much better idea. Maybe go and see your dad?" she said, walking over and sitting on his lap, arms around his neck, her fingers running through his hair. "I do worry about you."

"Me? What for?"

"There's so much going on in there," she said, tapping his head. "So much you keep inside. It's okay to let things out once and a while. We are a team and that works best when we share our thoughts."

Tom was gripped with a mixture of fear and love. Love for this woman who was everything to him, everything he had ever wanted. But fear was also there; the fear of her knowing what he was going to do, the fear of rejection, the fear of destroying all that he had gained. He so wanted to tell her everything; to come clean so that she could stop him, stop the madness before it starts, before he tumbled back down that rabbit hole with no clear way of getting out. At the moment she had a beautiful image of their life in her mind, of him; an image he didn't want to shatter. But although the weight of his actions was a threat, the consequence to his brother would be fatal.

He began to move his mouth, to speak, but the words clogged in his throat, damming the sounds. All he could do was smile and pull her close, his head buried in her chest. Ali held him tight, stroking his hair as she felt his warm breath through her thin jumper.

"Shall we head up?" She eventually said.

"Sure," he replied, hoping that she was tired.

They went through their bedtime routine, Tom taking slightly longer than usual. When he left the bathroom Ali was laying there waiting. She raised her hand and guided him behind to spoon her, putting one arm under her head and the other hand she placed on her breast. She clamped it in with her elbow and snuggled into him.

"I love you," she whispered.

"I love you more."

They lay there for quite some time until Tom finally started to hear her breathing change to a slow, deeper rhythm as she drifted away. He glanced at the clock and decided to give it another half an hour before attempting to move. Laying here now, in his favourite place in the world, with the woman of his dreams, in a safe and secure house, the last thing he wanted to do was leave. The comforting embrace, the warm folds of the sheets were begging him to stay; pleading for him not to go. The primitive, subconscious parts of his mind were using every trick in the book, trying to push the right buttons for him to close his eyes and remain where he lay.

But no matter what they tried he ignored it. He had no choice. He had to move. Ever so slowly he began to slide his arm from under her head and roll over to his side of the bed. As he freed it and moved out, she rolled with him, her arm reaching out with a groan.

"It's okay honey, I'm just going to the toilet."

"Mmmm." She protested, twisted over, waiting.

Shit, she was not going to make this easy for him. He stayed in the toilet for a while, hoping that she would go back to sleep in the meantime, but as he came back in, her hand reached out and made a grabbing gesture and he was forced to return to his previous position. She could obviously sense the tension and the need for security. Tom lay there, unable to remove himself, the stress of the day and the warmth of his pillow started to overtake him. The rhythm of Ali's breathing made it impossible for his own not to follow the same slow pattern and it didn't take long for him to succumb to the sleep he so desperately craved.

# 11. OLD PEOPLE'S HOME

## 1982 – AGE 9

Neither of his parents had noticed just how much Tom had grown more independent in the year that followed and how he could take or leave the company of his friends. It had started slowly at first, walking to the boundaries of his world alone and pushing slightly beyond every time. Granted, it was still a tiny part of the area, but it was certainly bigger than the bubble he had lived in before.

On one of these occasions, he walked to Inns of Court, a place that consisted of a row of shops and a pub that surrounded an open area for buses to turn. He would accompany his mother to the shops there sometimes to get things like paraffin for the heater, vegetables and sometimes other bottles he couldn't identify. Just beyond these stood the tall spire of a church; it raised its slender collared neck high, straining to be seen and to see into the lives of its parishioners. Although Tom had only been inside for the harvest festival, he had been taught that the church's bell had hung in all the previous church buildings that had occupied the site and that there was a part of an old manor house this area was named after, still standing as part of the vicarage. He didn't really pay much attention to the details so had never bothered to look.

He wasn't particularly interested in it at the moment either as he walked past a large building just beyond that was obscured from the road by a tall concrete wall. The wall was made from wide slabs that were slid on top of one another between concrete posts. Their appearance reminded Tom of pleated skirts, but on the side. Their texture was fairly smooth, similar to the ranks of garages that he could now easily climb, the gaps between each slab afforded some grip and the slight fold between them helped too.

As he walked along, his curiosity grew. He crossed to the opposite side of the road to get a better angle, but all he could see were the top floors of what looked like an old people's home. The rooms looked similar to those in a hospital, clean and white, but these ones contained old looking furniture. He saw what looked like a nurse in a blue uniform passing by a window and an old woman opening her curtains in another and a feeling started to grow that urged him to try and find out more.

As he continued to move along, he noticed the top of two large green cylinders just on the other side of the wall that he guessed were tanks for holding gas or oil for the building. Looking both ways along the road, he quickly ran across and scrambled up to the top of the wall. Once there he could see that the two tanks were housed inside a raised, fenced-off area within the grounds of the building. Checking his surroundings, he deftly whipped his legs over the wall and dropped down the other side.

The concrete platform the tanks were on must have been about four foot from the floor, making the landing that side much easier and provided an effortless escape route back over if needed. The fence that enclosed the tanks was made of three wide planks of wood that ran along the front and sides and had a gap of a couple of inches between them; plenty of room to observe what was going on the other side without being seen in the dark recess.

He sat there for a long time just watching people move around the building, seeing them in one window or another and tracking their movements. After a while he began to recognise the staff as he caught glimpses of them. It gave him such a thrill to be watching all these people's lives without them knowing he was there. When the time came for him to go, he checked the windows and climbed up the side of the wooden fence, peered over the wall to make sure it was clear, and jumped over.

As he walked back home, he felt as if he had found something special, somewhere he could be alone with his thoughts; to feel the excitement of being hidden from the world whilst watching it unfold before him. He decided he had to go back that evening.

***

Within a week, there was a bucket in one corner for his toilet, a large bottle of water and a carrier bag of crisps and small Freddo chocolate bars. He made the place neat and tidy, not obsessively so, but ordered with each item easily to hand so that if he wanted something it was there. This kept his movements to a minimum so that anyone who happened to be looking in his direction wouldn't notice. These things meant that Tom could spend much more time here before having to leave. It was here that he now spent his hours, watching these characters carry out the daily routines of their lives without the slightest idea that they were being observed; that they were the players in a real-life TV show exclusively for Tom's eyes.

He quickly learned the rhythm of the place, the movements of the nurses and which windows they were likely to be seen in next. He was surprised that he didn't see the residents as often as he thought he would. Occasionally he would see one open a window or close a curtain, but he guessed that the main areas for them were further in or on the other side of the building.

As his knowledge grew so did his confidence. One night he saw the last nurse in the laundry room leave and turn out the light. He knew that this would give him about five minutes before another face was seen at a window. So, scanning the perimeter, he quickly climbed over the fence and dropped down onto the grass behind the corner of the tanks that was hidden in shadow. He could hear his heart beating as a car passed by on the other side of the wall. Checking the windows one more time he bent over and ran towards the middle of the building, easy and unseen. He felt exhilarated at this new game, his first steps in the grounds of the building he knew so well; but he wanted to take it further.

Keeping low, he slid along the wall until he approached a darkened window. He ducked underneath until he came to the washroom with its light still on. Turning to face the wall he slowly edged his eye up to the bottom corner of the window until he could see inside; his breath reflecting off the wall in his face, bringing with it the smell of wet brick and mortar.

What he thought was a washroom was actually another part of the laundry, a drying room where clothes and sheets were folded and stored. Two women were in there talking animatedly, the blonde haired one that faced him more so than the dark haired one. Tom knew these people and had seen them many times in the windows and although he had no names for them, he knew how each one moved and carried out their duties. The blonde haired one was quick and moved between windows at a pace. She tended to fling open curtains and talk to anyone who was close enough to listen. The dark haired one was smaller and slower, taking her time with her work, folding back the curtains with care and always seemed to have a smile on her face. She was someone Tom could imagine being very friendly and kind.

As they continued to talk, suddenly, without warning, the blonde-haired woman started unbuttoning her uniform at the top whilst continuing to talk. Tom's eyes widened as she slid the uniform off her shoulder and slipped her breast out of her bra in one deft move, lifting it up so the other woman could see something underneath.

Tom stared in disbelief, aroused and uncertain at what he was witnessing. After a few seconds the breast was safely secured back in place and Tom lowered himself back into the darkness below. He wanted time to fully get to grips with what he had just seen so, with a quick glance, he ran back across the grass and climbed over the fence, back into his lair.

As he slumped down behind the fence breathing hard, he replayed over and over again what he had seen; an actual physical boob, right there in front of him. He felt feelings down there that he had never felt before, warm feelings that grew the more he thought about it.

He had seen boobs before in magazines and catalogues, but not in real life. The thrill of being somewhere he shouldn't had increased his excitement. Knowing that he could see everything of them, and they could see nothing of him made it all the more thrilling. The idea of keeping to the shadows and observing unseen had produced an unexpected treat he would not have had if he stayed where he was. He contemplated the fortuitous nature of his timing and concluded that it was meant to be. Smiling to himself he reached for a Freddo while his eyes returned to the building.

## 12. FRIDAY

Ali was already downstairs making breakfast by the time Tom's alarm woke him up. For a few seconds he lay there disorientated. He was unable to tell if he was home, lying in his barracks, waking in a prison cell or coming round from a dream as a child. The nightmares of his sleep spun around him, and it wasn't until the gentle smell of Ali's perfume helped guide him back to reality that he realised where he was. But the tumultuous fears that had enveloped him all night still clung to the folds of his mind as his eyes adjusted to the brightness.

Dread gushed into his gut like the breaking of a dam as he remembered that today was the day. This was mixed with feelings of failure at having fallen asleep when he should have been out preparing for it. Now he was left with no information and no time to get it. He berated himself for sleeping instead of ensuring the successful completion of the task, given the stakes were so high.

He languished in the bathroom; his energy having been drained by the unusual dreams he had had that still danced around the edges of his mind like a spectre. He dressed in his work clothes and headed down to the kitchen where he was surprised to see both Ali and William dressed and finishing off their breakfasts.

"What's all this?"

Ali rolled her eyes and looked at William who began laughing. "Didn't I tell you that Daddy would forget we are going to see Nanny and Pops today?"

Tom had no recollection of that conversation at all. He had been so wrapped up in his own issues that he had no idea of what was happening around him.

"We'll be back later this evening but won't be late. We'll see you before you have to head off with your brother."

Tom froze, trying to remember the lie he had told, "Okay, cool."

"There's some bacon on the side for you. You've got a long day, so you'll need the energy!"

"Thanks baby."

"Come on monkey, grab your coat and say goodbye."

William jumped down from his chair, hugged his Daddy and said goodbye. He was excited to see his grandparents. He didn't get to see them very often as they lived almost two hours drive away, but he loved it when he did and was spoiled rotten.

Tom followed them out to the hallway.

"Have a great time with your folks and say hi from me."

"Will do." They kissed and hugged all too briefly and then they were out the door.

As it closed, a wave of silence echoed around the empty house that made the transition even more surreal. He was the only one here who knew the significance of the day ahead. It made him want to tell her even more. They never had secrets, and this one was killing.

He turned and made his way out to the man-cave. Lifting the unused rucksack onto the bench he removed some of his equipment; much better to use a clean set of tools that couldn't be traced back to him. He opened the chest once again and this time took out black combat trousers and a jumper. There wasn't much from the top layer he needed and nothing from the bottom layer would help; he didn't want to delve that deep. He closed it up and stuffed them in the rucksack.

Returning to his bedroom he grabbed a T-shirt from his sports drawer and opened up his wardrobe. At the bottom neatly lay his shoes in colour order. He reached into the back and pulled out his black combat boots that still had a gleam to them.

Packing everything in the boot of the car he went back to the kitchen to polish off the bacon and as he stood at the counter, he looked around. He couldn't recall the last time he was here alone, without the noise of his son, without the activity and presence of his wife.

He scanned the kitchen and saw traces of them everywhere. William's drawings on the fridge, Ali's knick-knacks and framed prints on the wall, sprigs of dried flowers in an antique vase, inspirational quotes; she was everywhere. He walked through the hallway with his eyes open as if for the first time and saw the pictures of the three of them from their holiday last year and another one of just the pair of them before William was born; a happy couple and family.

He then moved into the living room and saw Ali again; pictures of her with friends, her graduation photo, pictures of her parents and family, even old black and white images of ancestors gone by. The only thing that Tom could claim was the single leather armchair, just as his father had had when he was a child. That and a photo of their wedding day. Where was his life, his history?

He walked upstairs and found no traces of life from before Ali. There were no pictures of Tom as a child growing up. No pictures of him in uniform with his buddies. Not even his graduation photo. It looked like his life had started the day he met her, which in a way it had. He found he was able to compartmentalise huge swathes of his life at a single stroke and simply box them up and keep them locked away. When one section of his life was over, he simply packaged it up and moved on. He had maybe a dozen memories as a child, none that he wanted to immortalise in an image on his wall. His time in the service had been eventful and the decision to leave painful, but once it was made, that part of his life was then over and so too was stowed away as well.

His bachelor and masters degrees felt like a blur of libraries, books and lectures. He was a mature student by then, so the party life was not really for him. He found it hard to take in the learning and reading, especially after his experience of school, so had to work harder to keep up. And now here he was, in a new part of his life that, and according to the walls, the only part of his life he had ever had. He began to wonder that if it all went wrong tonight, if he lost it all, would he be able to box it all up again and move on?

This felt different somehow, like home, a real home, and even though it was hard to dispel the demons of the past, he knew it didn't get any better than this.

He ended up outside William's door, he paused before going inside. The room was neat and tidy; a chest of toys with a framed image of Ali and him, a large bookcase of favourite stories with William's first attempts at drawing stuck to the sides. He tried to think back to when he was that age. His own room wasn't so different, maybe sparser on the personal touches. He tried to place William in his own childhood, to see how he might have been, but he didn't like the feedback he got so quickly stopped. There's no way he wanted his son to go through anything that he had and yet he knew that those battles, those experiences, made him the person he was today. They had given him the resilience and skills to be able to cope in situations where most people would fall apart. Perhaps adversity is needed to a degree in order to build those tools needed for adulthood. But there was surely a balance required between not enough, which could lead to being a spoilt brat, and too much, that might lead you to be an emotionally closed hermit. Tom felt that his was toward the later end of the spectrum which was maybe why it took so much effort to step outside of himself. He would much prefer to watch from a distance.

He closed William's door behind him and headed downstairs. He checked the windows and doors before picking up his satchel and heading for the car. He looked down at the leather bag he was carrying, at the clothes he had on and suddenly understood that these were just parts of a costume that he wore to feel like the person he wanted to be at that time. Now, he looked the part of a senior lecturer so he was one; later he would wear the clothes packed in the boot of the car and look like a criminal, but wasn't he that already? Wasn't he all of those sides of himself? Maybe the clothes just allowed different parts to come out. Like someone suffering with dissociative identity disorder, their multiple personalities and faces buried deep inside and all it took to draw them out was a simple change of clothes.

*\*\**

Friday mornings were always a little busier than usual on campus. Everyone wanted to get their tasks done early for the day before slinking off in the afternoon to enjoy a slightly longer weekend. The Professor's car was back in its usual spot which was nice to see; at least some things were back to normal. He hadn't even looked for it yesterday when he got back from his morning recce.

He made his way up to his office with a need to keep today as calm and as smooth as possible. He didn't want any dramas, any issues, just a regular day at work. Sitting behind his desk and firing up his computer, the wall between his outward persona and how he was really feeling inside felt pretty firm. As long as he didn't do anything too emotionally demanding, it should hold.

He began by reading what he had written the last couple of days and found that it made no sense at all. His mind must have been in turmoil to write such drivel. He deleted most of it and began again with a fresh sense of ability and focus when there was a knock on his door.

"Come in!"

The door opened and in came the Professor a little sheepishly.

"Professor!"

"Hello my boy. I thought I'd come up to the higher levels and pay you a visit." He moved into the room and sat down on the chair opposite.

"This is a nice room," he said looking around. "Reminds me of my office forty years ago," he said with a chuckle, then a frown as he looked around again. "In fact, I think it did used to be my office at one point."

They both laughed.

"I would offer you tea, but my facilities are rather lacking," offered Tom.

"Yes, well the luxuries in life are often reserved for those who simply take them."

He was, of course, talking about the university's policy that forbade kettles and unnecessary personal electrical items to be used in the building. Tom of course adhered to the rules while the Professor had started to take a more flexible approach.

"I'm just working on the analysis of my work so far for the review meeting next week," pointing to the screen.

"I'm sure it will be a great piece of work. I'm rather looking forward to it and to having an outsider in our midst! But I wanted to talk to you about Wednesday."

Tom's heart jumped; his internal wall shuddered.

"I spoke to Evelyn, and she told me that you were more than a little concerned about me?"

Tom flushed and he found his tongue was too tied to respond.

"I know I'm no spring chicken, but I'm more than capable of looking after myself. I know it must have been a bit of a shock for you, me not being here; it was a bit of a shock for me as well to be honest. But I'll tell you something, I feel so much better for it. The clear sea air and the open space to the horizon certainly had a way of blowing away the cobwebs and putting our insignificant specks of carbon into perspective. You know I hadn't been to the coast for almost five years, not since Maureen started to go downhill. Before that we were always there," he paused as those memories came flooding back. "It's funny how the things that are most essential in your life are often the things that go unnoticed. Some Fridays we would head down to Burnham-on-Sea, get a bag of fish and chips and walk out past the low lighthouse with a large blanket and just sit together and stare out to sea. It may not have been the most luxurious of locations, but it was our little piece of paradise."

His eyes began to fill with water at the thought and the loss.

"I couldn't venture to that spot yesterday, but I could see it from a distance. Looking over at that place was like peering back through time where so many years were spent thinking; thinking about what was, what could have been, and I realised that there had been a double loss."

Tom looked at him unsure of what he meant.

"You know Maureen and I never had any children. I always joked to people that the research was my baby, but that wasn't quite true. Maureen had cancer when she was much younger, in her teens, a rare form that affected the spine and meant that by the time I met her in her twenties, she had already undergone two major operations that had removed vertebrae and placed a titanium cage around what was left. You would never know of course, she kept active, riding her bicycle and gym classes, but there were days when I would wake up and look across and see her in so much pain, having spent the night in quiet agony so as not to wake me. Those mornings broke my heart and made me love her even more. The doctors' advised that pregnancy was too great a burden on the body and would likely cause major paralysis if carried to full term, so we decided not to risk it. You know, she tried to leave me one year when the cage had shifted after she was hit by a cyclist. She was walking through the park when he came out of nowhere and crashed into her back, her of all people. I was in a lecture when I got the message and ran as though my life depended on it. She needed another operation to straighten and probably rebuild the frame and she thought that it would be too much for me to go through as well. The months of her just lying there, unable to move, to feed herself, to use the bathroom. Perhaps she felt it was too embarrassing, too much of a compromising position for her, too much of an imposition for me; we hadn't known each other long at the time. It came close, but there was no way I could let the love of my life disappear and go through this alone, without me. So, our lives were spent together, sharing everything while both of us secretly wished for a child of our own that could never be."

Tom sat there staring; he didn't know any of this of course, but could see a deeper picture of the man before him now as if the colour and contrast had been turned up suddenly.

Their eyes met. "You know, I've always thought of you as a son, at least the son I would have liked to have had. I know it sounds crazy, but I care for you Tom and just wanted you to know that before...before I didn't get the chance to say it."

"Professor..."

The old man waved his hand at any response that might have been forthcoming and slid his chair back to stand. Tom stood also and moved around the desk towards the door where the Professor was heading.

"Not that I'm going anywhere, or you have to worry, but I just wanted to let you know that I'm here for you."

They hugged like father and son.

"Thank you. I feel the same way."

They broke off and the Professor headed out the door, his head turned to avoid showing the tears in his eyes.

Tom's wall was shaking and reverberating as if it were caught in an earthquake that extended around his entire world. He could feel the cracking and splitting of barriers that fell into the abyss. He held back the tears in his eyes and sat back down, taking a long shaky breath, looking at the work in front of him. He couldn't make out a single thing through the build-up of liquid, and if he wanted to continue, he had little choice but to let them flow.

***

After the flood gates had been restored somewhat and the current reservoir depleted, he managed to hold the wall in place with a finger here and there plugging up any gaps. Apart from a text message from his brother about the time and place for their rendezvous, he was undisturbed. For this he was grateful, and it meant that a fair proportion of the work outstanding had been completed.

He saved it all on the University's online drive, the remote server that would allow him access to it at home to finish it off over the weekend, ready for his Monday deadline with Evelyn. He wondered how much of what he had said to her had been relayed to the Professor. Either way he was glad that it didn't come up in the conversation.

Shutting off his computer and gathering his things together he headed for the door. He looked back at the desk and wondered if it would ever look the same again? If there were some things that happen that alter your perception irreversibly.

He walked along the corridors, deserted for the weekend, without seeing another soul. He had stayed a little longer than usual. Knowing that the house was empty did nothing to encourage him to expedite his journey. The drive back was traffic free and uneventful; it felt that the rest of the world had headed home early to watch an event, like the World Cup or a royal wedding. Maybe they all got back early to watch what would unfold later; like they all knew what he was going to do and had a pay-per-view subscription to watch it. Whatever the reason, it felt like the calm before the storm.

Pulling up in the drive he didn't wait, he got out and went straight in. The house felt as empty as the university building as he made his way along the hallway to the kitchen. The pictures and images seemed more colourful and obvious after he had seen them this morning. In fact, the whole house seemed to be fuller, and yet empty, as he continued to recognise things he had never noticed before. The pressed flower in a tiny square frame, the piece of ribbon tied around a cream vase on the kitchen dresser, the cookbooks with paper and notes coming out of their tops where Ali had tried favourites and adapted recipes; meals that he had simply eaten without knowing the effort behind them.

How could he have been so blind? He loved the bones of her without doubt, but he had never seen the wealth of life and colour she had brought into his life so clearly, making this house a home, making their life vibrant and meaningful, making him a husband and father. William was the bundle of energy that brought his life such focus, such joy. Maybe it was the thought of losing everything that made him suddenly appreciate just what he had. He should be spending all of his waking hours with these two amazing people who filled his life with so much meaning instead of risking it all for his fuck-up of a brother.

He pulled out his phone and called Charlie, determined to put an end to this madness.

"Tommy, what's up? Everything alright?"

"No Charlie, it's not alright. I can't do it. It's too risky and the dangers are too great, especially with as little information as we have."

There was a pause on the line.

"Um, I'm not sure that's an option anymore."

"What do you mean?"

"The equipment you requested and the assurance that it will be done has been passed to Stan, so this thing has your name all over it."

"What the fuck do you mean has my name all over it? I'm doing this to help you!"

"Yes, but Stan wanted reassurances that I wouldn't fuck up again, that it would be done; he wanted you involved, made sure of it in fact, to ensure everything would go to plan. He was quite insistent on it."

"Why the fuck would you do that? Why did you bring my name into it? You've screwed me!"

"Listen Tommy, all we have to do is finish what we've started and it's all good."

Tom's mind was reeling.

"And what happens if I say no?"

"That's not something you want to think about. You know what Stan's like, and anyway, this is just between you, me and him. It's too risky for anyone else to know so once it's done, it's done."

Tom couldn't believe that he was neck deep in this now. Like a Chinese finger puzzle, he had slid into it and there was no way of backing out.

Tyres crunched on the driveway as a car pulled up. He was out of time and options.

"Fine, I'll be there. But this is it for us."

He hung up, getting a sense that Charlie was starting to believe that now.

The sound of a key sliding into the lock and the change in air pressure as the door opened helped switch his focus back to the room.

He rushed out and held Ali tight, pulling William into his side.

"Well, hello! Maybe we should go out more often?" Ali joked.

"Missed you," he said, kissing her. "And missed you too monkey," he said, picking William up and giving him a squeeze. "Did you have a nice time with Nanny and Pops?"

William brought up a new toy car to show his father. He recognised it instantly as a customised Ford Shelby Mustang GT500, made famous by that movie with Nicholas Cage, the one where he had to steal a huge list of cars to protect his brother; this car was his nemesis.

Tom didn't know whether to take this as a good sign or a bad omen but found the irony pretty unamusing. He looked at Ali to see if she also recognised the car and she just rolled her eyes. Her parents were huge film buffs and there was no way they got it for him without knowing where it was from.

"That's a great car," Tom said.

"It's Eleanor," William said, clambering down and running off to test it out.

"Eleanor?" Tom said to Ali.

"Don't ask," she joked and leaned in for a proper kiss. "So, you've missed me have you?"

He gathered her up in his arms and held her tight. "Yes," he replied, unashamed.

"Good."

They kissed deeply, emotionally, until Ali leaned back and took a breath. "I'll definitely have to go out more often."

"I don't want you to go anywhere."

Ali smiled, feeling the love. "Not even to the kitchen to start dinner?"

"No, let's get takeout."

"I like your thinking, mister. Shame we can't have a bottle of wine with that seeing as you're leaving me for the night."

"We'll make the most of it until then," he replied, drawing her closer for another kiss.

\*\*\*

Dinner and bedtime for William flew by all too quickly. Ali was in the kitchen when he came down, preparing food and a flask of coffee to keep him going. She had made enough for him and Charlie. *'If only she knew,'* he thought.

"You didn't have to do anything; we could have picked something up from the services."

"I don't mind," she smiled. "This way you get back to me quicker without having to stop." Then she thought about it for a second. "Unless you're tired and need to stop of course, then do that."

"I will," he replied, moving up behind and wrapping his arms around her as she packed everything into a carrier bag.

"Don't start that or you'll never get going!"

Tom wished with every bone in his body that he could; that the paths around him weren't all culminating into the event ahead; the event that had no diverging options to take him around. He squeezed her tighter and resolved to get this thing done and get back quickly and cleanly.

He kissed her neck. "Right, I'll head off then." He grabbed the bag and leaned in for one last kiss.

"Drive safe baby, and say hi to your brother from me!"

Tom gave her a sideways look as he went. "Sure." He grabbed his jacket and keys, put on his shoes and was out the door.

117

The cool evening breeze felt refreshing as he stood there for a moment, trying to mentally make the switch from where he was to where he was going. The sky was still hanging onto the last shades of blue before the long black of the night took over.

They had arranged to meet at Twyford House Cricket Club in Shirehampton, a tiny clubhouse nestled away from the local residents only nine minutes away from the station.

Tom drove the short distance with care, his mind beginning to make the switch, letting out pieces of his past. When he arrived, he found his brother already there, sitting in the driver's seat of his van. He pulled up alongside and got out. Charlie looked ashen white with his cigarette hanging from his lips as if he had eaten something bad that was requesting an exit. Tom ignored him and went to the boot of the car. He began undressing, allowing his mind to transform with each piece of clothing; permitting a deeper persona to come to the fore, until there he was, black boots, trousers and jumper, black beanie and gloves; mission ready.

Moving around the boot he saw Charlie exiting the van dressed in black trainers, black jogging bottoms and a black hoodie. He didn't know which one of them looked the most ridiculous.

"Did you get everything?" Tom asked.

"Yeah," Charlie replied and opened up the back of the van.

Inside a large sports bag lay a pair of used bolt croppers, a new bag of industrial zip-ties and two handheld devices with the word 'Taser' printed up the side in white. Tom opened the bag of zip-ties, feeding half a dozen through his belt for easy access and storing the rest in a zipped pocket by his left knee. He picked up a taser and examined it for a moment. He squeezed the button on the side and an arc of blue electricity shot from one electrode to the other in a satisfying chaotic dance. He placed this in a zip pocket on his right thigh. He pulled out the bolt croppers and took them back to the boot of his car, placing them in the rucksack that now only housed the scope. He grabbed the trousers he had taken off and folded it around the contents to cushion their movement and prevent any jangling sounds from escaping.

"Where's the drill?" Tom asked, his tone flat.

"It's in the front."

He walked to the passenger door and opened it up. A battered turquoise box laid waiting. Tom opened it up and tested the battery; it seemed fully charged. He took the smaller drill bit from the top section of the box and placed it in the drill ready, putting the larger bit in his left back pocket. He put the drill in his rucksack, closed it up and shut the door. He grabbed the food bag from his front seat and walked over to a tin-roofed shed in the car park and hid his keys behind it.

Charlie was still standing there next to the van, having not moved a muscle. Tom took the other taser from the van and handed it to him.

"Here, you'll heed this."

Charlie took it and put it in the pocket of his jogging bottoms, but its weight pulled them down on the side, the drawstring missing, so he had no choice but to hold it.

Tom swivelled the backpack on, clipping both the waist and chest straps to prevent excess movement and looked at his older brother. He stood there like a frightened rabbit, his eyes wide, his leg jittering. Tom couldn't help but feel sorry for him to some extent.

"Right, all you have to do is follow me. Move when I move, stop when I stop. If I say 'cover', then you dive into the nearest bush or lay flat where you are."

"Okay."

"If there's trouble, I need you to step up and help take care of it. Use the taser if needed but no excessive force. We don't need the police after us as well as whoever's in there."

"Okay."

Tom made an assessment of his brother's condition and said, "Get in, I'll drive."

He handed the food bag to Charlie as they both climbed into the van's cabin, Charlie sliding across the drill empty box to sit in its place.

They headed out, the drive taking them past the dock entrance as before. Along the road, Tom pulled off and parked a little past the bridge to the station; leaving a clear space for them and the sack-trucks to run across and into the storage yard opposite.

They got out of the van, removed the sack-trucks from the back and headed over to the storage yard. There was a tall orange streetlight in front of the van which threw shadows around like a paint splatter, creating a sense of menace as they moved further away from it, their shadows growing ahead of them. Tom tapped in the pass code to the lockup's yard and pushed the gate open. Charlie followed pushing the sack-trucks, one hand still awkwardly holding onto the taser, the food bag dangling from the other. Tom searched around the floor until he found a discarded piece of cardboard on the ground. He picked it up and folded it several times into a long rectangular shape. He moved back towards the gate lock and placed the cardboard on the magnetic strip that secured it. It bounced at first. Tom took off a folded layer and replaced it. This time the gate held closed, the cardboard holding the magnet far enough away to stop it from making contact and locking but close enough to keep it in place. He removed the cardboard and kept hold of it, allowing the gate to close.

Charlie watched in awe at his little brother and the things he did seemingly without thought. They made their way to the container. Once inside, only a fragment of light found its way through so before they closed the door, Tom slid off the backpack and opened up the front pocket to retrieve his head torch and a strip of chewing gum from a very old and battered packet. He then pulled the container door closed, slipping the gum into his back right pocket and turned on the torch on his head.

They put their gear down and Tom looked at his wrist, palm up, to see the time. He had no recollection of turning the face around and was more surprised that he looked for it that way automatically. They settled down; it would be a while before it was late enough to begin.

They sat opposite each other, their backs leaning against the cold metal folds of the container. The torch was pointed to the ceiling, but any light was quickly lost to the darkness, barely any falling back down.

"How long will we be waiting?" Charlie asked.

"A couple of hours ought to do it," Tom replied.

A few moments of silence was maintained before Charlie spoke, "Thanks for doing this Bro, I appreciate it."

"It's not like I had much of a choice, did I?"

"Well, you could have said no and dealt with that, but I'm glad you didn't."

Tom sighed, "It's my own fault; I should have left a long time ago after I came back, but I just can't seem to get away. No matter what I do or where I go, I'm stuck with you, where I come from and who I was."

There was a heavy pause.

"Why do you think you're a cut above the rest of us, something different, something better? You were hardly around as a kid. When you got away to the Marines that was the last we saw of you; then when you came out and got your degrees and your job you may as well have been still in, Moving to Henleaze to be all snooty; forgetting who you are, practically disowning your family."

"I've never thought I was better than you. I just didn't feel a part of it, it wasn't me. I wanted something different for myself than the shit that we grew up with, the narrow boundaries and low expectations. Can't you see that there is more to life than dealing drugs, doing shitty manual labour for neighbours and the petty crime that seems to be a daily way of life for you?"

"I do what I have to do, to get by!"

121

"But you don't have to do that. You're trapped within the limits of your mind; within the narrow borders of Knowle West so much that you've never tried to find something different, something better."

"I go out of Knowle West!"

"To where? Hartcliffe? Hengrove? For what? To commit more crime or to look for a fight? Have you ever drunk anywhere except The Fighting Cocks or The Inns of Court? You feel safe within these borders, within that white, working-class mindset that you're determined to maintain even though it does nothing for you except keep you down."

"We can't all be geniuses like you!"

"But that's it Charlie, I'm not a genius. I've just tried to find a different way. It wasn't easy going to university when school had been so chaotic, when my mind kept wanting to return to the safe confines of the past. Trying not to believe all those things my head kept telling me about myself. That I'd never amount to anything; that I was from Knowle West so shouldn't expect anything but crime and poverty; that I didn't belong anywhere else so I shouldn't even bother. Do you know how difficult that is? To be standing in front of a hall of graduates giving a lecture knowing the things I've done; the place that I came from?"

Charlie remained silent.

"Christ. By the time we were their age, what hadn't we done?" Tom took a breath.

Charlie giggled. "You remember the time we stole that car from Tavistock and drove it onto Filwood fields? Driving it past the cop shop, we couldn't get it out of first!"

"I remember. You set it on fire to stay warm. When the police came, we legged it over to Whitchurch and hid in the sports centre."

"Yeah we did," Charlie laughed out loud.

Tom remembered the fun it had been and the thrill of the chase, but he also knew the other side and what pain that would have caused.

"Did you know whose car it was?" Tom asked.

"No, but I'd never seen it before, so it was fair game."

Tom sighed, "Don't you see how stupid and moronic that was?"

"It was only a bit of fun!"

"But to the owner it may have been their lifeline, their only form of transport. We could have left them without a vehicle that may have cost them their jobs, their livelihood, cost them their life savings to replace, their insurance going through the roof."

"We were only kids."

"But you think it's still funny now!"

"I haven't burnt out a car in a long time!"

"But you still have that frame of mind. That stealing and burning a car out is just a bit of fun with no mind at all on the consequences of your actions."

"Don't talk to me about consequences of your actions!"

Tom stopped dead and stared across the blackness into Charlie's eyes that he knew would be staring back at him. "That was different."

"Was it?"

"You know it was."

"Well, just don't forget it."

"That's the problem Charlie, you won't let me forget it. *I* won't let me forget it. Would you be happier if I just let that weight drag me down and go to work for Stan-The-Man like you? That I lived back on Novers Lane and got drunk and played darts in the pub with you every weekend? Getting by on benefits, cash in hand jobs and stealing?"

Tom knew that some of that Charlie would have liked for him. A brother in arms as well as in blood.

Finally, he answered, "That's not what I want for you Tommy. I'm proud of what you've achieved. Maybe it makes me feel bad as it shows me what a shit show I've made of my life. I didn't have much of a choice you know. I'd been working for Stan since he ran weed and glue from his car. Life at home was fucked up, you know that. I had to get out and make some money and that was the only way. Before you knew it Suzie was

123

up the duff and I had to make more money to pay for our own place, then Emily came along. I couldn't run off to join up and get out."

They both sat there in the silence with the echoes of their words reverberating off the metallic walls.

"If only things were different," Charlie sighed.

"Yeah," Tom agreed without the energy to figure out what that would need to be.

"You know that Knowle West could have been a very wealthy area?" Charlie said.

Tom snorted, "Really?"

"Oh yeah! Back in the day, when the old airport was running, it was the main one used in Bristol, during the war. It was involved in training pilots and testing new planes. It was so popular that the surrounding area kept growing with new estates shooting up, but then that's what eventually killed it. When the airport needed to be expanded, an extension of the runway was impossible with all the new housing, so they decided to open a new one where it is now; a million miles away in the arse end of nowhere, which makes no fucking sense. That sealed the fate of Knowle and Whitchurch. The old airport closed, the jobs dried up and the only industry that stayed was the tobacco factory."

"How do you know all of this?"

"Old Mr Hedges was part of the Knowle Historical Society, the 'Knowle-edge'. While I was fixing his plumbing, he told me all about the area. You know in the Victorian times it was supposed to be a place for Bijou villas of the local businessmen! But the housing estates put paid to that, again."

"I had no idea."

"You should learn a little about the area before you run it down so much!"

Tom hadn't wanted to know anything about the place he grew up in; all he'd known was that he wanted to get away from it as soon as possible, but he must admit, his interest had been piqued.

"Round the back of the vicarage at Inns Court there's even a fifteenth century stair turret that's still attached! And there are remains of old Iron Age and Roman settlements."

"I had no idea."

"Neither did I! It just goes to show."

They both sat in silence again, their minds playing on the events to come that neither one wanted to talk about if they could help it.

The hours passed until Tom checked his watch again, the light from his wrist illuminating his face, "Okay, it's time."

They walked to the door and as Tom turned the light off on his head, he gently pushed it open, his ears grasping for any sounds of danger before his eye could join in the search.

All clear, they stepped out.

"Charlie, you can leave the bag of food in there."

Charlie looked down and was surprised to still be holding it. "Oh yeah," he replied, tossing the bag inside.

The yard was still, darker shadows etched the floor as the last of the sunlight had passed away. They opened the gate and Tom placed the cardboard over the magnetic lock and pulled it to. They walked across the road to the bridge, their heads swivelling with every step to ensure they were alone. Tom grabbed the bottom of the sack-trucks as they got to the stairs and helped lift it up. They walked along the top of the bridge, the docks beyond looked dark and still. There were streetlights dotted around, but it was mostly quiet. The ship from before had gone which made their vision across the area and beyond a little easier.

When they reached the bottom of the steps on the other side Tom let go of the sack-trucks and took the lead down the platform, Charlie jogging behind to keep up.

When they reached the section where the fence turned, they stepped into the overgrown bushes and stopped. They crouched still for a moment to listen for any signs of people or vehicles. All that could be heard though was their own heavy breathing and the pounding of their hearts.

Tom slid off the rucksack and took out the drill. He quickly placed pilot holes in the bottom two and top one rivets of three of the panels. Switching out to the larger drill bit he waited again to check for any risk. Nothing. He then completed their removal with ease, replacing the drill to the backpack.

Waiting again. No sounds.

Tom pulled aside the strips of fence and slipped through, turning to hold them open for Charlie who struggled to get the sack-trucks through without knocking against the sides. There was an open area between them and the silos, and a green covered pond just inside the fence. *'Must remember that's there'* thought Tom, not wanting to be chased back to the exit only to fall in.

Keeping low they ran across the grass and concrete and stopped between the first silo and the green building. Kneeling, Tom took out the scope to scan the area ahead. There were a few buildings along the way and storage areas sealed off with tall concrete walls. He tried to find a way through without using the road, but he couldn't see one. They would just have to risk it and find cover wherever they were able.

He spent a while there, gathering as much information as possible. There was some movement of trucks to the left, near the entrance, but nothing deeper inside.

"Now what?" asked Charlie?

"We wait."

Charlie sat down next to his brother. Minutes went by like hours as he wondered what he could be looking at. He couldn't see anything going on.

After a while Tom finally spoke, "Get up. Be ready"

Charlie got to his feet, his heart racing once more.

"Okay, move," Tom whispered as he left the safety of the darkness and began jogging across the forecourt towards the road. Tom took long skipping strides to minimise his foot falls, camouflaging the sound by making it unlike the usual sound of running. It also allowed the maximum time in the air so the quiet between steps could be used to pick up any external sounds from the environment. It didn't matter much as the short-stepped pace and rattling of the sack-trucks behind him gave it all away.

They ran around the first docking area and turned left to follow it along the back edge. A pair of menacing red cranes loomed ahead like giant sentinels creating a sense of dominance over their small and insignificant frames. They turned right just before reaching them and went around the second dock. When they turned left again the building in Westland was almost in sight. They slowed down as they passed a tall white structure with large pipes stretching overhead to join a maze of others to their left; their precise turns and weaves looked almost beautiful.

As they passed and got to the start of the storage items, they ducked in between to catch their breaths. This road led straight to the building, but it was too open to use as an approach. Instead, they headed in towards the maze of storage containers that littered this huge yard. Here they moved slowly, almost at a strolling pace, no noise, no excessive movement of air.

They weaved their way through gaps and around tight corners until the building was in front of them. They stopped again to regain composure.

Tom looked around the edge of the container and scanned the surrounding area. He lowered himself and crawled on his stomach, keeping his shoulder pressed into the dark corner of the container wall until the entire width of the building was visible. It appeared to be the back of it with the fire exit doors on either side; those would be difficult to use for an entry. The front of the building faced away from them. They wouldn't know what was waiting for them until they walked up and met it.

He lay there for a while, just watching the building and getting a feel for the place, looking at the dark windows to see if any shadows crossed or lights flickered. He had almost forgotten Charlie was there until he slumped down next to him.

"So, what's the plan?" He asked.

Tom looked sideways at him. "The plan? The plan is that we have no idea what's inside that building, we can't see the entrance because it's facing the other way. We can't see how many guards are outside and the windows are blacked out, probably because they open to different rooms with who knows what in them."

"So…"

"So basically, we'll be walking into a nightmare with no plan on what it looks like until we are neck deep in it."

They both lay there for a while, thoughts of the unknown in front of them sinking in. The way back looked a hell of a lot more inviting than what was ahead, but the consequences were less appealing.

Regaining some composure Tom finally spoke. "Okay, we'll move across the space and head right towards the back left of the building."

"Wait, are we heading right or left?"

"We are heading right," replied Tom, remembering to keep it simple. "There should be a small space down the side for us to use which will give some cover and allow us to see something of what's there before we go rushing in.

"Okay."

A sudden thought flashed across Tom's mind; *'how the hell would Charlie have done this without him'?*

"Ready?"

"Ready."

Tom picked up the end of the sack-trucks again to prevent any noise.

"Move!"

They rushed out from the containers and across the yard. All was still and quiet, but the feelings of dread and anticipation grew with every metre they crossed. They reached the back of the building without issue and crept to the right to look down the side. It was dark except for a small yellow light piercing through a side window.

"Leave the sack-trucks here," Tom whispered as they began to creep quietly along the wall towards the light.

The window was quite high up and allowed plenty of room to crawl underneath, but Tom stood up and slowly began moving his eye around the bottom edge of the corner to peer inside.

Sweeping the room as he moved, he could see filing cabinets in the corner, a couple of desks, one below this window and another underneath a window to the front. With his ear so close to the wall he could make out muffled sounds of movement and talking from inside. His eye continued its path until he saw an open door to a room beyond and in that he could see two pairs of legs sitting on what looked like a sofa, blue light of a TV came from in front of them. The talking from the TV speakers was dull and tinny with the real voices low and deep. Tom moved his head a little further round until suddenly, a third figure walked through the door and entered this room.

Tom froze, any sudden movements would draw attention to the window, so against every instinct, he slowly began rolling his head back away.

"Well?" whispered Charlie.

Tom placed a finger on his lip with a look that said, *'shut the fuck up'*.

He waited a few seconds until he heard the louder voice and footsteps leave the room and move away.

Kneeling down he motioned for his brother to come closer.

"There looks like three people. Two sat down watching TV and one moving around. We need to get that one outside to take care of without alerting the other two. Then we will need to go in fast and take them."

Charlie nodded. "How do we get him out alone?" He asked.

There was no easy answer. Usually there were three scenarios that could be played out; one where they would create an unusual commotion to draw out the people inside, but that would alert all of them which was no good here. Second, where you would observe the guard pattern and the paths they took and take them out silently along their routes; but they had no way of knowing if they would ever come out to do a sweep of the building let alone which way they would move. Third and most aggressive, they would simply use flash bangs and storm the building with overwhelming force.

Tom looked over at his brother who was crouched down fingering the electrodes of the taser in his hand. That was definitely not an option. Perhaps a combination of one and three; a small noise that would attract only casual focus to draw out one to have a look; then rush the other two.

Tom stood back up to see if he could spot where the front door was in relation to the TV when he heard more 'real' talking from inside. He moved his eye back in place and saw four other men walk into the TV room from deeper inside. He heard muffled laughter and talking as they moved around.

That made seven men with who knew how many more inside. That changed things completely. Charlie was looking up at him with expectant eyes.

Tom crouched down again shaking his head. "There is now a count of seven inside plus more potentially unseen."

Charlie's eyes widened at the new information, his mind searching for a solution and coming up blank.

"What do we do?" he finally asked.

"Nothing. We can't do it under these circumstances and to do so would result in complete failure and probable death."

"But we have to!"

"No Charlie. Unless you can tell me a way to take care of seven men, probably armed, with only the two of us and a pair of tasers, it's not happening."

"Can't you use some of that Marine shit?"

"That Marine shit would involve trained soldiers with proper equipment, resources and intel. What that Marine shit would tell you in this situation is to remove yourself as quickly and as quietly as possible to reassess for another day."

"But we don't have another day," Charlie's voice began getting louder than a whisper.

Tom frowned heavily and put his finger to his lips with force. He pointed behind Charlie, back the way they had come and began to move.

Charlie led the way back to the rear of the building. With a quick scan Tom pointed back across the yard to the maze of containers. Charlie went to grab the sack-trucks, but Tom stopped him and shook his head.

They ran back across the open area and into the darkness of the narrow corridors again. Once out of sight they stopped.

"What the fuck are we going to do now?" began Charlie.

"We go home"

"And then what?"

"Then you tell Stan the situation and work out another way to pay off your debt."

"He's not going to like that."

"He's going to like it a hell of a lot more than both of us being tortured to give up his name and the war that follows on his doorstep."

Charlie thought about it for a second and nodded.

They retraced their steps back to the fence and climbed through, replacing the posts as straight as possible. They walked over the bridge calmly, back in the safety of an unrestricted area, but still feeling like they shouldn't have been there.

They threw their stuff in the back of the van. Tom walked over to the storage gate and opened up with a simple push, kicking the cardboard away as it fell. He retrieved the food bag from the container and locked up, closing the gate behind him.

As he crossed the road, he saw Charlie sitting in the passenger seat again looking dazed. He walked around and climbed in the cab handing him the food.

"Eat something."

Charlie reached inside the glove compartment and pulled out his tobacco tin, removing a cigarette already prepared from inside. He lit up before looking into the bag.

The drive back to pick up Tom's car was silent; a mixture of disappointment, anxiety and relief swirled around the cabin of the van like the smoke from Charlie's roll up. Pulling in next to the car, Tom left the engine running and got out.

Charlie came around and they met at the back. "Thanks for trying," he said.

"No problem," Tom answered, and they hugged for the first time in probably decades. There was nothing more to be said. Charlie moved into the drivers cab and closed the door.

As he pulled away Tom retrieved his keys and stood by the rear of the car. He paused, leaned forward to place both hands on the car and threw up; take away noodles and peppers sprayed the floor and his boots. He wiped his mouth and opened the back, changing as he stepped around the pile of puke at his feet. Each piece of clothing brought him back a little more from the edge.

He drove off feeling empty. The worry of the last few days and the relief at not being able to do the job was immeasurable. He had shown up for his brother and had gotten away with not having to go through with it. He could return home safe to his beautiful wife waiting in bed for him, and his amazing son all snuggled up under his duvet. The thought brought tears to his eyes again, but this time they didn't flow. They sank back inside with the thought of his brother telling Stan that they had failed. What would be the result he wondered? Would Charlie get a proper kicking or assigned another impossible task? He didn't know, and at that moment he didn't care. He would drive home slowly, wasting some of the time it would have taken to return from Southampton before finding his way home.

# 13. THE PRISON

## 1983 – AGE 10

Gradually, Tom spent more of his time at his secret hiding place and continued to watch the goings on inside with fascination. Sometimes he would leave it a while and hang around with his friends just to change things up a little. He had considered telling them about the place so that they might enjoy it together, but they were not the type of people who could keep things to themselves and before long he knew everyone would know about it and it would be ruined. So, he decided to keep it to himself. He liked secrets; they were a silent way of exhibiting power; a way of having control over something when everything else was out of his control.

He spent so much time away from the house that he was as barely aware of the activities of the rest of his family as they were of his. That changed drastically though when one day he returned home from school to find his mother sitting at the kitchen table, sobbing in a way that Tom had never seen before. His mother's best friend, Helen, was sitting next to her, rubbing her back and speaking soothing words. Tom froze at the sight before him, wracking his brains to work out if his mother's tears were connected to anything he had done.

Through her cries, his mother spotted him and in one motion sprang from her chair and hugged him tightly, wailing, "Oh Tom, oh Tom!"

Tom's next thought was that someone had died. He hadn't seen his brother or his father in a while and only now wondered where they had been. If one of them had died, would he be expected to cry as well?

Helen moved over and continued rubbing Tom's mother's back, as if it was the only thing to do in such a situation, but what situation?

After some time, Tom's mother relinquished her grip on him and slumped back down into her seat. Tom sat opposite her and waited for the explanation of what was going on. His mother tried to keep her sobs under control long enough for words to come out, but only managed a series of unintelligible consonants, punctuated by sharp intakes of breath that ended with a descent into more crying.

Tom looked to Helen, who seemed remarkably calm considering that a possible death was about to be announced to an unsuspecting child. She wrapped an arm around his mother, stared at Tom and took a deep, dramatic breath.

"Tom," she began. "Your father has been arrested."

"What?" He replied.

"He's been arrested and charged with fraud. Apparently, he has been renting out the company trucks without them knowing and pocketing the money. Although, god only knows where he's been spending it 'cause it certainly ain't here!"

Tom's mind spun. His dad had been arrested? When? How? He searched his mind for the last time he had seen him and thought maybe it was a few nights ago.

Tom's mother reached out her hand, over the table and took Tom's, an unusual position. She tried to smile through the make-up streaked, tear-soaked face as she whispered, "it'll ... be ... okay." She squeezed his hand, "it'll ... be okay".

Tom smiled back and nodded. "I'm just gonna get changed," he said, pointing to the door out of the kitchen. His mother nodded back and let go of his hand. As he left the table and closed the door behind him, he could hear a new bout of crying erupt.

The next few days and weeks were stressful for everyone in the house. His brother appeared more often as did old friends, family and concerned neighbours all turning up to show support, but mostly to just get the gossip and be a part of the drama. During this time Tom kept himself out of the way either in his room or in his den. He didn't want the company of these people, preferring the places where he felt safe. His mind was filled with the thought of his father behind bars and what might be happening to him. He had seen American TV shows where prison was a form of torture, where you were beaten, murdered or worse. He couldn't believe his dad would be in such a place.

\*\*\*

On the day of the court case and sentencing Tom's house felt like it was hosting a wake. Everyone in suits and dresses, bringing dishes of food and taking it in turns to console Tom's mother, and just like a death, nobody knew what to say to the child. They just looked at Tom and smiled; some apparent family members who he had never seen before ruffled his hair.

Tom hated every second of it and had to steal himself away several times in order to maintain his outward calm. He so wanted to get his knife out of his pocket and tell them all to piss off. However, he did begin to learn more about what actually happened and how his father had been caught by the numerous quiet and not so quiet conversations that were being had around the room.

Apparently, his father's best friend, who also worked at the same place, was in on the fraud, but when the company started to find anomalies and ask awkward questions, he squealed to the police and put it all on Tom's dad's, claiming that he himself had little to do with it.

This complete act of betrayal stabbed at Tom's heart; he couldn't believe that a friend would do such a thing. True, he hadn't experienced friendship like that himself, but he had seen it in the movies so knew what it was supposed to be like to have a best friend. Tom vowed that whenever he had a best friend, he would never do that to them; he would make sure that they would never do that to him either. It would be a brotherhood, a bond closer than anything. He would do anything for them; they would look after each other no matter what.

\*\*\*

It wasn't until a month later that Tom and his mother were allowed to visit the prison where his father was being held. For the visit, his mother had bought Tom a toy car to play with. It was a big white sports car with stripes down the side that you could control with a clicker that made it go forward and back. It was something to keep him occupied while they talked, no doubt.

Both Tom and his mother were dressed in their smartest clothes. Tom's mother had spent a long time just staring at herself in the mirror whilst putting on her makeup. When they finally began to drive, it was in silence. Tom's mum stared ahead as she drove, and he suspected that she wasn't really seeing much of the road in front of her. He stared out of his own window and tried to picture what he was about to go into, what his father might look like and how scary it might be; the images of TV shows and movies filled his mind with horror stories. Still, he had his toy in his lap and his friend in his pocket.

Pulling into the parking area, the prison front looked relatively small and unimposing, not overly threatening at all. As they walked towards the entrance, Tom could see that it looked clean and relatively new. This relaxed him a little until they reached the guard station. A man with a very serious face came outside to check the papers his mother handed over. Looking down at Tom, he said he liked the toy car. He bent down and took it from Tom's hands, inspected it and returned it to him with an attempt at a smile. Tom just stood there, frozen to the spot and only jolted back to reality when his mother pushed him forward towards the building. He suddenly wondered what would happen if he was searched for weapons. The knife in his pocket suddenly started to burn, as did his face.

Past the guard station were a series of paths that led through to a large courtyard with flowers and walkways that made it feel more like a country garden than a prison.

After being led into the visitor's area and sitting at a table for a while, Tom saw his dad enter in a pair of matching blue trousers and jacket, smiling. After giving Tom a hug and asking how he was, his father began to speak to his mother. Tom was told that he could go over to the children's area and play with the car. Reluctantly he did as he was told.

Whilst he was playing alone there, he had the opportunity to really look around at what a prison actually looked like on the inside. It wasn't as bad as he thought. There weren't any bars on the windows and doors, the carpets and walls were brightly coloured. The guards, although tough looking, smiled and didn't appear to be like the thugs he had seen on TV. His father didn't look beat up or anxious about his surroundings and his mother had calmed down considerably. He was the only child in the play area, so he just drove his car back and forth over the floor, slowly making his way over to the window where he was able to look at the grounds beyond. The buildings seemed fairly new and the lawns and plants in the beddings were all healthy and happy. There were people, prisoners he assumed, walking around from one building to the next as if they were simply strolling along the pavement. They were unaccompanied and trusted. Tom thought that there must be a way of keeping an eye on them and thought maybe that there were towers and guards that he had not seen, barbed wire fences just out of sight. The more he looked however, the more he could see none of these things; he couldn't understand what kept the prisoners from simply running away.

When it was time to leave, Tom was allowed to give his father another hug and then he and his mother walked back out to the car park, Tom all the while continuing to look around. On the drive back to their house, Tom sat in the back to give himself a little space with his own thoughts. He was contemplating the experience of the day and found that he had to seriously adjust his view of what an actual prison was like which differed so vastly from what he had been led to believe. It didn't seem like such a bad place.

# 14. SATURDAY

Clutching the bedclothes around him, Tom woke with a start. He had been having a nightmare where everything was being taken away from him and no matter how tightly he tried to hold on to them, they just slipped through his weak and powerless fingers.

He relaxed his head back on the pillow when he realised where he was, frustrated that his sleep kept being taken by monsters. His breathing returning to normal, he heard soft feet coming up the stairs as Ali flowed in with a cup of tea.

"Good morning sleepy head!" She sang, placing the tea on the bedside table.

"What time is it?" He asked.

"It's almost eleven! You needed a lie in after your busy night."

Tom remembered his night and as he did so, an unusual feeling started to develop in the pit of his stomach. He couldn't tell what it was; it wasn't anxiety, fear or relief, but there it was, like an oversized orange, heavy and uncomfortable.

Ali moved over and sat on the bed. She looked at him worried, stroking his face. "Everything go ok?"

"Yep," he lied. "No problem".

She continued tracing her finger over his face for a while as if unsure to take the answer given or to press further. Finally, she decided and said, "Come down when you're ready. It's almost lunch time. We've only had a bit for breakfast so a hearty brunch would be great about now."

She stood up and backed out of the room.

"Thanks honey. I'll be down in a minute."

She smiled, nodded and turned, heading back down the stairs.

Tom's focus returned to the growth of the feeling inside him, trying to get a handle on it, but not being able to. He got up and started his morning routine.

Downstairs, life carried on as normal. The sound of the radio playing, a cool breeze floating in from the patio doors that carried with it the noise of William playing in the garden. Tom came into the kitchen to see Ali standing there looking out through the window. He didn't know what he expected to see that morning, the morning after, if he expected to be able to see anything at all.

He moved around behind her and kissed her slender neck; her hair was up in a bun and gave him easy access.

"I love you," he whispered, continuing his volley of kisses.

She turned and placed her arms around his neck.

"I love you more," she replied.

William came running in to break the momentary lovefest.

"Come and play!" he yelled, grabbing hold of Tom's hand and dragging him outside.

Tom willingly allowed himself to be pulled out to the patch of flowers growing in the borders to the left. Here, William had placed several of his toy figures and cars in a sort of battle formation; one team versus another in the jungled overgrowth of hydrangeas, monkey grass and hosta. Further along, on the rocky section, where the creeping thyme filled the gaps like moss, stood Eleanor, like an overseer of the kingdom, the newest and therefore most important toy in the garden.

They played there for a while, moving the toys around and doing battle, hiding behind stems and cloaking under leaves. It didn't take long for William to move on, to grab the cars, including Eleanor, and take them to the patio area in front of the man cave, a much smoother surface to drive over. As they pushed the cars along, they made skidding noises as they drifted around corners, Tom could see the faint boot prints from that morning's return and reversed his toy car away, spinning 180 degrees to avoid the thought of it.

They were just getting a little bored when a wonderful word echoed around the garden.

"Food!"

They both scrambled to their feet, Tom scooping William up as they ran in.

On the table waiting were steaming hot omelettes filled with sausage, onion, mushrooms and small flecks of black pudding. A fry-up in one. They devoured every mouthful; Tom savouring the flavours like it was either the last meal of a condemned man or the first meal of a prisoner released.

With their stomachs full and energy high they decided to spend the afternoon at the local park. Walking there, hand in hand with William between them wanting to be swung every few steps, felt like heaven. They began singing a song, *"...and I would walk five hundred miles and I would walk five hundred more..."* He couldn't remember the last time they had walked like this, taking the afternoon to just enjoy the late summer sun and each other. As they approached the park gates, William shook off his parents and rushed in, leaving the empty hands behind to find each other.

There were numerous benches dotted around the edge of the play area and Tom and Ali found one that was pretty central. They snuggled close as they watched William climb the frames, scoot down slides and balance across ropes. The sun was fairly high but was being filtered through the leaves of the tall oaks and hawthorns that surrounded the park and created an atmosphere of peace and tranquillity.

After a while, Tom couldn't contain himself; he kissed Ali and ran off towards William. William saw him coming and screamed, running off to find shelter atop the nearest climbing frame. Tom stayed below, like a giant, looking for the little boy who had snuck into his lair and stolen his golden egg.

William giggled madly as he jumped down to be chased, only to climb another frame, safe from the giant's reach. Tom was lumbering around exclaiming loudly, "where is this little boy!" The other children looked at him a little weird, but the mothers were all staring, a little in love with this playful father.

Ali sat there and watched the scene unfold before her. Each time Tom looked over she was just staring and smiling at them. It wasn't too long before she couldn't hold back any longer herself and raced over to William just as the giant was getting close and offered him a helping hand of escape.

They ran around laughing and joking for hours and it wasn't until a cold breeze ruffled their sweaty necks that they realised the sun had fallen so low.

They gathered themselves together and were making for the exit when Tom said, "Do you fancy heading to The Victoria for food?"

Ali's and William's eyes lit up at the thought of staying out and they turned around and headed in the opposite direction.

The Victoria was a cute little pub that had a lovely rural feel and great food. It was very 'woody' inside, with smooth wooden floors, stressed wooden planks on the walls and a tiny wooden panelled bar. They found a table on the back wall and sat. There were a few people in here already including a group of eight in the 'snug', celebrating a sixteenth birthday. Balloons, presents and cake were tied up and dotted around the table as happy sounds of laughter filled the air.

The table where they sat was another one of Tom's favourites. Behind him were several almanac books of years gone by, one of which was the year Tom was born. He loved flicking through and seeing what was happening at that time, which countries were in turmoil and what celebrities had died. He didn't look today though, he was too busy scanning the menu and enjoying time with his family. They talked about William's nursery; his teacher was Miss Freeman, a twenty nothing angel who was the loveliest person in the world, apart from his mum of course. She read them stories, took them outside and taught them about worms and snails, and played them music on her guitar while they painted. It did sound pretty idyllic. His friends, Sebastian and Toby, were in Blue Group like William. They sounded a little crazy, but certainly helped bring William out of himself and meant that he couldn't wait to be there for the whole day on Monday.

Ali told them about the bridge project on Gypsy Patch Lane; that after years of complaints about the narrow tunnel under the railway line with near misses and the regular destruction of wing mirrors, they were finally going to expand it, that meant the tunnel, road and rail line would be out of action for a year, which then caused even more complaints. You just couldn't win! People didn't understand that you couldn't simply carve away the opening of an active train line above a live road while it was still in use. That the whole section of track would need lifting up including the sleepers, sidings and tonnes of earth and gravel and that to actually build the replacement bridge would need a manufacturing plant on site to mould the hundreds of tonnes of concrete and steel frame. And then to store and replace all the earth they had removed, expand the road and align the tracks including all the testing took time, planning and skill.

She was in her element telling them about the engineering details, the weights, the processes and people involved. William and Tom spent most of the time just staring and nodding without even knowing what questions to ask.

The food arrived along with a couple of beers and a juice as their conversation continued. The warm air gently strolled in through the door and casually made its way around the room bringing a Mediterranean feel to the evening that reminded Tom of their honeymoon in Venice; the stroll across St Mark's square, the warm early evening breeze, the chatter of happy people; a perfect time.

Finishing off their meal they headed up the narrow hill towards home. The temperature was probably colder than it felt as they happily meandered along, warm in the glow of the day. They fell through the door ten minutes later feeling the effects of their play and full stomachs, William yawning as he slipped off his shoes. They put on some music and sat on the sofa and in no time at all William was fast asleep, his head tilted back at an impossible angle, mouth open wide catching flies.

Tom picked him up gently, bringing his head back to a more comfortable position and carried him up the stairs. Although he felt hardly any weight at all he could tell that he was getting heavier, growing older. Pulling the duvet back with one foot, delicately balanced to avoid any sudden moves, Tom placed him in his bed, removing his socks for good measure. Covering him up, he sat there for a while, reflecting on the day they had had; the perfect family day that could have been so easily missed. He leaned over and stroked his hair before leaving him to sleep.

When he went back down, Ali was returning from the kitchen with a bottle of wine. They smiled and sat facing each other at each end of the sofa, legs entwined in the middle. It was still relatively early but somehow felt much later after their activities. This time twenty-four hours ago Tom was heading out the door with a completely different evening before him. The surreal nature of the past day was not lost on him. Laying here now it felt more like a dream than reality. He marvelled at the mind's ability to adjust and adapt so quickly to wholly opposed situations, to be able to return to a normal state without effects.

Of course, he knew that there were effects; that the PTSD so many of his colleagues faced daily was no illusion. He felt something himself, the heavy ball that was still knotted in his stomach had remained with him since this morning. He still wasn't sure what it was; it wasn't post-traumatic stress or post situational comedown. It was an emotion still to be identified. The feelings he had from his service in the military, the things he had seen, the emotions that could overwhelm him were kept locked away, safe and secure so he knew it wasn't that.

"How you doing?" Ali asked from across the way, seeing his mind whirring.

"I'm good," he replied, bringing his focus back to her.

"That was a great day," she smiled.

"It sure was."

"Hope you didn't have any other plans that were interrupted?"

"Well, I was hoping to catch up on some work," Tom said half-jokingly.

"Well, there's still time!" she replied, moving her legs out of the way for him to get up.

Tom grabbed them and brought them further onto his lap. "Not a chance."

He began massaging her feet as she leaned her head back and closed her eyes. "Are you getting saucy Mister?"

"I'm just giving you a foot rub," he replied innocently.

"Just a foot rub, eh? Perfectly innocent!"

"Exactly."

"So, you'd give a guy a foot rub?" She said, mimicking that movie line.

Tom held her ankle and switched from using the front pressure of his thumbs to the narrow tips of his fingers.

Ali sat back with a start, "don't you dare!"

At that he tickled her feet even more fervently, eliciting shrieks of laughter and annoyance. Ali's body went through fits and spasms until finally she broke her legs free of his grasp.

"Right," she said, curling her legs underneath her, arching her body forward like a lioness ready to pounce.

"Now don't do something you'll regret," said Tom, seeing the change from victim to hunter before him.

She pounced before he had time to lift his legs or arms in defence, her fingers clamping to his sides, to the weak points she knew so well; her fingers moving like the legs of a centipede, crawling along the soft space below his ribcage. He was helpless, unable to find the strength to counter this attack, laughter with tears rolling down his face.

"Okay, okay! You win!" He managed to pant between gasps.

She paused for a second. "Really? I win?"

Tom took too long to confirm her victory, so she started again.

"Yes ... Yes ... Really, you win!"

She relinquished her grip and brought her knees higher to straddle him, pinning him below her.

145

"Well, I'm glad that you've finally seen sense; that I am in charge!" She said and took hold of Tom's wrists.

"Is that so?" He giggled, eyebrows raised.

Ali lowered her head and brought her lips close to his, teasingly. "Are you questioning me?

Tom shook his head.

"Good." She kissed him, keeping his hands above his head, holding tight to his wrists to show him she was really in control.

He was not going to complain in the slightest as they continued kissing, lips together, tongues searching until Ali suddenly moved lower and bit his lip. She kept it between her teeth for a few seconds. Smiling, she gently kissed it better before teasing him with her tongue on his lips, running it along the top and bottom, driving him crazy.

He tried to move his hands to take hold of her, but she stopped and pushed him back down, raising her eyebrow. She brought his hands together and clasped them both with her right hand, freeing her left. This she lowered and began unfastening his belt and unzipping his jeans. He was as hard as a rock, so it didn't take much for her to free him. He lay there, not about to move a muscle. She lifted her dress up and slid her pants to the side and with a skilful manoeuvre raised herself up and fed him into her.

She replaced her hand back on his wrist and used them as a solid anchor with which to move. She was incredibly lithe and rolled her body as good as any dancer, sliding him from deep to deeper. Tom could feel the opening of her cervix like an internal kiss with every roll. Each time bringing a gasp of pleasure from her, a pause, then another roll, until they became quicker and quicker. Her clitoris was being stimulated by his pubic hair as her thrusts began building to a powerful sensation. The deep penetration, the movement inside and the rubbing brought her to climax with a deep guttural moan as her body shivered and twitched for ten/twenty seconds; every little move that Tom made sent waves of pleasure throughout her body. After thirty seconds she managed to gasp after holding her breath. She looked down and began moving her hips again in a motion that made Tom's toes curl. Moving faster now, thrusting, sliding, riding. Tom could feel himself building up, building up, and finally spreading his fingers wide above her grasp as he came deep inside, gasping, back arched, hips raised.

Both of their heart rates would have caused hospital machines to go haywire. She released her grip on his wrists and lowered herself onto his chest. Tom's now free hands found the skin around her neck and under her hair.

"I love you," he whispered.

"I love you more."

They stayed like that for a long time, neither one wanting to break away until the deflation inside began to become apparent.

"Better clean up!" she said, dismounting him and sliding her pants back across to keep some of the mess intact.

She skipped to the kitchen and grabbed a roll of paper towel from the side, unwound a few sheets for herself and threw the roll to Tom.

"Thanks!"

"Anytime," she said, walking up the stairs and heading to the bathroom.

Tom took the roll and peeled off a few sheets to wipe himself down, pulling his pants up and fastening his trousers.

As he pulled his belt back together, he felt a buzzing from his pocket and took out his phone. Charlie's name appeared on the screen. He contemplated rejecting the call but thought that he would rather take it now, while Ali was in the bathroom, than him ringing all night and having to answer it while she was there.

"Hey, Charlie."

Charlie's voice was jagged, as if he had been running or crying. "He's got her," was all that came out.

"Who's got who?"

"My beautiful girl," he answered, not holding it together at all. "My beautiful baby girl."

"Emily?"

Only sobs replied.

"Who's got Emily, Charlie?"

147

"Stan! Stan-The-Fucking-Man!"

"What do you mean? You aren't making any sense."

"He's got her, for failing to deliver the goods. He's fucking got her!"

# 15. THE BULLY

## 1984 – AGE 11

In the final year of junior school, Tom was relatively happy and confident. His father had returned home after a few months at Her Majesty's pleasure, but things seemed to be worse between his parents; more arguments and the start of violence. At least he was able to get out and be free from the battles that had started to become frequent.

Being in the eldest year group at school brought with it many benefits such as the ability to push in at the dining room queue, being trusted by the teachers a lot more and also the threat of older bully's all but gone.

By the Easter of his final year the realisation that these glory days would soon come to an end made Tom try that much harder to make and keep friends, friends that would transfer with him to big school. He would often be out at their houses or playing with them in the streets around the neighbourhood. He joined in their games and tried to fit in, even though it was difficult at times. His father's exploits had earned him notoriety and after a growth spurt, he was a good deal taller too which meant that he stuck out wherever he went. This sometimes led to the people he called friends teasing him and ganging up against him, even Justin at times, but Tom went back to them after everything, he tried to get along. He never trusted them though with what was going on inside his head or his home or even with the knowledge of the den, but he hardly ever went there anymore so it didn't seem like a massive secret to keep.

Outside the bottom gates to his school were a series of bars that were probably once used to keep the children from running into the road, but was now used by the local kids, those at the top of the school, to climb on and hang around at. It was common parlance to 'meet at the bars' in the evenings. For Tom it was an ideal place, mid-way between his house and Justin's that allowed him an extra 30 seconds before having to sprint home. His father had become even more meticulous on the times which meant that Tom still had to set his watch to the kitchen clock every evening before he left to make sure he could squeeze every second out of playing without incurring his wrath.

This Friday Tom was at the bars on his own. He usually arrived earlier than everyone else, as soon as he had finished his dinner. He would practice walking on top of the bars, trying to make it all the way around without falling off. His balance was good but making the jumps between the gaps was pretty tricky. He had been practicing for a while and for the last three times had managed to make it all the way. He wanted to show his friends later to impress them.

As much as he tried, he never felt like he fit in somehow, that he was always on the edge. Sometimes he was in and a part of things, but then sometimes we wasn't, and he could never tell which it was going to be. When he was shunned, he would feel like there was something wrong with him, that he was to blame for them pushing him away, that he had done something to make him unworthy. Although he was used to being alone and keeping everything inside, when it came to his 'friends', he tried to be more, to do more to be accepted. So, the dangerous act of walking around a series of slippery metal bars that could just as easily toss him off and cause real damage was an easy price to pay for their attention and the feeling of inclusion.

As the first few kids arrived, they just sat on or swung their bodies over the bars, circling round and round. Tom was waiting for more of the crew to arrive before he revealed his latest ability to amaze them. He could feel the burning desire to show off welling up inside. He kept it in check, just, which made him appear a little too happy and over animated.

Within the hour everyone was there. Justin, who lived the closest, was the last to arrive. Conversation and laughter flowed in the relatively warm evening air. Now was the time, thought Tom. Without warning or any pomp, he walked over to the start of the course and climbed up. He made a bit of a show of balancing there for a second before he took a step, just to get a few people's attention. When he reached the first gap, he leapt across without stopping, keeping his balance under control. All of the group stopped and were now watching as he turned corners and jumped again. The last jump was the most difficult and as he approached it, he could hear their shouts and cheers, some encouraging and some telling him he was going to fall and crack his head open.

Reaching the edge of the gap he paused, more for effect than a need. He let his peripheral vision take in all the eyes that were on him, all the attention. Then he leapt! Landing, his back foot slipped, he wasn't as focused as before, which caused a collective gasp from the audience. He regained his balance, stood up and strolled easily to the end and jumped on the wall.

Everyone cheered and clapped at the thrilling event, the near fall making the whole experience even more tense and exciting. He climbed down and basked in the glow of the group while others had started to try the course for themselves. He had inspired them to achieve greater things. He felt amazing.

From far up the street a number of kids came walking towards them. As they drew closer their identities became clearer. Well, not all of them, but it only took the recognition of one to know who they were as a collective.

"Shit, it's Hancock!" someone yelled.

All the kids froze in place, unsure whether to run or to play dead. Hancock had been the school bully a couple of years before. He had moved up to the big school, releasing his reign of terror on the kids below him. Tom often wondered how he coped being the small kid in a big school having been the master of the playground before. Seeing him stride towards them now with his gang of disciples he guessed that things hadn't changed much. Or maybe he felt the need to come and pick on the little kids again as he didn't get the chance much these days. Whatever the reason, here he now appeared, back in his old stomping ground.

"What are you doing you little dickheads?" he said. He had a slight lisp which further amplified his character.

Nobody answered.

"You still hanging around here like little pricks trying to walk across these fucking bars?"

"Not trying," someone replied. "Tom walked all the way around just now!"

Tom's stomach dropped.

"Who the fuck's Tom?"

All eyes turned to focus on Tom as he looked up, not able to answer.

"You walked around these things, did you?" It sounded more like a challenge than a question.

Tom was just about to answer when someone did it for him.

"Yeah, it was so cool!"

*Just hand him a fucking shovel*', thought Tom.

"Well then, looks like we got here just in time," Hancock said to his gang. "Let's see it!"

Tom shook his head, but all of his friends started mouthing words of encouragement. That's how it felt to start with until it became clearer that they had suddenly switched sides and were all now focused on Tom as the target, joining Hancock and so keeping out of his sights themselves.

Tom had little choice. He walked towards the starting wall and climbed up. Hancock followed and kept close as Tom began. His nerves were amplified by the proximity of this bully. He got to the first gap and considered not making the leap on purpose in order to get this ordeal over with, but with all eyes on him he decided not to. He leapt across and balanced easily on the other side. Every step along the bars seemed to make Hancock angrier, making him move closer to put Tom off. When he reached the middle gap Hancock walked through and stood there for a moment, making Tom wait. When he moved, Tom jumped across with ease, revelling in the dissention he was now engaged in. He could hear whispers below of how cool he was, doing it in front of Hancock, that he was braver than they thought; all of which was pissing Hancock off even more. At the last gap Tom paused again. Hancock had moved to the inside and held his hand out a little too unnaturally which made Tom think that he might try and swipe his legs out if he landed. The instruction was clear, fall yourself or I'll make you fall.

Tom had a choice; obey the bully or not. He decided.

Tom leapt across the gap and landed safe and secure on the other side. Almost instantly, Hancock's hand came swinging for Tom's legs as expected. Tom saw it coming and simply skipped over it and leant on the finishing wall while everyone started clapping and whooping. He turned and looked down, seeing steam blowing from Hancock's ears.

"Come here you little shit!"

Tom jumped down to the other side of the bars as Hancock reached over. There was a pause, a Mexican standoff, a collective holding of breaths as to what would happen next. Hancock suddenly moved towards the gap in the bars to get to him, but Tom had already made the decision to get the hell out of there as fast as possible.

He ran from the bars as Hancock found the exit and gave chase. He was close. Tom leaned forward, he was used to racing home at speed and started pulling away. But the excitement of the evening had taken its toll and he felt like he was getting tired and slower with every step, like he was being pulled backwards. He glanced behind and saw Hancock closing and knew he wouldn't make it home in time. He looked ahead and saw the first house on his road. He sprinted towards its open gate, slamming it shut behind him as he ran up the steps and grabbed hold of the door knocker.

Hancock crashed into it, but it held firm. They stayed there for a few seconds, Hancock contemplating running in and punching him before he had time to knock and the man inside to come out; Tom ready to knock the hell out of that door to get the man out here fast.

As they stood there, Tom realised that his other hand was in his pocket, clasping onto his penknife. Surely this was the perfect opportunity for him to pull it out and use it, or at least to flash it around and stand up to this bully.

With his thumb, he unfolded the blade in his pocket, ready to bring it out, but something stopped him. What if Hancock just laughed and took it, using it on him instead? Tom felt paralysed and unable to do what he wanted.

Before he had a chance to persuade himself to do anything different the door knocker was thrust from his hand as the door swung open. Tom turned in shock to see an elderly man standing in the doorway staring at them both. He had heard the commotion outside and had come to investigate.

"What the hell are you doing? Clear off the both of you!"

Tom looked at Hancock, not prepared to leave the safety of the garden until he had gone. Hancock could see this. He pointed his finger at him. "I'll fucking get you."

He walked off, the man at the door beginning to understand what had happened.

"Are you alright? Do you want to come in for a while?" The man kindly offered.

Tom shook his head. "No, thank you."

He walked back towards the gate and stepped out, watching Hancock in the distance being surrounded by his now adoring fans, all of them shouting at Tom for being a pussy.

Tom turned and began walking up the road to his house. Why hadn't he just fallen off the bars? Or even better, why hadn't he pulled out the knife and showed Hancock who the fuck he was. That he wasn't afraid of a dickhead like him. But he had been too afraid to do anything but run. What was the point of this knife if he was unable to use it?

He got home and went straight to his room, throwing the knife at his bed in anger, seeing it disappear into the dark recess underneath. He felt useless, powerless and utterly humiliated.

# 16. SUNDAY

Knowledge is a strange beast. Sometimes things appear before they are fully recognised, like a creeping tiger in the jungle; glimpses of stripes moving through the shadows, circling, assessing, waiting to make itself known; the crack of twigs and the low menacing growl fuelling an air of anticipation in the night.

So too with Tom, he now knew with absolute clarity what the knot in his stomach was; it had been circling his conscience, thriving on his mounting anxiety; it was the feeling of concentrated, hard-boiled dread. The understanding that just because they couldn't finish the job didn't make it all okay now, all over and done with; that there would be consequences and fallout from their failure. The heavy sphere in his stomach had grown to a bowling ball, pressing against his stomach creating a sensation of nausea; crushing his lungs and stifling each breath; constricting his heart, the pressure unbearable.

He had managed to end the call with Charlie with an arrangement to meet the next morning. He forced as relaxed an end to the evening as he could manage and lay on his back in bed all night; the weight in his stomach drawn through the mattress and almost scraping the floor below.

He lay there in the blackness, in the silence, feeling the world spinning beneath him like a rotating fairground ride, but instead of being pressed against the walls of a spinning cage he was weighed down by the gravity of the situation, experiencing every single one of the Earth's thousand miles per hour as it spun.

There was no stopping to get off, no change of address or destination that would place him anywhere but on this rock as it continued its path around the black void of space.

His mind had been running through different scenarios on what might come next; testing out hypotheticals, judging conclusions and consequences; examining and adjusting parameters.

This involved whether to tell Ali everything, most of it, some of it, or none. To pull away from his brother and let him deal with the fallout completely, somewhat, or to stay fully involved.

He had managed to find and eliminate the options that gave the worst outcomes, the ones where the people around him got hurt the most, but he had yet to find the one way, that one narrow path which left everyone unscathed. Maybe it didn't exist. All the paths forking ahead of him led to the next inevitable point with the casualty count unchanged.

He began to notice the dark recess of the ceiling above become softer as the morning moved closer, the light shade becoming visible, floating in the sea of darkness. It didn't take long before the faint sign of its shadow began to stretch and yawn across the ceiling as the Earth went about dragging the day into existence.

The shadow became his focus now; it was a distinct reality that helped push the unknowns of the night away. He concentrated on the thin dark line of the light chord as it was drawn out towards the far wall where the demon fingers of the shade, knotted and grotesque, hung down and moved as if they were groping for someone, for him.

Hours passed; the hand became clearer but didn't venture further than the wall. The slow introduction of orange softened its effect until it morphed into more of a flower petal, a drooping bluebell hanging on to the first rays of the last days of summer.

He stretched his head to the side without moving his body to see the time on the alarm clock. It read a disappointing six fifty-five. He had arranged to meet Charlie at eight so that he would be able to slip out before Ali woke up, but the painfully slow

157

years that had passed that night left no patience to lie there any longer.

He took a deep breath and forced his frame upright, knot and all, and slipped out of bed. He stepped on the corners of his slippers and stood up, replacing the duvet as softly as possible. His jeans lay next to him, so he thankfully didn't have to open the closet, but his T-shirt and jumper were in the drawers at the end of the bed. He moved around silently, and with effort he tried to break the inertia of the wood without a sound. He failed.

Ali stirred beneath the covers, her breathing changed as he retrieved the items and pulled them on. He moved around to her side and whispered, "I've just got to pop out. Be back in a bit."

He kissed her head and didn't wait for the reply. He walked out and downstairs as quickly as possible before his words floated into her consciousness.

He put on his shoes by the door, grabbed his jacket from the hook and keys from the box and left. As he drove out of the driveway, he saw the bedroom curtain pull back, but he was gone before he could see Ali's confused face looking out.

He drove straight over to his brother's house and knocked on the door. After almost a minute he heard shuffling from inside as Charlie opened it, unshaven, with eyes as bloodshot as an alcoholic's last hoorah. He smelled like whisky and there was a bright red mark across his left cheek. He pulled the door open and stepped to the side to let Tom in.

The air inside was heavy with cigarette smoke and sweat. Charlie followed him in and returned to the chair he had been living in all night; the coffee table filled with empty cans and bottles and an overflowing ashtray.

Tom sat on the sofa staring at the pit his brother had been crawling into all night.

"Tell me what happened," asked Tom.

Charlie leaned forward and rolled a cigarette from what was left in his tin, licked the edge with a shaky tongue and sealed it shut. He lit up and placed his head in his hands. Tom waited.

"Yesterday morning, after we got back, I called Stan and told him what had happened. I told him about us getting to the building, that there were at least seven men inside, probably armed and there were just the two of us with shitty tasers. I said that if we would have gone ahead and got caught and tortured, we would have little choice but to give his name up. That really, we did the best thing in the circumstances."

"And?"

"Nothing, he just listened and when I had finished, he hung up without saying a word. You know what Stan's normally like for hearing his own voice, but he said nothing, which made it worse."

"So, then what?"

"So, then nothing. I thought that he was probably brooding because he knew we had made the right choice which left him without the goods and with me still in debt. I went about the day as usual; a bit or garden clearing, a few runs to the tip. I stopped off in the pub on the way home for a couple when Suzie called asking if I had seen Emily, that she went out with her mates downtown but had suddenly disappeared when they were walking around the shops."

He took another long drag, letting it out slowly, shakily, like a meditational breathing exercise.

"I came home and tried calling her, but no answer. I called her friends and spoke to them, but they didn't know anything except that they were looking around the shop at the time; that they went to show each other something and she was gone. They looked around the place and outside, but she wasn't there."

"Okay, then what."

"Then I got a call from her phone. So, I picked it up, about to have a go at her, but it wasn't her voice on the line, it was Stan's."

He leaned forward and poured himself another shot of whisky, necking it with a look of pain.

"He said that I had fucked up, that there were consequences to my actions and if one consequence couldn't be fulfilled then another one would be. I shouted at him and swore, but he just laughed. He said he'd give me one last chance to get the stuff or Emily would be sent away and used at a tenner a time until all the money plus interest had been paid back. Then I would get back whatever was left of her."

He broke down and cried at the thought. "Suzie knew I had done something. She went ape shit on me, hitting me, calling me names. She left. I told her I'd sort it. That's when I called you."

He finished off his cigarette and reached for the bottle once more. This time Tom placed his hand on his. "That's not going to help."

Charlie pushed his hand away but didn't pick it up.

"What the fuck are we going to do?" He asked.

"We? This is your mess, Charlie. I tried to help you out, but it didn't work."

"This is your niece we're talking about. I get that you don't want anything to do with me, but you've got to help her!"

There was a pause, then a change of tack, "How will you explain to Ali where Emily has gone? To William where his cousin has disappeared to? Why Uncle Charlie and Auntie Suzie spend their days crying and drinking and shouting? Telling him where you were the other night?"

Tom stood up, angry at the position he had been forced into, the weight in his stomach threatening to burst through at any moment. "You're putting that on me? Charlie, you're a worthless piece of shit that has brought the whole fucking world down around him, crushing not only you but everyone around you and now you want to make sure that I'm under the rubble as well?"

He began pacing the floor, the anger welling up inside and finding its way out through his throat.

"It's always been this way. You just can't help it, it's who you are. I should have got the hell out of this town years ago and never looked back. You've screwed me and my life, you know that? You've fucked it all up!"

A cold stare was carved on Charlie's face as he took this rant. "So, what you gonna do about it?" He asked.

Tom stopped and looked at him, contemplating beating the living crap out of him and leaving him to deal with his own mess. But he was right; how would he explain it to Ali? She was bound to hear about it from Suzie or his mother sooner or later even if Charlie kept his mouth shut. No matter the choice he made, she was going to find out.

He picked up the bottle and threw it at the wall, "Aaarrrggghhh!"

Charlie just sat there as the shards of glass scattered around his head like rain, watching Tom slowly regain his composure, his breathing return to normal.

"Now that's out of the way, what are we going to do?"

Tom sat down again and began thinking out loud.

"The job just can't be done with just the two of us and the tools we have. Two versus seven is not the odds of success. We would need at least four people, trained in CQB, to take the building cleanly. We don't have that, or the equipment needed. We could get them all out with a distraction, but they would come out armed and prepared and we wouldn't be able to get the package out undetected. We could switch that around and lock them in and use gas to render them unconscious, but we have neither the gas nor the information on the building to accurately administer it."

His mouth shut as his mind whirled, reliving the previously discarded options from the night until finally he looked at Charlie and asked, "Where would Stan be keeping Emily?"

Charlie's eyes widened and shook his head.

"No way man, no way are we doing that."

"Do you have a better idea?"

"No, but even if we get her out, what's stopping him from taking her again or even coming after yours?"

Tom felt sick rise in his stomach.

"We have to make it clear that it would be in his best interest not to. How much money do you owe him?"

"About fifteen grand."

"Get twenty, that will sweeten the pill. We can get her out cleanly, leave the money and move on."

"Twenty! Where the hell am I going to get twenty grand from?"

"You said you could get hold of the money; that you had already offered it to Stan, but he turned you down!"

"I offered it to him, but I didn't say I had it!"

Tom looked at his brother with incredulity. "What the fuck Charlie! What the fuck did you do with the drugs you stole?"

Charlie looked away.

"Talk to me."

"I gave them to a mate who took them up North. I would get the drugs, he would take them to sell and we'd split the profits."

"And?"

"And I've not heard from him since."

Tom slumped back into the sofa, defeated by his brother's utter stupidity.

"I've tried calling, but his phone doesn't even ring anymore."

Tom had questions forming, but he knew they would be as worthless as the answers he got.

"So, to summarise," Tom began. "You stole drugs from a bad man and gave them to another bad man who has gladly taken them and disappeared. Now the first bad man knows you stole them and told you to steal more drugs from an even badder man to make up for it. The even badder man is almost impossible to steal from so the bad man kidnaps your daughter and you have neither the money nor ability to do anything about it. Does that sound about right?"

"Tommy..."

"No, no. Is that about right?"

"Yeah, that's about it," Charlie sighed.

They both sat there, leaning back and stared at the yellowing ceiling and praying for a divine intervention to appear from between the cracks around the light fitting.

"What about the police?" Tom said finally.

Charlie frowned at him.

162

"Look, if you tell the police they can get Emily, make arrests and nobody is hurt, for now. You'd probably do a little time, but it won't be that bad; you'll be out soon enough, especially if you told them about the stash of cocaine at the docks. You can leave my name out of it and everyone's happy."

"That sounds real nice, but you're missing a little bit there Tommy boy. If I tell the police, there are no guarantees that they will find Emily, and more than likely Stan will bury her somewhere just to get rid of the evidence. If they actually did find her then Stan and his boys, Ry-Man and whoever fucking else is at the docks plus me will all be inside together. Like a cosy little family. And even if we're not in the same prison, how difficult would it be for one of them to find somebody who is and that's the end of me. Then they will still grab Emily and even Suzie, maybe Ali and William and even Mum, all for good measure simply for being my family. I'm not sure I heard that bit in your plan Einstein."

Tom just stared at him. "So, what's your plan then you fucking moron?"

Silence. What plan could there be? Tom continued to stare at him while his eyes simply fell to the floor. There was something he could do, but it would be a gamble. Hell, anything at this point would be a gamble.

"Where will Stan be now?" asked Tom.

"We're not going to grab Emily."

"Just tell me where he'll be right now."

"He'll probably be at his shop in Filwood. He's always there"

"Right."

Tom stood up and headed for the door.

"What are you going to do?"

"I'm going to have a little chat with Stan-The-Man."

\*\*\*

The drive wasn't far and almost took him back to his old house where his mother would be sleeping soundly no doubt. He turned right at the roundabout and headed up past Inns of Court. He hadn't been here for many years and was surprised to see the extent of the changes that had happened in his absence. The pub had been knocked down, which made him feel a little stupid accusing his brother of always being in there before. He drove past where his old den used to be, the concrete slatted fence was still there but the big green containers were gone. He felt an urge to jump over and have a look at what was there now. Everything appeared to be so much smaller than he remembered it; much closer together as if it had all shrunk in the wash.

He carried on up the road and past the football club on the right and the road left that led to the police station. He looked down at it as he passed with a feeling of both distrust and need. When he turned left onto Filwood Broadway he was shocked to see the swimming pool had been pulled down. Many hours of PE and a countless number of verrucas had been shared inside that building. Out of the whole area, that had been the most popular and most used, so why had it been the first to go?

He was pleased to see that the library was still standing at least. The Broadway was a wide street with a tree lined centre splitting the two directions of traffic. He slowed as he drove up past the church and saw more buildings had been pulled down just past it. He felt bad that he couldn't remember what had been there before. The old theatre still stood, graffiti covered and empty. Here is where the shops started, an off licence, body piercings, bookies, newsagents. Directly in front was the imposing Filwood Community Centre; a wide rectangular building with a large garden courtyard in the centre that wouldn't have been out of place in an upmarket Victorian neighbourhood. It had always seemed to Tom to be out of place here. He recalled what Charlie had told him about the area's history and some of it started to make sense. He parked on the corner and got out. Stan's shop was on the other side of the Broadway, so he first crossed over towards the community centre to maintain some distance.

His old school was only five minutes away and he recalled how his class would file up here in a long narrow row for swimming lessons in their younger years and how that had changed to a slow swagger as they got older, without the need of a teacher to chaperone. But you had to be careful, that's when Stan and his gang would grab you. It wasn't difficult to spot which shop was his. It was the only one with the shutters up and not a smudge of graffiti on it.

As he walked past, he couldn't see inside. There was a white film across the widows making it impossible to know what was going on. The door was closed. He continued walking and crossed back over once he had passed. Around the corner was a driveway through the building that took you to a car park behind the shops and access to the houses above. As Tom turned in, he was met by a black metal gate with a key code blocking his way. It was only a little shorter than him, so he walked up to it, placed a foot on the crossbar and jumped over with ease.

Above the dilapidated shops were two storey accommodations that from this side actually looked quite nice, like shiny white teeth sprouting from black and diseased gums. There were stairs leading up in the distance to a walkway that snaked around the first floor. Below were the plain brick backs of the shops, their solid metal doors were all closed, apart from one.

Outside that door was parked a small white van with its rear doors open as well. As Tom approached, a man came out carrying a large heavy box. He saw Tom and continued to put the box in the van, shut the doors quickly and turned to intercept.

"Can I help you there mate?"

"I'm looking for Stan," Tom answered calmly yet firmly.

The man let his eyes wander over Tom, getting the measure and decided that he didn't fit. "Stan who?"

"Cut the shit, I'm Charlie's brother."

At this the man's eyebrows raised. Tom couldn't tell if he was shocked or impressed.

"Wait here."

He disappeared inside and was gone for less than a minute before he poked his head out and beckoned Tom in.

Inside was bright and open, not the dark seedy location Tom had imagined. He followed the guy past the storeroom. He pointed to an office door along a narrow hallway and kept on walking. Tom made his way down and knocked on the solid door at the end that felt as secure as Evelyn's.

"Enter." The voice rang, deep, almost like a growl.

Pushing the weighty door, a waft of cigar smoke rushed out around the edges, eager to escape the confines of the room. As the door slowly swung open, he first saw a wall of shelving that housed rows of lever arch files, each one with a code and a date on the front. Next, he saw a large industrial paper shredder and behind that, a garden incinerator. Clearly, he had no issue with burning down the building to protect whatever was in these folders. Then came the desk, with a paper tray neatly on the corner, a telephone and notepad and behind it sat Stan.

He was a large man with a shaved head and bushy eyebrows. He had the presence of a giant, but instead of being strong and firm, he was fat and grotesque like a melted ice-cream on its cone, wide at the bottom and pointy on top. Tom noticed a lower piece of his left ear missing from having had an earring pulled out in a fight once and a disfigured nose; not bent and twisted, more like flat, all the cartilage inside having been punched out.

He sat there with a cigar in his mouth, focusing on the papers in his hands. He took the cigar out with thick fingers almost the width of the cigar itself and without looking up gestured to the seat in front of the desk.

Tom walked in, eyeing up items that would make good potential weapons if it came to it, but knew that it would take a hell of a lot more than a stapler to put him down.

He sat.

There were no windows in the room so when the door clicked shut behind him all that took place in here was private.

A minute passed before Stan put the papers down and looked up. He stared at Tom and eventually smiled; dark yellowing teeth blinked in the first light they had seen in a while.

"You know what the trouble is with the world these days?" he began. "Too much damn bureaucracy." He spoke with a deep timbre and broad Bristolian accent.

"Used to be that running a successful business was about reputation and honour; I could simply say something would be done and they could trust that it would; that a handshake was as good as a signature. Now it's all about paperwork, keeping track of everything, holding people to contracts. I swear I feel more like a stock control agent these days than a ... a man of business. Working with manufacturers, imports and exports, transportation of a whole range of items from the mundane to the sensitive. But it does have its upsides. You build up a good network of storage locations worldwide, the contacts to ship and move delicate cargo undetected. Last month I brought in a whole litter of Japanese Tosa. You know what those are?"

"It's a dog bred for fighting."

"That's right, clever boy. I kept one myself, beautiful dogs, amazing golden coat. I'm looking to train it for the ring and am in need of good live pieces of meat for it to practice on."

Tom looked at him unimpressed. Even Evelyn had better scare tactics than this guy although she probably didn't have the means to carry them out.

"I understand that you're in academia now, so you must know what it's like. Pen pushers running the world and holding the purse strings. You must have found the change difficult from a decorated soldier to a university pussy?" Stan leaned back taking another puff, waiting for the response.

Tom simply stared at the man, his heart rate dropped below normal, his breathing smooth and calm.

"I'm not here to talk about the pros and cons of being an asshole gangster or my change in career. I think there are more important things to discuss."

Then there was silence; Tom began to question his tactical approach. Stan simply burst out laughing that quickly changed to a guttural cough as he went on.

"The notorious Tom Hook. It's been a long time!"

"It has."

"I have to admit that I'm surprised to see you here, like this."

"Like this?"

"Well, considering the situation I might have expected a siege with all guns blazing!"

"That's not really what I do anymore, not if I can help it."

"Yes, so I'm learning. So, what can I do for you?"

"I believe you know what you can do for me. You have my niece, and I would like her back."

"I see, so you have come to discuss your brother's debt to me and the terms I have set out for repayment?"

Tom couldn't believe that he was talking about his niece, a child, as though she were a commodity.

Stan continued. "Well, I have no issue with the arrangement. Sure, it's a longer-term investment, but it's one that serves multiple purposes."

"Such as?"

"Well, I get to recoup the cost of the items stolen and even if that falls short, I get to create a whole new story for my reputation. I know it's old school, but it still holds some sway and I'm an old fashioned kinda guy."

"Have you considered the downsides to the arrangement?"

"Downsides?" Stan chuckled, his jowls quivering. "What downsides? Charlie is like a limp dick in my hand. I can squeeze the life out of it, but it just can't get hard. It just doesn't have it in it."

He took a draw on his cigar.

"Now *you* were an unknown. I remember the skinny kid that used to run past here scared shitless, but I've also heard stories, mostly from your brother, about what you got up to in the Marines. Which is why I gave you a test, to see what kind of man you are, now that you wear a tweed jacket. Unfortunately for you,

you passed which has given me enough information to draw some conclusions from."

"What do you mean a test? I didn't go ahead with stealing the drugs so how is that a pass?"

"It shows me that you're very versatile, that you can plan and adapt at short notice, that you have the skills to get into and out of difficult places and assess the situation rationally. It tells me that you weighed up all the options of how to respond to your niece being taken and concluded that a face-to-face discussion was the best way forward."

Tom sat there confused.

"If I had sent any of my men to do that job they would have carried on despite the obvious outcome. They may have done it out of fear or stupidity or an over inflated sense of ability, it doesn't matter. What matters is that they wouldn't have the knowledge and experience to assess and walk away. And they certainly wouldn't have the balls to walk in here afterwards."

Tom was slowly catching up.

"Do you know how many people I have working for me? There's a folder here somewhere with the number. But do you know how many good people work for me? If I want something picked up, that's fine. If I want someone removed, no problem. But if there is anything more complex that requires a deeper understanding and methodical approach then I'm shit out of luck. And in today's competitive market that just won't do."

"Are you offering me a job? After what you've done?"

"Your niece is safe, probably having a relaxing time, for now. It's not her I want, it's you."

Tom let this revelation sink in. The cunning of the man opposite had thrown him completely off guard. He was expecting to bargain and barter for the life of his niece, not his own, not like this.

"But I already have a job," said Tom, almost as if it were a normal headhunting interview.

"We can work out the details later. I'm sure your lovely family won't know the difference."

The mention of Tom's family snapped him back. "My family?"

"Yes, that beautiful wife of yours and little son. They are important factors in this too."

Tom's focus was now sharp. "My family have nothing to do with this."

"On the contrary! I take the wellbeing of my staff and their families very seriously and would never let any pain or harm come to them." He smiled wide at this.

"I can see I've thrown you somewhat?" Stan interrupted Tom's thoughts. "It's a lot to take in, I know. Why don't I give you a couple of days to consider the proposal? Shall we say tomorrow to mull it over and we'll meet back here on Tuesday morning?"

An idea had started to form in Tom's mind. "And what will your other people think of me coming in and stepping on their toes?"

"No one knows anything about this yet. We will manage the onboarding process carefully."

*'Wow, he really did sound like a businessman'*, Tom thought.

"Tuesday," said Tom.

"Tuesday," repeated Stan.

They stood, neither one offering their hand. Tom turned and headed for the door. He could feel Stan's stare boring into him, trying to penetrate his mind to gauge the answer before it was spoken. He walked out and back through the building, this time looking into the front of the shop as he passed. There were a couple of men at a table boxing up bags of something and stacking them to be picked up by the man in the van who appeared behind him now.

"Okay?"

"Yep, all good," said Tom smiling, attempting to convey a sense of a happy conclusion to the meeting. He walked back through the open door and headed out. As the fresh air hit his face his phone buzzed several times. There had obviously been no signal inside that room as notifications came flooding in. He took out his phone and saw several missed calls from Ali and Charlie. As he wondered what he could say to her the phone rang again. It was Ali. He stared at it and contemplated cancelling it. His heart rate clicked out of its composed state and hit the accelerator. He pushed the green button.

"Thank god! I've been trying to get hold of you."

"Sorry honey, I didn't have a signal for a while."

"What's going on Tom? I called Charlie to try and find out where you were, and he sounded in a bad way."

"I need to talk to you about something, but not over the phone. I'm on my way back now. Just know that I'm okay."

There was a pause on the line, "are you okay okay or just okay?"

"We'll talk when I get there."

Tom hung up and walked towards the gate. He called his brother, "Charlie, I need you to get me some things, not through the usual channels. Do you still know that guy from Bristol Batteries?"

"Yeah, what do you need?"

\*\*\*

Tom sat on the driveway for a few minutes before getting out, trying to regain some control over his breathing. He had formulated some kind of way out of this, but it meant telling Ali everything. He opened the door, but there were no tiny footsteps racing his way. Instead, there was silence. As he walked through, he could see Ali sitting in the kitchen with a cup of tea held in both hands.

"I've taken William over to Mrs Fitzsimmons. Thought we needed some quiet time."

Tom walked over and sat down opposite her.

"Cup of tea?" She offered.

"Yes, please," he said, suddenly exhausted.

They were both silent while she made it, until it was placed before him.

171

Tom took a deep breath as she sat down, expectant.

"Okay, so I'm going to tell you something and I know you'll have a lot of questions, but please let me get to the end of the first bit before you ask any. Is that okay?"

Ali nodded and took a sip.

Tom began to tell her all that had happened, from the lunch he had with Charlie to lying about going to Southampton the other night. He told her about not being able to do what was asked and that Emily had been taken as a result. He said that he had been to see Stan that morning and what he had offered as a solution. He laid it all out there.

Ali just sat and listened. She didn't speak; she didn't flinch or avert her eyes at any point. When Tom had brought her up to the present morning, he paused.

She sat there for a while, eyes lowered, running her thumbs along the top of her mug while she thought. The wait was excruciating, and Tom felt every second that went by as if it were a year. Finally, she spoke.

"I have some questions."

"Okay."

"Firstly, why the hell did you agree to do this with your brother in the first place?"

"I didn't have much of a choice. His life was on the line, so I had to help. I know that's difficult to understand. You know he saved me when I was sixteen, and although Charlie and I don't exactly see eye-to-eye, he is still my brother. I couldn't turn my back on him."

Tom's mind returned to that time; he saw Charlie's face disappear into the back of the ambulance at Wills's; he saw the look on his face that other fateful night.

"So why lie to me?"

He sighed, "That I'm sorry about. I figured that if I could just get it done then it wouldn't matter; I didn't want you to see that part of me. If I told you then it would somehow make it real, and I didn't want my past to be a part of our future."

"But it is, already, even more so now."

He just nodded.

"I know about your past, Tom, and Charlie's. You've trusted me with that and although it was hard to understand and accept, I kept it safe. I know it was difficult for you to talk about, to open up like that, it was difficult to hear, but we got through it, together. That should have told you that nothing was off limits for us. You need to trust me."

He recalled now the night he had told her. The fear in his chest was like nothing he'd ever felt before. Knowing that he had to share all of himself with her; hoping that she would understand and not run. The meal he had cooked, the glass of wine, the more than usual nervousness that must have looked strange after their months of dating. The look of sorrow in her eyes and the intensity of her holding him after he had finished was something he would never forget.

She reached out her hand, placing it on top of his with a squeeze and a look of strength.

"So, now that we're in this mess, what are we going to do about it?"

"There is a plan, one that requires you and William to go to your parent's house for a while, just in case. Do you want to know the details or just the main points, because it won't be pretty?"

She looked at him, "I want the details."

"Okay," he said, hoping that the plan itself didn't show a side of him that would drive her away despite her knowledge of his past.

# 17. FLORENCE BROWN

## 1985 – AGE 12

Since his birthday and change to big school, Tom had moved away from the people he had hung around with before. He stopped going to the bars and that side of the neighbourhood. Instead, he began exploring his world in the other direction. He started turning right out of his driveway instead of left, and then right again as he moved through familiar looking streets to the narrow lanes of Camberley that were a series of mazes and dead ends. This fascinated Tom and he would eagerly take new turns and directions through these cave-like passages, between white houses he half remembered.

On one occasion he had found the back entrance to a field with a large single storey building in the distance that looked like a school. The gate was unlocked so he went in with caution to explore. There was a fenced off area just inside the gate that had a concrete tennis court laid out. The wire fence had seen better days with holes and gaps easy enough to climb through and the court itself sparkled with tiny bits of broken glass. To the far left spread open fields, but directly ahead, past the tennis court, he could see some play equipment.

He started walking towards them, keeping close to the fence to minimise the chance of being spotted and as he got close, he saw a small brick playhouse that looked like something from a children's book. Further to his left was a tall metal slide and in between a narrow spiral staircase that wound around a thin central column from which sprouted four poles that bent down

174

to the floor at a forty-five-degree angle; to Tom it looked like a strange four-legged spider. It was to this he went first. He wound around the steps as he went higher and higher, then he grabbed hold of one of the bars as it drew close, threw his legs up and slid down with an enormous sense of pleasure.

'*That was pretty cool*' he thought as he ran up again to try another bar. He tried them all and was especially excited about one that was nearer the top and angled away from the step which meant that he had to take a leap of faith in order to grab it. He jumped off, soared through the air and reached for the bar before gravity took hold and he plummeted to the concrete below. That was it, he had to test himself further. The lower down you jumped the harder it was to grab them as they were that much further away. He began around the tenth step on each of the four bars and then stepped down upon completion. He made it to step seven before one of the bars became out of reach as it was around the other side from where the spiral step lay; his fingers reached, but not quite touched. He made it all the way down to step four before the last one evaded him.

His arms had begun to ache, and his palms were red, so he looked around some more. Behind the bars was a partly covered courtyard with narrow slats in the brickwork. Peering through he could see steppingstones of different heights dotted around so his next challenge was to leap across them all without falling off. That wasn't too difficult, so he tried doing it in different patterns to test the limits of his leap.

Next, he wandered over to the brick playhouse he had first noticed. There was an entrance with no door and a narrow window on each side. There was only space for a single room inside, but it felt cosy. He could see what looked like the remains of a fire in one corner and he imagined people snuggled up around it in the dark. It was an inside camp that was a better version of his own den but with a less interesting view. On the roof was a pretend chimney and after walking around the building he could see an easy way to climb up. So, he did, using the brick window frame, the roof overhang and the chimney to gain leverage.

Once there he suddenly felt like a great explorer conquering the highest peaks. He looked all around at this new vista; at the land he had discovered. From his unique vantage point, the main building's roof didn't look that much taller, and an idea suddenly sparked; that's where he would go next.

He slid to the lowest eaves on the roof and jumped down with ease and ran back over to the courtyard. Once inside he began to scout the edges and corners for foot holds and ledges, but no matter how he tried, the metal window frames were just too slippery, and made them impossible to use. He walked back over to the partly covered area and slid through one of the gaps in the wall and as he stepped through, he looked up. This part had a slightly lower roof than the main one so perhaps he could just wedge his feet or legs into the gap to help him shimmy up.

He turned to face the gap and stepped up, sliding his toe on one side of the slit and forcing his heel down on the other until it held. *'This could work'* he thought as he lifted his weight onto the foot. He placed his other foot in the same way and stepped up again. Another step and he could reach around to find the lip of the roof. He leapt up, pushing from his feet, simultaneously releasing them and throwing himself out to get a proper hold with both hands. Once his fingers were solid, his feet began scrambling up the wall until he could cock his leg over and pull himself up.

He rolled over onto his stomach and stayed there a while. If he was caught up here, he would be in serious trouble, even police trouble, so he would have to take it slow. He looked around and saw no one and nothing that could be an issue. So gingerly, he rose to his feet, walked to the end of the covered area and stepped up to the main roof.

From here the roof looked like a strange, tessellated shape with weird angles and pieces that jutted out masking the shape of the rooms below. He could see a few dome-shaped skylights running through the centre of a large rectangular section in the distance so he wound his way over to see if he could peer inside.

When he got to the first one it was impossible to see through. There was condensation all over the inside and on the outside had grown a good layer of moss. The next one along looked cleaner, so he walked over to see. There was a small patch of clear glass here and as he cupped his hands around his eyes and lent forward, he could see shimmering blue ripples of water beneath. A swimming pool!

Tom was amazed that a school could have its own swimming pool. He had to walk through Filwood for his swimming lessons during PE which, although led by his teacher, didn't feel particularly safe.

His eyes became adjusted to the gloom below and he made out a net on the side that held a wide range of floats and toys, a strange crane-like contraption in one corner and a series of steps along the far end to walk into the pool.

He suddenly felt the heat of the sun on his neck and wished he was able to dive right in. The cool waters below, the toys, the private experience of having the place to himself began to overtake his mind. He strained his eyes to see where the doors and windows were that led to the pool. He got a good idea about the space below and where it might lead before he moved to the edges of the building to look over at the windows below to see if they matched up. As he tight-roped around the perimeter he suddenly noticed that one window was reflecting more of the sky than the others. He got above it and laid down flat for a closer look. The window was open, just a touch, from the bottom.

His heart skipped a beat as he looked around for where that window was in relation to the building and grounds. He noticed that it was in a sort of enclosed garden space with overgrown grass and flowered borders around the edges. If he jumped down, there was no way out apart from in or back up; and there were no easy windows or ledges to make that climb.

He thought for a while and then concluded that if the window was open as it looked like it was, then all he had to do was walk through the building to find another window back to the playground, open it up and climb out. He didn't have to convince himself too hard.

Sliding backwards, he swung his legs over the side of the building and shuffled down until he was dangling at arm's length. He let himself drop, falling backwards as he landed in the flowers. No damage done apart from a few broken hydrangeas.

He walked over to the open window. As he got close, he could see that the metal arm of the lock inside was secured in a hole which held the window open at this angle. Tom slid his hand underneath but didn't have enough strength to prise it from its slot. He looked around and saw a broken piece of wood from the flower bed border and so, with a little effort, he managed to use it to pry the arm up, releasing the window. He pulled it open he pushed himself up, his stomach folding on the window ledge, as he crawl-slid in headfirst, hands grasping for the floor, his knees and shins scraping on the frame.

When his legs finally dropped to the floor the window slammed behind him, shaking the glass. He froze at the noise, wondering if there was anyone in earshot that would come running. He held his breath and waited. When no sounds were returned, he stood up and noticed where he had landed. He was in a classroom, one about the same size as his own but with only enough tables for ten students max. *'This must be some school'* he thought *'to have only ten kids in a class and a swimming pool!'*

He walked over to the door and stopped short before he got there. He hadn't thought about the doors. He flashed back to his own school where the teachers locked everything and panicked; he could have just trapped himself inside.

He reached out his fingers to the handle and gently twisted the knob. It turned smoothly; then he pushed, but the door didn't move. He pushed a little harder and still no movement. Fear began to well up inside as his eyes widened with horror. This may have allowed a slightly clearer image into his retinas as he then noticed the door frame; then pulled. The door opened with ease and a flood of relief washed over him as he chuckled at himself for being an idiot.

The corridors were clean and narrow with a ghostly air to them, images of children and teachers that walk these hallways he now trespassed. He turned and headed toward where the pool should be and less than a minute later, he was staring through a door at the water beyond. He stepped inside and the warmth of the humid air made him gasp. Filwood pool was never this warm.

He looked up and saw where he had first laid eyes on the water and congratulated himself on a job well done. He had discovered the treasure, planned a way in and had executed it thoroughly.

He knelt beside the water and dipped his fingers in. It was warm, but not too warm, inviting even. He stood and walked over to the floats and toys that were stored haphazardly in a net and took one out; a faded red rectangular slab of foam, and tossed it into the pool. It landed with a slap as ripples began to disturb the peaceful surface and echo around the solid walls.

He slipped off his shoes and socks, slid under his T-shirt and stepped out of his jeans. He stopped with his fingers in his pants and decided to keep them on. Despite being alone, he didn't want to be naked.

He walked over and sat on the edge of the pool, his legs dangling in the water and with a quick look around, he let himself slide in completely. The water felt heavenly as he turned on his back and pushed off from the side, sailing to where he had thrown the float. Reaching it, he tucked it under his head and continued to lay there, the quiet and solitude penetrating deep inside him.

His mind began to wander, thinking about his own school. Most of his teachers were pretty strict, especially his maths teacher, but he kept his head down and tried to disappear into the crowd of other boys as much as he could. Even Hancock hadn't noticed him around the playground or fields which he was thankful for. He kept vigilant for trouble which allowed him to steer clear of it. He guessed he had learned that from his home life. The arguing had continued, but the violence had managed to settle into some equilibrium with pushes, slaps and bloody noses only happening a couple of weekends in the month.

He kept out of the way of any of that and would lie on his bed at night and just listen to it happening below, picturing who was doing what based on the screams and bumps. The bruises and fat lips the next morning showed if he had got it right or not. When he couldn't escape outside, he found solace in the music of his record player, stories from his magazines and pictures from his colour TV that used to belong to his brother.

He only now realised that he hadn't seen him in months. The last time was when he was walking to the swimming pool at Filwood; he was going into the bad shop with a fat guy. He had wanted to shout out, but there was something about the way they were talking that didn't feel like it was the right thing to do. If in doubt, keep quiet.

As these thoughts swirled around his mind a new sound began to enter it. He couldn't recognise it at first until suddenly he did. It was whistling.

His body froze as he listened to this tune getting louder. He flipped himself over onto his front and made his way to the edge of the deep end, trying not to make any splashing noises. When he reached the edge, he could clearly hear someone moving closer towards the door he had come through. His head bobbed just above the water line but barely below the level of the floor. He floated there, heart pounding, thoughts racing. The door opened and the tune echoed around the room with a ghostly reverberation.

Tom took a deep breath and pushed himself under the water as deep as he could. From here he could see a dark shadow move along the side of the pool, its outline distorted and morphed like a demon from the ripples. It stopped halfway along and started doing something on the wall there.

Tom knew he couldn't stay under forever. He had watched a program on a deep-sea diver once who was able to go so deep for so long by slowing his heart rate and controlling his breathing.

He had worn long flippers that looked like a fish's tail. Tom now began willing his heart to slow, his mind to calm, thinking about the flippers moving back and forth, seeing the gentle wave of a tail. It was helping as he felt calmness begin to spread throughout his body, his pulse slowing.

The dark figure was still on the side, not moving.

A burning sensation began to appear in Tom's lungs now that was trying to draw his attention away from the calmness. His mind started to join in the rebellion with thoughts of drowning or flapping to the surface and being caught, getting beaten up or hauled away by the police. The image of the flippers and tail began to disappear as the burning started to take over. He couldn't go to the surface, but he didn't want to drown either. He was stuck. He tried to let a few bubbles out of his mouth to fool it that he was breathing again, but it did little for his lungs. Then, when he knew he couldn't hold it for many more seconds the shadow began to move, he followed it slowly, willing it to hurry as it went along the bottom edge of the pool and disappeared from sight.

He couldn't wait to find out if it was still there or not; the air had all run out. He kicked up as panic burst at his rib cage, his head and neck straining for the surface. As his face erupted through, a gasp of air was sucked deep inside. He didn't care if he made a noise as his lungs struggled to work as deep and as fast as he needed them to. He stared at where he had last seen the figure but saw only a door they had obviously disappeared through. He expected them to return at any second with the sound of this wheezing and spluttering and was thankful when they didn't.

He pulled himself along towards the ladder in the corner and climbed out. He didn't have time to get dressed now so simply scooped up his clothes and ran out the door he had come in. The floor beneath him was being drenched in drips and footprints as he sped along the corridors. It would have been an easy trail to follow. He rushed to the very end and turned left, an overview in his mind of his location to the building shape helped navigate him to the far end and as close to the playground as he could get.

He looked through the doors as he ran to see if he could spot where he was and what was outside, but they were all dark, closed blinds over the windows until finally he skidded past one room that had them open, the sun shone in like a heavenly body and showed him the way out. He opened the door and rushed to the window, still gasping for air. He sat on the floor and stuck his legs into his jeans. His damp skin sticking to the material, and he had a real fight to wriggle and squirm them on. He rolled his T-shirt on and reached down for his socks. Where were his socks? He looked inside his shoes and around the floor, but they were nowhere to be seen. He sure as hell wasn't going to go back and get them, so he crammed his soggy feet into his shoes and laced them up.

He stood and looked out of the window. On the other side of this transparent barrier, he could see the playhouse staring at him, surprised to see him inside, its door making a 'oh', its windowed eyes wide. He unlatched the arm lock of the window and pushed it open, the fresh breeze of freedom swept in. He dragged a chair from behind a desk, stood on it and fed his legs through the opening and slid out. He closed the window behind him and ran towards the gate. His lungs were returning to some kind of normal as his legs pounded over the grass, leaving his fear in the building behind him. *That was awesome'* he thought, his feet squelching as he ran.

# 18. MONDAY

Pressing the button on their alarm, both Tom and Ali were already awake. Neither had slept that night with thoughts of everything that had been shared. After William was put to bed, they went through the plan again and again, looking at its impact, the details and the consequences together. It was good to be able to share this thing, even though it felt surreal. They got out of bed and went about their morning routines in a stoic silence, a resolute air to their actions.

Tom went in to wake up William who had cried most of the evening when he was told that he wouldn't be starting nursery full time the next day, but instead he was going on a holiday to Nanny's and Pops' house. As much as he loved them, they were no substitute for his friends.

Tom woke him up with a gentle kiss, "Wake up buddy, time to get up and dressed."

William stirred and smiled at first until he remembered where he was going. His face fell into a frown and his lips pouted out extra hard to make the point.

Ali had packed their bags the night before and they were waiting by the front door. No coffee or breakfast that morning, it was agreed that the sooner they head off, the safer they would be. Tom carried the bags to the car and put them in the boot while Ali strapped William in his seat. He was silently protesting by squirming around, making it difficult to clip the belt in.

When he was finally secured, she closed the door and walked around to Tom who was waiting by the driver's door. They held each other close for a long time, swaying to some unheard music, knowing that the next time they embraced, things would be different.

She pulled away and stared at him straight in the eyes with a steely glare. "Get this thing done."

"I will."

"Safely but without compromise."

"I will."

"I'll be waiting."

"I know."

"I love you."

"I love you more."

They kissed.

She got in the car and pulled away. Tom could see her eyes looking back through the rear-view mirror until she turned and was gone.

He walked back inside and went to the kitchen to put the kettle on; he needed all the energy he could muster. As he stood there, stirring a hole in the bottom of the cup his mind was clear, focused. He had a checklist of jobs to do and the resolve to see them done. The understanding that Ali had shown gave him the strength and clarity to feel like he could switch from who he was to who he needed to be, with the knowledge that she would be there to help bring him back, if he came back. He continued to stir as thoughts of all of his demons being released from the box they had been secured in all these years flowed around his mind. What would they bring with them he wondered?

Draining his cup, he headed out to the man-cave. He moved the chair from in front of the chest and opened it up. The top layer was a bit of a mess from having been rummaged through. He moved the contents aside to find the handle to the lower compartment. He lifted it up to reveal what was just below the surface.

This was a much thinner section that most people wouldn't even realise was there. This part was much neater only because it contained three simple items. Tom picked up the Browning nine-millimetre pistol on the left. It was held in a holster along with two spare magazines. He placed this on the workbench for cleaning and servicing. To the right he picked up two thin holsters in which were sheathed a pair of double-edged knives. He placed them on the table next to the pistol to be sharpened. Then he looked down at the one item remaining. It was black and charred and rusty in places, the cheap metal barely glinting through. Tom picked up the small penknife and stroked it with his thumb, revealing some of the pattern below. It felt delicate and light in his hand, but it carried a weight that was known only to him. For anyone else it was a useless piece of metal whose blade wasn't even sharp anymore, but to Tom it was something else, a talisman, an amulet, an object that could help him be who he needed to be, to do what he needed to do.

He put it in his pocket and moved over to the table to begin his morning's work.

*\*\*\**

When he had finally finished it was lunchtime. The pistol had been dismantled, cleaned and oiled and now moved with silky smooth precision. He did the same to the magazines, removing the rounds and cleaning the mechanisms and springs so that there were no pieces of debris that could cause a jam. The knives took a little longer; not because they were dull; no, it was because the action of sliding the edge up and down, up and down the whetstone was almost hypnotic and allowed some peace to enter his mind for a while.

When he returned to the house, he brought out the laptop and fired it up. He needed to do a little research on routes and maps but as soon as he had logged in, emails began to arrive. He could see by the pop-up notifications that they were mostly work related. Then one pinged from Evelyn, politely reminding him of the need for the master copy for photocopying. Then another more stern on the deadline and finally a message that was as pointed as the knives he had just sharpened.

185

'*Shit*'. Work had completely gone from his mind as things had unfolded over the weekend. He hadn't finished the master copy and wouldn't get the time to either. He opened the email fully and clicked to respond to Evelyn's last message.

*Dear Evelyn,*

*I am so terribly sorry to have missed the deadline for submission of the documents for copying and binding ready for the review meeting on Wednesday. Please accept my sincerest apologies. A family emergency has occurred that needed, and still needs, my full attention. I have attached the documents as they are in the order that they should appear. I would appreciate it, if you and your team still have the time, if these can be completed as requested.*

*Warm regards*

*Tom*

He copied in the Professor and began adding the files he had sent himself, but never finished and hit send. Then he thought another message was in order.

*Dear Professor,*

*As you can see from my message to Evelyn, something has occurred at home which means that I won't be able to be in the university for a little while. I don't know how long this emergency will take to resolve, but I will do my best to be there on Wednesday for the review. I know how important it is. Would you please be able to arrange cover for my lectures I have scheduled this week and as soon as I know more about my return, I will let you know.*

*I'm sorry to have to ask.*

*Tom*

He sent it and tried to push the thoughts of the Professor and his disappointment out of his mind. He hoped he wouldn't react the same way he had when the Professor took the day off.

He closed down the emails and brought up the map. He didn't want any search to be stored in the history, so it took him a while to scroll around and find the area he was looking for. Once the information had been noted he closed everything down and went back up to his bedroom. He changed into his combat trousers, boots and old T-shirt before returning downstairs and heading for the door. As he took out his keys from the box he stopped and looked at himself in the mirror. He could only manage as far up as his neck; his eyes were unable to meet themselves, maybe out of shame, maybe out of disgust. Either way, he didn't want to look at who he was right now.

As he drove off and along his street he switched on the heater. It was the first time he had used it since the Spring; the sun had hidden its face as well it seemed, too was ashamed of what was being done below and wanted no part of it.

It wasn't long before he was parked up outside Shirley's cafe, the lunch crowd was in and the place was busy. '*Good*', thought Tom as he got out and walked past it, along the pavement towards the Bristol Channel. As he slowly walked along his eyes were scanning the vans and trucks, inside the cabs and on the open trailers behind. After a few metres he had spotted what he was after. He walked all the way to the end of the street before turning back. Five cars ahead was a pickup truck with tools and boxes in the rear, the windows open. When he was three cars away, he moved out into the road, hugging the vehicles close. At one car he slowed his pace whilst still looking casual. Then at the pickup's passenger seat he jumped up and leant into the cab and snatched a high-vis jacket from the seat. He slid it out and allowed it to droop low from his fingers as he dragged along the floor. Anyone looking from the cafe wouldn't be able to see anything through the windows of the vehicles blocking their view.

Reaching his car, he climbed in and tossed the jacket in the back. He started up and drove away. The journey took less than seven minutes and as he pulled up to St Andrew's station, he had flashbacks to the other evening; him and Charlie running over the bridge, across that street and into the storage yard.

He got out taking the jacket with him. He folded it inside out so that the bright yellow was hidden by the dark blue of the interior. He crossed the bridge, went down to the empty platform and walked to the end of the fence to the overgrowth. He checked around to make sure he was alone and stepped in.

The space inside was a little more open than before after he and Charlie had trampled it. He looked at the empty rivet holes and drill marks on the bars and gently slid them to the side and stepped through.

On this side he donned the jacket and walked towards the road by the two large silos, along the same path they had taken a few nights before. The daylight, the movement of trucks and the noise rendered the environment in a completely different light. There was a ship in the dock again that looked like it was having its liver removed in some giant game of operation by one of the cranes that had loomed so large. Despite the people walking past and trucks driving along, he was not given a second look; it is truly an amazing contradiction that a high-vis jacket could make you so invisible.

He wound around the second dock and could now actually marvel at the pipe work that weaved around itself like a giant game of snake.

Instead of darting into the tower of containers as they had done before, he continued up the main road, bold as brass and brazen in his approach. As he neared the rear of the building he could see the sack-trucks still in the same place they had left them. He chuckled to himself at the thought; he didn't know what to expect, but it amused him that after the drama of that evening, they should still be there waiting.

He continued around to the front and walked over to the narrow steps that led up to the door and knocked. He could hear a sudden shuffling come from inside and a face appear at the window that quickly darted back out of sight.

After a few seconds the door opened and a large guy came out, obviously the one with the most bulk of intimidation to ask what he wanted.

"Hi, I'm looking to talk to Ry-Man if I could please."

There was another sound of shuffling inside as the guy in front of him was unsure how to answer.

Eventually he replied, "I don't know what you're talking about."

'No', thought Tom, 'you probably don't exercise that part of your body much'. He decided to make it easier for the poor man.

"Look, I know who you are, and I know what you have stored in there. I need to talk to Ry-Man about a threat that's coming his way and what he can do about it."

The eyes of the mountain in front darted away and began scanning the horizon and nearby road as if the danger was an immediate and present. When nothing appeared, he grabbed Tom by the scruff of the neck and hauled him inside.

Once in, a skinny guy in an orange tracksuit spoke first, "Who's this then?"

"He said that he came to threaten Ry-Man," replied the mountain.

"No, that's not what I actually said."

The orange tracksuit stepped up to Tom and put his face in his; the odour of bad breath and cigarettes oozed out, "Are you stoopid or sumfingbruv? You come in 'ere and freaten us?"

The tracksuit was something, but the London gangster accent was worse.

"What I actually said was that I needed to speak to Ry-Man to tell him about a threat that was coming, you know, to warn him."

The orange tracksuit stepped back and eyed Tom up in his work jacket. "You work 'ere or sumfin?"

"No, I am an acquaintance of Stan-The-Man and I have information that Ry-Man would find very interesting."

After a few seconds of hard contemplation, he pulled out a phone and walked into the back room. There didn't seem to be any other people in here now, just these two. That must mean that the goods had been moved. A muffled voice found its way into the room; from the syntax Tom could tell that he was trying to explain as best he could what Tom had said. A few seconds of quiet before he reappeared in the doorway again, the phone to his chest.

"Yo, what's your name?"

"My name is Tom Hook, the brother of Charlie Hook."

He returned into the depths to relay the names. Tom looked at the enormous bulk of the guy next to him and thanked whatever gods may be that he didn't try to storm the place the other night with him inside.

Moments later the orange tracksuit came back and simply said, "He's got you. He'll be in touch shortly."

Tom didn't quite know what that meant. "You mean is he going to call back, should I wait?"

The question seemed to throw his cool off a little. "Nah, he'll be in touch shortly. You can go." He nodded to the big guy who stepped back and opened the door.

Tom smiled and left the building. *'Well, that was weird'*, he thought as he made his way back towards the gate. He was expecting something a little more dramatic perhaps, or at least to speak to the guy. He was disappointed that he wasn't even frisked for weapons, amateurs.

He recalled what Stan had said about good help these days and pulled out his phone.

"How did it go?" Charlie answered.

"Well, a little weird. He wasn't there but they spoke to him on the phone, and he said "He's got me. He'll be in touch soon"."

"What does that mean?"

"Beats me!"

"So does that change anything?"

"No, go ahead as planned. I'll just wait for contact."

"Ok...how was Alison?"

"That's not something I'm going to talk about with you Charlie."

"...okay."

As they hung up Tom's thoughts floated back to Ali in a daydream-like haze until the last words she spoke to him echoed clear 'get this thing done'. And that's just what he intended to do.

*** 

The house was cold and dark by the time he eventually made his way back. He had been driving around in order to avoid returning home for as long as possible. It wasn't that he had never been home alone before, but just not like this, not with this much weight hanging in the air.

When he got there, he made himself some food and began to eat it at the dining room table, but the chairs around him began to speak too loudly of their emptiness, so he picked it up and went to the living room. He slumped in his chair and turned on the TV for some company, but the blast of noise that erupted from the speakers shattered the silence around him too much and he quickly switched it off. He never sat in front of the TV to eat like he knew others did; he ate at the table as a child, then either in the NAAFI or in the field. Ali had insisted on eating at the table when they moved in together, even when it was just the two of them, so that meals and the day could be shared. He had no complaints and it had proved to be a worthy routine.

They would eat and talk at the table, share breakfasts, even have sex on it. They had to switch the chairs around at one point due to damage being done to one of them from an overexerted lap dance and appreciated response. That chair was now Williams; it didn't have to bear much weight.

While his fork played with the noodles on his plate his mind returned to the day they had met. He had recently joined the faculty at the university and was invited out for a few drinks after his first week. They had gone to the Vittoria, probably the thinnest pub he had ever been in. It opened out a little towards

191

the back so that was where they sat. It was hammering with rain that afternoon, but they all felt warm and snug by the radiators. It was Tom's round so he got up and went to the bar. Just then the door was flung open and three burly men in thick orange jackets carrying hard hats fell through the door laughing. Coming up the rear dressed the same was Ali, laughing the loudest and shoving them all in. She had black smudges over her face and her hair was tied back in a low ponytail to keep it out of the way. He had never seen anything so beautiful in all his life and he became unable to pull his eyes away from her. Even the bartender had difficulty trying to yank him out of his trance long enough to get his order. He lost all ability to think and had to ask his table twice what they had wanted.

The guys she had come in with noticed him staring and started ribbing her about her admirer. She said nothing but simply blushed whenever she looked over at him. They finished their pints quickly and got up to leave. Her movement created an electric shock that shot through Tom and forced him to his feet. His colleagues jumped as his chair scraped back. It was so loud that the whole pub stopped. Tom walked over to her, the floor beneath his feet felt unsteady as if he was walking across a ship's deck in a storm. He was unused to feeling this petrified in a situation and it took her speaking first for him to find his voice.

"Hi."

"Hi."

"Can I help you with something?"

"Yes...I was wondering if you'd like to go out for a drink with me sometime?"

The guys she came in with nudged each other in amusement; they wanted to take in every part of this so they could take the piss out of her later.

"Sure, here's my card."

From her pocket she brought out a grubby, oil smudged card that read 'Alison Elliot – Civil Engineer'.

This filthy piece of cardboard had suddenly become the most precious thing on the planet and as she left, he continued to hold it in his hand, not trusting his pockets or wallet with such a valuable and delicate artefact.

She was a tough woman, something that he had forgotten over the years as she became a wife and a mother before his eyes. He had seen it that morning though, and the day before when this all came out. He didn't know anyone who would have reacted that way; she was one of a kind.

He looked down at the congealed lump sitting on the plate and wished he could have a drink. A nice whisky would go down a treat about now, but he had to keep his head clear, his focus sharp, at least for a little longer.

He slid the contents of his plate into the bin and washed up, taking his time, but the solitary pieces of cutlery didn't take as long as he wanted before they were nestled back in the drawer. He couldn't do this for the next few nights and resigned to pick up some ready meals from the shop tomorrow so that he had food to hand that required him to be in the kitchen as little as possible.

His mind began to focus on the meeting with Stan the following morning, running through all the things he needed to get from it and how he was going to get them.

He checked the doors and windows and headed up the stairs, walking quickly past William's room and into his own. All he wanted to do was to collapse on the bed and sleep, but he forced himself to maintain discipline and complete his bedtime routine. He emptied out his pockets and his heart leapt as his hand felt something cold inside. He withdrew the knife and placed it on the table beside his bed. It looked out of place there, like an ancient fossil amongst freshly poured cement.

When he was done he pulled back the covers on his side of the bed he slid in; they were as cold as sheets of ice; unwelcoming and lonely. He closed his eyes and fell into a fitful sleep and dreamt of witches and crushed cars.

# 19. THE FRENCH MAN

## 1986 – AGE 13

Secondary school seemed much smoother by the second year. Tom had retained his height advantage from the earlier growth spurts and his increasing confidence had started to show in his personality. Although he went to an all-boy's school, there were never really many fights, none that he had seen anyway, so he felt he was able to use his size to get things he wanted without the threat of violence. He had seen enough of that at home anyway to know what to do if it came to it.

He never considered himself mean, but he could easily cut in line at lunch or make sure his favourite seat in each class was never taken. His ability was even more pronounced in his PE lessons. He was easily the fastest runner and his strength at throwing events such as shot-put, and discus was impressive and earned him the school record for both. He wasn't particularly skilful at football, but in defence there were few that could (or even tried to) get past him. Rugby was a different matter altogether; this he loved more than anything. The ability to be aggressive and take people out all within the confines of the game was a revelation to him. He eagerly threw himself into tackles and would run at others with the ball without slowing, daring them to take him down. He had already gained his school colours in cross country, rugby and basketball and felt pretty good about himself.

His school had a reputation of being rough, so when it came to playing against other schools, it actually helped in beating them mentally before they did so physically. He did notice however that other schools were quite different to his own. For starters they had girls. A concept Tom thought of as exciting. He remembered them in class from junior school, but now they had taken on a new dimension. The schools' he visited also had much nicer buildings and grounds than his own which had a pretty run down feel to it; cracked windows, broken doors and litter all added to its ambiance.

There was a main block where you learned maths, English, science, history, geography and languages. There was a separate block for art, design and technology and a separate sports hall to the side. There was a courtyard of sorts in the middle where kids would run around if the field was too crowded or rough.

Tom didn't really have a place he preferred to be and would often just wander around at break and lunch having fun where he could.

The sun was hiding behind the clouds today creating a bland feeling of greyness as he walked across the courtyard alone. Ahead of him he could see a few of his friends throwing a bag around to each other, a younger kid in the middle trying to get it back. Tom walked up and yelled, "Over here!" The bag was duly thrown his way and he held it high above his head, the small boy unable to reach. He laughed and began walking backwards, making the boy follow. With a bit of a gap between them, he now leapt forward into a run being chased by the boy and the gang of kids who were enjoying the new action, whooping and cheering. Tom ran around the courtyard and headed towards the art block, ensuring he didn't go too fast as to lose the boy. He circled back around and returned to the top part of the courtyard where two large cylindrical rubbish containers stood. As he raced past, he tossed the bag up high and into one of them, hearing it land inside with a satisfying clang.

The boy stopped and looked up at it. He could neither climb in to get it nor seek help from any of the other boys who were now taunting him.

Tom walked away laughing at the fun, leaving them to continue the game. As he walked, he heard a loud banging on a nearby window. He looked up and saw Mr Greaves staring at him, beckoning him inside to his room, a menacing glare in his eyes.

'*Shit*' thought Tom as he headed in, *'I'm in trouble now'*.

Mr Greaves taught French which Tom was neither good at nor interested in. He was an elderly man with bushy white hair that made his red nose and cheeks stand out even more than usual. He was pretty firm with kids, but also had a kindness to him that made him likable.

Tom knocked on his door and went inside, his stomach in his mouth.

Mr Greaves was standing with his back to the window, waiting for Tom to come in. When he opened the door Mr Greaves pointed to a spot on the floor in front of him where he wanted Tom to stand.

Tom walked over like a dog that had been caught chewing his master's slippers.

"Do you think it's funny do you?" Mr Greaves began, anger in his voice, a slight French accent. "Teasing and bullying a smaller kid like that? Huh?"

Tom just stood there.

"How do you like it, hey? How do you like it?" At this Mr Greaves began poking Tom in the shoulder causing him to step back. Fear and anger began to swell up within him at being called a bully and being pushed around. He wasn't a bully! He didn't deserve this!

"Not nice, is it? Being pushed around by someone bigger than you. How do you think that boy feels? What do you think he's going to go home tonight and cry about?"

Tom had never given a thought about what others did, felt or thought. Now he was being forced to confront the consequences of his actions. How would that kid feel? Powerless he guessed; small and insignificant, unable to stop the forces in front of him from doing just what they wanted. Tom recognised how that felt and tears of guilt began to form in his eyes at being the cause.

Mr Greaves saw them and stopped pushing, his voice a little softer. "Don't you see what you are doing, Tom? You're a good lad and one who doesn't need to do things like that. Why don't you use your size to help people instead of hurting them?"

Wrinkles formed on Tom's brow at the thought of the words coming out of his teacher's mouth; being able to help people had never entered his head and the idea of it felt like a foreign body invading neutral ground. How could he help others? He could barely help himself. He didn't understand what his teacher was saying to him. What could he see in Tom that he couldn't see himself?

There was silence in the classroom as these thoughts swirled around Tom's mind until eventually Mr Greaves said. "Go on, get out of here."

Tom turned and walked out confused. He had never thought of his size as being useful for others and had never considered that he had the ability to do good. The heroes he saw on television were never as afraid as he could be, but perhaps that was something he could change? A resolution began to form in his mind that transformed these questions into statements. I can do good; I can help people. It was like a switch had been flipped, a clear direction of intent that had been laid before him where once there was none. He would do these things; he would seek out the weak and help them if he could.

Memories of all those heroes he had watched on TV came flooding in to try and help shape his new persona. Buck Rogers, The Dukes of Hazzard, The A-Team, Knight Rider, all of the shows he watched and loved without ever knowing that he too could be like them.

He stepped out into the courtyard in a daze, his mind frantically trying to reform its thoughts and behaviours into this new character. He kept walking without direction until he suddenly heard shouts coming from up ahead. He looked up and saw in the distance a small boy at the bottom of the muddy slope to the side of the sports hall. There were bigger kids at the top, refusing to let him up, pushing him back down every time he scrambled and slipped his way to the top. He was covered in mud. The kids up top were laughing.

'*This is it*' thought Tom as he strode over, barging past the boys at the top and holding out a hand to the kid below. He managed to reach out, grab the small hand and yank him up unceremoniously. The other boys just looked in shock at someone daring to spoil their fun. Tom turned around and looked at them, looked straight into the eyes of Hancock.

Fear and dread exploded in his stomach as if it had been dropped from a great height, splattering his insides.

"Who the fuck do you think you are?" Hancock shouted.

Tom's throat was suddenly too dry for any sounds to slip past. He just stood there like an idiot.

The two guys either side of Hancock began laughing and jeering. Hancock stepped forward and suddenly Tom was looking over to the right, at a window to the building in front of the field, a sting beginning to form on his left cheek. He turned his head back toward Hancock in time to see him swing his fist again, returning Tom's gaze to the window like a whip.

'*Did he just hit me*'? Thought Tom, unable to believe it. He returned his eyes back to Hancock trying to figure out what had happened.

Hancock just stood there, the boys to his side staring open mouthed. This kid had taken two straight punches to the face and barely moved a muscle. Hancock undoubtedly felt his grip on power wavering and decided to retreat, shouting, "And don't fucking interfere again!"

He turned and walked away, dragging his friends with him who continued staring back. Tom looked at the little boy beside him who took off and ran.

'*Great, not even a thanks!*' thought Tom; but something else was left behind apart from the pain that was erupting in his jaw; a feeling of having done something good, something worthwhile. He *was* able to do good, he *was* able to stand up to people who scared him. He stared across at the distant empty window where Mr Greaves had been standing and wished he had seen that! Had seen who he had now become instead of who had been only moments before.

# 20. TUESDAY

Although the night had not been kind to him, Tom awoke with the first tone of his alarm. The covers around him had been through hell and were damp with sweat. He looked over at Ali's side, the crumpled-up duvet made it appear as though there was a body below it. He knew it was empty, but that didn't stop his hand from flattening it down just to be sure.

He slid on his slippers and pulled the duvet back to air. His morning routine done, he headed down for a coffee and breakfast. The house around him had shifted somewhat overnight and had become like an alien version of his home. It was close to the original, but something was missing.

As he stood by the patio doors looking out at his man-cave, his phone rang.

"Hey, Charlie."

"Hey, how you doing?"

"That's a bit of a stupid question."

"Yeah, right. Sorry. How are you feeling about the meeting with Stan this morning?"

"I'm feeling fine."

"I've had Suzie on the phone to me all night threatening to go to the police if Emily isn't back. I've told her that I was on it, but she doesn't think that I'm capable."

Tom let the silence speak for itself.

"Well, anyway. We still okay to meet up later? Mum is cooking dinner and I said you'd be there too."

"Why did you go and do that for?"

"Because...it might be the last time we're all together."

Tom was about to tell him off for talking like that, but he might have a point.

"Okay, I'll meet you there at six."

"Great. Good luck. Speak later."

Hanging up his mind lingered on the thought of the three of them together, alone. He couldn't recall the last time they had been in each other's company without partners or children there. Perhaps they brought the others to use as shields and defensive positions to hide behind when the questions and emotions began flying?

He finished off his coffee, checked the windows and doors, grabbed his keys and headed out.

The drive took just over twenty minutes but felt like he had barely pulled out of the drive before he was parking up at Filwood again. As usual the shutters were up as he headed for the front door of Stan's shop this time. He pushed it open, and a little tinkle sounded above him. Tom looked up and saw a small brass shop keeper's bell on a short spiral; it gave the impression that you were entering a grocers or sweet shop perhaps. Maybe that was what it had been once or perhaps that was how it was now treated by the customers that entered.

The shop front was empty, the room bare apart from a couple of tables pushed to the sides with hand roll tape machines laying on top, underneath piles of flat boxes waited. The lights were off here, but a dim glow from the back had managed to bounce its way from wall to wall and find its way out.

Tom made his way toward it and noted that the back door was also shut and that there were no sounds coming from the storeroom in the back. He reached the short corridor to the office door and walked down, an uneasy feeling making itself noticeable in the pit of his stomach.

He knocked.

"Enter."

Tom pushed the door open, prepared for the weight of it this time. The scene before him hadn't changed in the slightest and he wondered if Stan ever left the room at all. With the shop front open and his office door unlocked Tom thought that Stan's confidence may have been a little inflated.

"Ahh, Tom. I'm glad you came around early. I'd hate to be waiting all morning for you."

"No problem," replied Tom as he sat down. "A little quiet out there."

"Yes, new shipment needs to be delivered. No need to keep a crew around while they waited; besides, plenty of other things to keep them busy."

There was a momentary silence shared between them, like a full stop or the end of a paragraph, the pause before the start of negotiations. Tom knew what he needed to get from him and some idea of how to get it, but Stan was a slippery character, and his cunning was not to be underestimated as before.

"So, I hope the wife and son are enjoying their holiday away," said Stan.

Boom. Straight for the jugular.

"So, you've had me watched?"

"I like to keep an eye on my investments."

"I thought you said that no one would know I was coming on board until we had spoken?"

"They don't need to know the details to be able to keep a lookout."

'*Fuck*', not a great start. '*What else does he know*'?

"In that case they are fine, thank you for asking."

"Good, good. And what of your thoughts on our last conversation?"

"Well, it was certainly an unexpected turn of events."

Stan smiled at having played well enough to have surprised him.

"But I have some concerns and questions before a final decision is made."

"Naturally. Ask away"

"The first thing of course is Emily. How is she?"

"She's fine; actually, she's been giving the people looking after her a pretty hard time. I think they'll be glad to *get rid* of her."

Tom could imagine that, but the double meaning wasn't lost on him.

"And when will that be?"

"Well, after we have concluded our discussion, it should take a day or so to get her back with us."

*'A day or so? Where the hell did he take her?'*

Stan could see the question falling from his eyes and decided to let it rest there without answer.

"So tomorrow?"

"Mmmm, more like Thursday...evening."

"Okay. Next is the type of work expected of me. There are lines I will not cross."

"I understand that completely and as mentioned already, I have people for the messy side of things. What I need is a leader, someone who can teach and guide as well as go into the field and assess; to strategize and plan; to streamline and solidify."

"Sounds more like a troubleshooting type of role."

"It is in a way. To bring people and roles together and get things into shape. But it's more than that. I know you may think of us all as gangsters and evil villains, but in reality, we're just people trying to get by. There are some really vulnerable lads working for me who wouldn't be able to get of or hold down a job anywhere else; some just out of prison. You know what that's like, with your father. And they too have families that they're trying to support and improve things for, so their kids don't follow in their footsteps. You think the education system over this side of town prepares these kids to succeed in life? In order for the world to work as it does and the rich and powerful to stay where they are, there needs to be a clear hierarchy, otherwise who are they going to stand on to be at the top of the pile?"

"Uh huh."

"Your naivety is surprising. You're a product of that very system are you not?"

"I am a senior lecturer of psychology at one of the top universities in the country!"

"That you are. But how many other senior lecturers do you know that can break into secure locations, hotwire a car or kill a man?"

"That's just my training."

"Is it? I'm sure the training helped shape and supplement your knowledge and ability, but what were you capable of before you joined? What trouble did you get into and out of? What did you experience growing up that meant that the core of you will always be here, will always have that foundation no matter how many degrees you try to wallpaper over it? This is the crucible where young men are shown violence, cruelty and told that they need to suck it up and deal with it. Throw in a concoction of poverty, unemployment and a culture of drugs and alcohol and you have a perfect mixture to mould the lower class in a way that ensures they stay where they are. They make us cannon fodder, the lowest of the low and then vilify us when we act accordingly."

Tom listened, agreeing with a lot of what he had to say. He knew that few people ever got away from the area and when they did, they carried with them this dirty part of their history everywhere they went, trying to hide it, make excuses for it and in Tom's case, even try to deny it exists in the first place. But things are never as simple as they seem and there will always be people who will take advantage of the downtrodden and needy to further their own lives hiding behind the guise of help. It's easy to blame the government, corporations or even the illuminati for that matter. Perhaps they do this to ease their own conscience or maybe they actually believe it; whatever the case, Stan was certainly not running a charity for the hard up.

Tom decided not to argue. "I see, so would my role be mainly office based, consultancy or on the shop floor so to speak?"

"I would say it would be a mixture of all of them. I would oversee your tasks and guide you to the roles that need fulfilling and the activities of the organisation that need completing and it will be your job to make sure they are done in a way that is timely and efficient."

"I see, so I would be your lackey?"

"No no, more like the right hand of god."

"Will I get to choose the people and method of execution?"

"You most certainly will, with my agreement to begin with."

Tom thought about this for a few minutes, mulling this over and trying to form a shape of the role in his mind.

"Okay, that's something that will adjust as we go, I'm sure."

"I'm sure it will."

"So where will I be based? Here?" Tom couldn't imagine them both sharing an office or hot-desking in this room.

"You can choose. Here is relatively central, but it may be beneficial to rent a commercial office; you know, give a decent face to the organisation. Not all of what we do is illegal!"

"Okay, I'll look into the options."

Stan nodded.

"Next is the salary."

"Of course. What are you making at the moment?"

"What I'm making doesn't impact on what I should be earning with you. Despite the threats, I am not a monkey that will work for peanuts."

"No one would ever convict you of that. What number did you have in mind?"

"For that I would need to look at your financial overview. If I am going to add value, I need to see where and how much. That should be the basis of what I'm worth."

Stan stared at him, the wheels turning at this request. He stood up with a groan and went over to the shelves. Using his thick index finger as a guide, he traced along until he found the file he was looking for, opened it up and took out the stapled pile of paper from the top. He stepped back to his seat and paused before handing it over.

"That is the accounts for the last tax year. On pages three to five you'll see a breakdown of areas and costs."

Tom was impressed. Although he was sure that this version of the accounts was not what the tax man saw, it was all documented. Drugs, broken down into type, cost, price, transport; Sex work, Theft, Body Contracts, Disposals, Bribery, Fraud, Cyber Crime and Salaries.

"What's Body Contracts?"

"Those are activities involving the human form, ranging from knee-capping to things a little more severe."

"I see!"

Tom examined the whole document several times including the more detailed discussions and commentary that followed. When he had finished, he closed it up and began tapping it in his lap as he thought.

"Three hundred and fifty thousand," he said.

Stan choked, "and where did you pluck that number from?"

"There are several areas in your portfolio that require a lot of input with minimal value, these need to be cut. The high profit/low input areas need to be solidified and expanded. Cyber-crime is hardly even mentioned. This is the twenty-first century so that needs to be addressed. Overall, I think I can save or make three hundred and fifty thousand pounds in the first three months. So that's where I plucked the number from."

Stan leaned back letting out the air in his lungs slowly. "Where the hell have you been all my life?"

He leaned forward again sharply, slapping the desk. "Okay, I will pay you that, but, after the three months are over it will be adjusted to reflect what you actually made. Deal?"

"Hmmm, will that also be the case if it's more?"

Stan burst out laughing. "You've got some confidence there, I love it. Sure, why not."

Tom remained emotionless and simply nodded.

As Stan's laughter abated, he asked, "So, anything else you need to work out?"

"Yes, two more things; how I will be announced and my start date."

Stan wiped his eyes with a handkerchief and motioned for Tom to continue.

"I am assuming that there is a hierarchy within the organisation?"

"There is."

"So, this would only be applicable to the senior and middle members of the group. If I am to be the *right hand of god*, then they need to know together, as one, so that there's no miscommunication, discussion or gossip beforehand. That will also allow me to address them and share the message and ideas for moving forward."

"That sounds great, but I don't think we've ever had a get together on such a scale before. It's not like we arrange Christmas parties!"

"Maybe you should?"

"Okay, leave that with me. I can get something sorted, which brings us on to the when."

"Well, I have a standard months' notice to give at the university..."

"No, that won't work at all."

"What do you mean?"

"This needs to happen now. I'm not waiting a month before you move over, who knows what may happen by then. This happens now or not at all."

His demeanour suddenly turned from jovial to serious in an instant. "There are things that are happening soon that will need your attention and other matters that have already taken place that will require you to be onboard before they are resolved. You'll understand soon and you won't want it dragged out."

Tom sighed. "Okay, but that's going to cause an issue. Can we say Monday at least? Give me a chance to smooth things over?"

"Monday it is. I will get everyone sorted for Monday morning, but I'm not sure where to house them all!"

"You can hire one of the lecture halls at the university. We let businesses do it all the time for presentations and showcasing. Why not do it in style? I'll book the Wills Hall for Monday morning at ten."

"Perfect," the smile returned to his face. "So, we're all set!"

"I guess so!"

ANTONY CURTIS

They both stood, this time their hands extended over the desk.

"I'll let you know what time on Thursday Emily will be ready."

"Thanks. Oh, and I may have some things that I want to move over before I find an office space. Will this place be free to store them in until then?"

"Yes, that will be fine. We can put it in the shop or in the storeroom behind. There'll be no one here for the next few days, but you can just leave it, I'll get them to move it when they're back on the weekend."

"Perfect."

Tom walked out with everything he needed.

\*\*\*

Driving around to kill time, Tom decided to head to an old haunt he hadn't visited in a very long time. Being here in his old neighbourhood and seeing the changes had made him curious. It wasn't long before he was reversing into a spot in the car park and walking towards the high street.

Keynsham had a very particular feel about it that was hard to describe, kind of like a small village feel with a large village attitude. As he rounded the corner, he was surprised to see an opticians in place of the old jewellers and across the road now loomed a Sainsbury's with part of the civic centre above. There was no sign of the Fast-Food Shack or the public toilets at the end that had once been a focal point. The walkways had been newly paved and as Tom walked across the road, he was glad that the old clock remained, even though it wasn't in its original tower.

He crossed the road again and headed for the park. Instead of walking down towards the main gates he walked along the high street knowing that there would be a little alley which would cut straight through and bring him out at the top end.

This place hadn't changed much, just some revamped play equipment and a new cafe. He tried to remember the old playground and the stunts he used to get up to in there, but it was difficult to picture how it was then, seeing it now. It was like the old picture couldn't be placed over the new. He walked down the hill towards the river where the ring road bridge loomed overhead to form a wide overpass. The bridge made the path and river it crossed into a kind of building without the side walls. The slopes up the side were a great spot for running up and sliding down. This time he walked up them and sat near the top eaves, listening to the traffic that raced just above his head. It had an almost rhythmic quality that helped Tom clear his mind.

He took out his phone to check for missed calls or messages, but there was nothing. He hadn't checked the answerphone at home, he had hardly been there, and it was never used these days. He sent Charlie a text message asking if he had heard from Ry-Man; he was getting a little worried that he hadn't made contact yet. He didn't even take a number! Was he just fobbed off?

He had wanted to call Ali as soon as he had left Stan's, but they had agreed to a no contact rule to minimise the risk of being heard or tracked. He knew that given Stan's cyber-crime income, he had neither the infrastructure nor the expertise to do so, but he still wouldn't want to risk it. He wondered what she would be doing now with William. Knowing her parents, they were getting a filmic education on all the latest releases and the old classics. He loved her parents and had hours of conversations with them about movies. They had made him watch all the films that he knew but had never actually watched; Lawrence of Arabia, Gone with the Wind, The African Queen and he was surprised at how much he enjoyed them. He felt particularly drawn to Humphrey Bogart's character in Casablanca. The loner with a dark past; the secret he keeps guarded as much as he guards his heart. But then Ingrid Bergman walks out of his past and blows all his defences to dust and the only way he can show his love is to send her away to be safe.

He stayed here for quite a while. He didn't want to return home to an empty house and couldn't bring himself to go into work. His office, the university, all seemed like it was on another planet, distant in body as well as in mind. The thought did remind him to book the Wills Hall though. He took his phone out and dialled the number as he walked down the slope and back to the path. By the time he reached the cafe at the top it was all arranged.

*** 

Tom stood outside the door of his mother's house, his family home, for nearly a minute, plucking up the nerve to just open the door and go straight in as was expected. He knocked.

"It's open!"

He went in and through to the kitchen where Charlie sat, and his mother was standing at the oven. He nodded to his brother as he walked over to kiss his mother on the cheek.

"Hello love. Put the kettle on, will you?"

Tom lifted the kettle to fill as the two continued their conversation.

"So, what's the matter with her?" His mother started.

"Nothing, we just had a falling out and she's staying at her mums for a while. No big deal."

"You been putting your dick in places where it don't belong?"

"Mum! I would never!"

"Hmmm. And what about you, eh?" To Tom. "What's happened with yours?"

"Ali and William are spending the week at her parent's house. They don't get to see her and William much, so thought it would be nice before he starts school."

"Don't know what's the matter with the pair of you. Can't keep a good woman at home," she said, glancing between them.

The brother's looked at each other then away. *The truth is worse than that',* they thought.

Tom sat opposite his brother and thought he had better say something vaguely normal.

"So, how's work going?"

Charlie looked up at him with a puzzled look on his face. Tom nodded towards their mother which helped him get the idea.

"Umm, it's a little slow at the moment. Just finishing off bits and pieces. How's yours?"

Tom thought for a moment and remembered that tomorrow was the day of the research review and a guilty bubble burst in his stomach.

"Yeah, it's okay."

A silence fell over them like a blanket floating down from the ceiling, having been thrown up at the corners; their mother busy and oblivious; the noise of the kettle now growing.

Tea made and shared, they all sat down.

"Have you heard from your father lately?" his mother asked.

His father was always a contemptuous subject. Tom still felt the anger in her voice when he came up, but also the love that was still there he thought.

"I spoke to him last week. He's doing okay, still in that little cottage overlooking the sea."

"Sounds horrible," she replied, her eyes saying something different.

"Yeah, I might go and see him next year."

"I can't remember the last time just the three of us were here on our own," she said, changing the subject. "Must have been when you first came out. Charlie picked you up and brought you home. You looked so good in your uniform. All the neighbours watching...you don't talk about it much do you?"

Tom looked at her, "Sometimes the conflicts and battles we fought are best left unspoken." He looked down at the chip in the table and ran his fingers along it.

She lowered her eyes and nodded.

*'Well, that was a mood killer'*

211

"So, what's for dinner," piped up Charlie, trying to bring the evening back to life.

"I've made a mid-week roast!" She said as she got up to check on the boiling cabbage.

"Yummy!" mocked Charlie giggling toward Tom who couldn't help but smile.

"You don't like it, you can bloody cook next time."

"I didn't say anything!"

She dished up the food and served, placing a bottle of white wine in the middle of the table. Charlie opened it up and began to pour.

"None for me, thanks," said Tom.

"What's the matter with you? You can at least have one to celebrate us being here together!"

He thought about it for a moment, "...okay, just one."

They ate and drank and talked. Well, Charlie and his mother talked mostly, but it was nice to watch. Tom had a sense of remembrance pour over him as the words flowed; the smell of the over-boiled food, the taste of the cheap wine all aided the recall of times gone by.

"You remember that time at that wedding in Pill?" Charlie threw at Tom. "You spent the entire evening snogging that bird from the other side."

"I did not!"

"I remember that!" His mother added. "I kept getting daggers from her parents on the other side of the hall!" she laughed.

"Well, it wasn't all evening!" They all burst out laughing at the shared memory.

"And besides, it was Charlie who disappeared with her older sister!"

All eyes on Charlie now, his face blushing. "Well, what can I say? They just couldn't help falling at my feet...literally."

"Eww...too much information!"

"You were such a lad back then and such a great artist," his mother said.

"You were an artist?" choked Tom.

"I drew a little."

"A little? You used to draw those amazing muscular women with their tits out, and the guys with their huge swords! You had those books by what's his name?"

"Boris Vallejo."

"You loved those books. Remember the one you bought for a fortune that was signed by him? You wouldn't open it up all the way for fear of bending the spine. You used to peer into it through little openings!"

Charlie glanced at Tom, "Well, it's all in the past now."

"What happened to them? One minute they were there, the next, gone? They might be worth something now?"

Charlie simply shrugged.

They finished off the bottle and opened another that seemed to grease the flow of stories remembered.

His mother shared, "I remember you, Tommy, being mesmerised by the TV as a child. We were one of the first to have Cable TV back then. It only had four or five channels that you changed by turning a switch on the wall, remember, but my god, was more than enough for you! The bloody movie channel that showed repeats twice a day for weeks before they changed them. What was that foreign one you used to watch with that football guy in it?"

"Little Giants," Tom recalled. "And that football guy was Pele!"

"Yes, that's it. You must have watched that every morning and evening for a month before they took it off."

"It was a great movie!"

"And don't get me started on MTV and those girls in black dresses with red lipstick!"

"Addicted to love," both boys said dreamily.

They moved into the living room for the third bottle which may have well been a time machine for how it made them feel. No, thought Tom, not a time machine, because he could never recall a time when they were ever like this. More like a portal to an alternate universe where they were a regular happy family. He

213

ANTONY CURTIS

sat there and listened to all the history they had shared together; fascinated by the different experiences they each had of the same events. How they were each coloured by their own biases and understandings; sometimes it was something as small as standing at a different angle that shed a new perspective on what had happened. He wondered, if we all took a step to the left, would our experiences alter that much to make us a different person?

Halfway through the fourth bottle things began to slow down somewhat, the memories that eased out before now became a jumbled mess or were lost in the swell of alcohol. He didn't remember talking about it, but they all found themselves staggering up the stairs after midnight, heading for their own old bedrooms as if no time had passed.

Tom slipped off his shoes and crawled under his duvet, the sheet smelled a little musty, his legs not able to extend fully. His mind was a haze as he took one last look at the sideways room he used to know so well before he fell into the deep hole of sleep.

# 21. THE SPLIT

## 1987 – AGE 14

Every Saturday followed a similar pattern for Tom. He had been trying to get into a routine each morning, but Saturday seemed like the only day he had time for it. School days were a mad rush and Sundays were for sleeping. Saturday was a bit of a lie in, but not a Sunday amount. He would wake up and shuffle off to the bathroom, splash water over his face to wake himself up, do his teeth and head back to his room. Then he'd select which clothes to wear and head downstairs to make a bowl of breakfast. Everyone else was either still sleeping or busy with other things.

He had made new friends in school, kids from different parts of Bristol, that were just as adventurous as he was, if not more so. He would often get on his bike and cycle up to Totterdown to see Carl and then hang around for the day, playing cricket, exploring the graveyard, and listening to music. He had been introduced to whole new styles and bands that he had never heard before such as UB40, Bob Marley and Madness.

From his newfound friends he also found an array of new food. He was used to meat, mashed or boiled potatoes, boiled cabbage, maybe even spaghetti if his mother was feeling adventurous, but here he could have a pot noodle, spring rolls and curry. He loved the new tastes even though the curry always made him sweat like a pig, a sight that always made Carl take the piss.

This Saturday though was meant to be different. There was a wedding of someone or other and it was going to be a posh affair. There were often family events he went to, weddings, funerals and christenings. He didn't really speak to his cousins or uncles and aunties much, but he did enjoy watching them all get drunk and cause a scene, and sometimes there was a pretty girl.

He got up this Saturday to the sound of shouting from downstairs. *'Great, they're at it already'*.

He went through his morning routine and chose a nice pair of trousers to put on and a shirt. He headed out of his room just as his father stomped up the stairs and disappeared into his bedroom without a glance in Tom's direction. Tom just waited for him to pass and headed down for his breakfast.

In the kitchen his mother was sitting at the table, red eyed and fuming mad. She stared at Tom as he entered and continued to watch him as he went about making his breakfast, her eyes boring into him. Before he had even poured the milk she spoke.

"I don't know why you're dressed nice, we're not going to the bloody wedding now!"

Tom turned his head, "Okay."

*'Great'*, he thought. *'I get to go out and play instead'*.

This was obviously not the answer his mother was looking for.

"Oh no, he doesn't want to take his wife and his son! HE WANTS TO TAKE HIS FLOOZY INSTEAD!" She shouted towards the stairs rather than at Tom.

He didn't know what to do or say. The revelation that his father was having an affair hit him like a punch to the gut. Maybe this would finally be the thing that split them up. He looked over at her now and wondered if she was trying to push his father's buttons on purpose.

Suddenly Tom heard his father's heavy footsteps banging across the ceiling, heading towards the stairs.

*'Oh shit, she's done it now'*.

In he burst with eyes like venom.

"What the fuck are you saying?" he shouted, leaning over her.

"What? You don't want your precious son to know that you're fucking someone else and taking her to the wedding and not your family?"

Tom's heart leapt from his chest. He wanted to get the hell out of here but they were between him and the door, so he was stuck, frozen to the spot. He had heard all of this before in one form or another, but he had never been in the middle of it.

"I don't know what the fuck you're talking about woman! You've gone crazy! Why the fuck would I want to take you to the wedding like this?"

"I'm crazy because you're a fucking adulterer! Sleeping with that bitch!"

Tom saw his dad's hand raise behind his head as if in slow motion, when it had reached its highest point it flew forward, smacking into his mother's head, causing her to fly off her seat into a crumpled mess on the floor, her legs pivoted up and crashed into the table above snapping off a chip.

His father stepped forward and wound his hand back for another.

'No', thought Tom. 'I can't allow this to happen', and without thinking he rushed forward and put himself between them.

"No dad, no more," he said, his voice quivering.

His father stopped still and stared at Tom for what seemed like the first time. He lowered his hand, his eyes regaining some of their focus, the red mist dissolving.

"Get to your room," he said, pointing towards the door.

"No dad, I'm not going to let you do this anymore."

From behind him a voice spoke. "Get to your room, Tom."

He turned around and saw his mother repeating his father's words. He just stood there stunned. Then almost in unison, voices raised, they repeated their command.

"Get to your room."

'What the fuck! I have stuck up for you, put myself in the middle to help and I'm being told to get to my room?'

"It's alright now," his father said as his mother got to her feet. "Go."

217

Tom stormed out of the room, tears filling his eyes making it impossible to see where he was going. He felt his way up the stairs and slammed his door shut, falling against the wall at the foot of his bed. The scene played in his mind over and over. He had finally stood up to his father, tried to be a hero and protect the weak in a situation that terrified him, and he was repaid by being sent to his room!

As Tom looked down, he saw a glint from under his bed. He reached out through waterlogged eyes and felt a cold familiar texture in his fingers. He held it in his hands, turning it over, reacquainting himself with an old friend. Anger was now boiling over as he flicked open the blade.

*'You want something to cry about! You worthless piece of shit, you can't do anything; you shouldn't even be here!'* the voice screamed in his head.

He took the knife firmly in his hand and placed the blade to his wrist, just above a solitary freckle. *'One cut, just one quick slice and it's all over'.*

His hand was shaking, adrenaline coursed through his veins, veins that he wanted to open up and release.

*'Go on, just do it; then they'll be sorry'.*

He took a deep breath and braced himself; holding the knife tight he pushed down.

*'That's it; now just pull it across, like a band-aid, better to do it quick'.*

His hand shook, his mind willing him on, but his body holding him back, stopping him from making the final cut. He couldn't even do that. He dropped the knife and put his head in his hands and cried. He cried until the tears had run out and then he cried some more until he heard the front door slam and his father leave the house to go to the wedding, no doubt. The morning had been just another episode to him and to his mother, but to Tom it had been as though he had gone to war and returned a failure. Like those movies of Vietnam soldiers returning home having put their lives on the line only to be spat at and have it thrown in their face.

\*\*\*

It was a month later when Tom returned home from school to find his mother waiting for him, her bags packed and waiting by the door. *'She only took those bags out to go on holiday, so were we going somewhere'?*

"Go and get your things, we're leaving."

Tom just stood there in his school uniform and stared at her.

"Now Tom! Just pack a bag with your clothes and hurry up!"

Her frantic voice shook Tom and he rushed upstairs to his room. A sudden realisation that this was it, they were leaving his father. But what if he didn't want to leave? He didn't appear to have been given a choice as he threw clothes into a bag without even looking at what he was grabbing. His mind was trying to grasp the situation as a real event and not something he was dreaming. He struggled. He couldn't comprehend not being here anymore. Then another terrifying thought emerged; what if his father came home now and caught them escaping?

At this, he zipped the bag, half empty, and ran downstairs. His mother was by the door on the starting blocks and as soon as she saw him coming, she opened the door and ran out, like a relay team member not even waiting for the baton to be passed.

They threw their bags in the boot and leapt in the front seats. Her hands shook so much she could barely find the keyhole to start the car. When she did, she instantly stalled it. Both of their eyes darted around at the roads and the windows of the houses surrounding them; trying to spot his car or the neighbours spying behind curtains, calling him to tell him they were escaping.

The car roared into life, and they were off. In less than two minutes they were parking up and getting out. Tom didn't know the address of his Auntie's, but he recognised it by the bright red phone box outside her house.

*'Here'?* Thought Tom. *'Surely not here, it's not far enough. If we're going to run then we need to go far away, somewhere they have never been, another country perhaps. Not here, this is the first place he'll look'!*

219

They got out and grabbed their bags. The door opened and his Auntie stood there ushering them inside before anyone could see. Tom felt like a criminal after a breakout.

He was taken upstairs to his cousin's room and told to put his stuff away in the two drawers that had been emptied ready for his arrival. As he started taking out old T-shirts, underwear and school shirts his hand fell on something hard. He looked down and saw the knife staring back at him. In his mindless state he had somehow wanted this above the useful items of clothing, toys and music; it had been this that had leapt inside. He placed it in his pocket and finished emptying out his bag. When he had finished and the quiet returned, fear began to build within him. He felt naughty, that he was doing something wrong, unforgivable. He stood at the top of the stairs unsure whether to go down or to stay up. There was an airing cupboard on the landing, small and tight. He opened it up and somehow managed to squeeze himself into the bottom of it, hoping to block out these emotions and thoughts; wanting to remove himself from the world. With his hand in his pocket, he closed the door. The soft red cover of the water heater next to him felt calming. He allowed the darkness and walls to close around him, holding him safe where there was no room for anything other than himself and the warm sensation beside him.

It didn't take long before there was banging on the front door. He could hear his aunt open it and speak, his father's tone clear, but it wasn't the explosion of anger and emotion he was expecting. He somehow imagined that when his father got there the whole house would tremble and shake, tipping the two of them out and back into danger, but that was not what was happening.

Tom opened the door of the closet and crept to the top of the stairs to listen as best he could. His father was talking, apologising, crying! He didn't know whether to feel sorry for him or his mother who was standing her ground. The conversation lasted less than ten minutes before Tom's father left; no fuss, no shouting, no fighting. Tom slumped against the wall, his body worn out from shaking, and slid to the floor. So, this was the end, the end that came without a bang, but with a whimper.

## 22. WEDNESDAY

Tom couldn't decide at first whether the thumping was coming from inside his own head or from outside his body. As his consciousness began to claw its way back to life, he mentally checked himself over. His knees ached and his legs were sore from being bent in the same position all night. His stomach felt as though an excavator had been at it and his throat was dry and coarse. He opened his eyes and regretted it instantly as the blinding white light of the day kicked at his head.

With a moan he swung his legs off the bed and sat up, his feet automatically searched for his slippers that were on a completely different floor. He remained still while his inner ear tried to re-establish the correct pull of gravity. Once it had settled on a general direction, he heard more banging from downstairs. That made him feel a little better, at least it wasn't all in his head.

He made his way down the stairs, grasping hold of the banister. In the kitchen Charlie was looking through the cupboards to try and find food for breakfast. When their eyes met, they both looked how each other felt.

"Coffee?" asked Charlie.

"Oh yeah!"

"Sleep okay?"

"I did until I woke up!"

Charlie chuckled, flicking the switch on the kettle.

"Have you..." Began Tom, but the noise it made began to grow too loud to continue, so he waited, rubbing the pain from his legs.

When it finally clicked, he carried on.

222

"Have you heard anything from Ry-Man?"

"No nothing."

"He didn't even take my number."

"He's cutting it close."

"He is. Stan said Emily will be there tomorrow evening so we don't have long."

Charlie nodded as he stirred the coffee and added milk.

"Mum still in bed?"

"Yeah, she won't be up 'til this afternoon."

Tom looked at his watch. "Shit, ten thirty already!"

"That's what happens when you're having fun!"

"Well, I wouldn't say that."

"What? Admit it; you did have a good time last night, even though it was with your shitty family."

"Hmmm, it was certainly a new experience for me."

"Maybe we'll do more of it when this is done?"

Tom looked at him without answering. They drank in relative silence, not wanting to upset their heads too much. When the cups were empty, Tom got up to leave.

Charlie spoke as he moved, "Let me know if you hear anything. I'll finish off the rest of the stuff today; it's not like I have far to go!"

"I will." As Tom left the house, he hoped it would all come together as planned, it had to.

***

Tom pulled up in his driveway and was surprised to see a familiar face staring back at him from his doorstep.

"Professor, what are you doing here?"

"Hello my boy. I thought I'd drop by to see how you were and let you know how the review meeting went this morning."

Tom flushed at having missed it; he opened the door and walked in. As he led the way through to the living room, he looked at the landline phone in the hallway; it was flashing with a message.

223

"Come in and take a seat. Can I get you a cup of tea?"

"That would be lovely."

Tom headed for the kitchen and pulled out the green tea and earl grey, his eyes drawn to the blinking light he knew was flashing away to itself just a few metres away. As the kettle flipped, it drew his attention back to the cups and he finished off.

"There you go," he said, walking back to the living room.

"That's wonderful, thank you."

They sat for a second or two, blowing their tea in silence.

"So how are you doing?" The Professor asked.

"I'm okay, just having to deal with some family things at the moment. Nothing too serious. I'm sorry for missing the review meeting this morning, how did it go?"

"It was fine. The research you put together and the outcomes of the latest tests were all they were interested in. I waffled around the topic for a while, and they left feeling satisfied."

"That's good. Thank you so much for covering for me, I know how important..."

The Professor waved his hand, "It's just work; nothing that won't wait. Family comes first."

It was such a relief to hear him say that and Tom instantly felt some of the tension ease from his shoulders.

"Are Ali and William not here?"

And then it returned. "No, they're away at her parent's house for a few days."

A frown formed on the Professor's brow, "Is everything alright with you two? You know, a relationship can go through some tough times, but it's important that you stick with it and figure it out."

Tom smiled, "Its fine, that isn't the problem side of the family."

"Oh, that's good then," he chuckled. "Did I ever tell you about my Uncle Stanley? He was a professor of engineering up in Edinburgh. He started a distillery in one of the basements making whisky! Called it the Northern England Whisky Still; wouldn't dare assign it to Scotland! He got really good at it until the still blew up one night, taking all the whisky and half the building with it!"

The professor laughed so hard at the memory that his face turned red. "Perhaps we could set one up in the bottom of..."

There was a loud knock on the door.

Tom looked over, and got up, "Excuse me a moment Professor."

The professor waved as he picked up his tea and began to blow on it some more.

Tom glanced at the red light again, teasing him as he passed, and opened the door.

Before him stood three men, the one at the front slightly smaller than the two behind, but still a decent size.

"Tom Hook, I presume?"

'Oh shit', thought Tom, 'not now'.

"That's correct, and you are?"

"I think you know who I am Mr Hook, you've been trying to get hold of me have you not?"

They stared at each other. "Well, aren't you going to invite us in?" And without waiting for the answer, he walked up and into the house, closely followed by his two colleagues, a waft of expensive aftershave and leather encircled them.

Tom closed the door quickly and entered the living room behind them all. The professor sat there wide eyed. "Hello gentleman."

"Hello yourself!"

"The Professor was just leaving. I'm sorry Professor, maybe we could do this another time?"

"Not at all," Ry-Man said. Let's all just stay and enjoy a little chat together, shall we?"

"It's ok my boy, I'd better get back to the office and see what trouble they've made without me."

The Professor moved to get up, but one of the other men stepped forward and placed a hand on his shoulder, preventing him from rising.

The Professor looked at Tom, then at Ry-Man and sat back in the seat.

"There we go, isn't that better?" Ry-Man took the space at the other end of the sofa while his two friends stood behind. Tom sat down in his chair struggling to come to terms with the disjointed parts of his life that had crashed together before him. His eyes glanced out towards the gun and knives that were sat in a rucksack in his man-cave. They may as well have been on the moon.

"So, what was so important that you snuck into my *less* than secret location to talk about?"

"Can't we do this in private? The Professor doesn't need to be here for this."

"I just made a house call, I didn't decide who was here or not, but now that we are, I think we'll keep it that way until we've finished. So..."

Tom looked at the Professor who seemed to have shrunk next to these men and tried to show him a look that was reassuring. He had no choice but to speak; perhaps he could keep it vague enough that it would be explainable afterwards.

"I'm assuming you know who Stan-The-Man is?" Tom began.

"I do indeed!"

"And I'm assuming that you know my brother works for him?"

"That I have recently been made aware of."

"Well, my brother made a mistake whilst in his employ and to make amends for it he was charged with going to your less than secret location to retrieve a recent shipment you were storing there."

"I see!"

"He asked me to help him in the task which I did, but we didn't go through with it."

"For which I am grateful, no doubt."

"Then something was taken from my brother and won't be returned unless something else is offered."

"And does this something else have anything to do with me?"

"No."

"Then how is this now any of my concern?"

Tom looked at the Professor again, "Because you and Stan are in competition, and a competition in your field tends to lead to disputes over areas and market share. This is something I can help you with."

Ry-Man considered these words for a moment. "Stan's business isn't really big enough for me to worry about or be interested in that much."

"Seven point four million pounds. That was his turnover last year with a three point two million pound profit."

Ry-Man's eyebrows raised.

"And he's not even that efficient or trying particularly hard."

"And you know this how?"

"I have seen his books and analysed his numbers."

"So you're telling me that you're going to give me that?"

"I'm telling you that I can give you Stan and all his business information, hell the whole business itself."

Ry-Man stared hard at Tom. "And what do you want for this?"

"I want you to take Stan and bring him to a location I choose."

"That's all? No percentage, no stake in the business?"

"No, I want nothing to do with it. I just want him."

"Take him? Just like that?"

"He is returning something to me tomorrow evening. He'll be alone in a place that's unlocked. I can go in and get the thing, make sure it's clear; then you can go in and get him"

"And what if you're lying to me? What if this is just a ploy to get me and my boys in there to take us out?"

"It's not."

"But how will I know?"

Tom didn't have an answer for this.

Ry-Man thought for a second before slapping his thigh, "I know. I'll take something as collateral, something that I'll return once this is all completed."

"I don't have anything."

Ry-Man looked across at the Professor gingerly sipping his tea.

"That's not entirely true now, is it?"

"No, you can't take him."

"Can't? Are you telling me what I can and can't do?" The men behind him leaned forward, their leather jackets creaking.

"No, of course not, but..."

"Good," he said standing up. "Here is my number. Give me a call later with the details and I'll see what can be done."

He handed Tom a business card with the telephone number punched out across the middle. No name, no printing, just the cut out numbers.

"Come on old man, you're coming with us!"

"I'm sorry, what?" The Professor said, spilling his tea as he was pulled up? "Tom?"

"I'm sorry Professor. It'll all be okay in a day or so. I'm so sorry."

The Professor handed Tom his cup as he was ushered past and out the room before he could voice any more objections. He was like a resident in an old people's home, being lifted to his feet and guided out the door with a look of bewilderment on his face, not knowing what was happening or why he was being moved. Tom followed; the feeling of guilt mixed with his hangover and left him feeling utterly helpless.

"Speak soon, Mr Hook."

Tom watched them leave the driveway and walk away. The professor looked so small between the men that it reminded him of William between him and Ali on their way to the park. He kept glancing behind at Tom with a look of desperation.

Tom closed the door and turned around, leaning his head back against the wood, staring up at the ceiling. What the fuck had just happened? What a fucking mess this was becoming. How did it ever get this bad? His eyes lowered until he saw the red light flashing before him. He walked over and hit the play button.

*"Hi Ali love, it's only mum and dad. We were wondering if you were coming to us or not, only we were expecting you and William yesterday and haven't heard anything. Give us a call back when you can. Bye...bye."*

\*\*\*

"Charlie, he's got Ali and William."

"What? Who has?"

"Fucking Stan!"

"How do you know?"

"He's had me watched and asked me about them yesterday, the slimy fuck. I'm heading there now to beat the living shit out of him."

"No, wait. You can't do that!"

"Can't I now? I'm gonna make him wish he had never been born."

"And then what? What about Emily?"

Tom thought about Emily and also the Professor. How will they be safe if he did what he so desperately wanted to do now? He swerved the car over to the side of the road.

"FUUUUCK! FUCK, FUCK, FUCK!" His hands were on the steering wheel trying to shake it loose.

It took several minutes before he could speak again, his breath strained.

"If Stan has Ali and William then he knows something's up."

"Or maybe he took them to make sure you'd join him?"

"He mentioned looking after the family of his employees. Fuck, I just don't know."

"Okay, so we just have to go through with the plan and get him to tell us where they are when we have him."

"And what if he doesn't? That's all our cards dealt. We have nothing more to bargain with."

"What else can we do?"

Tom had no idea what they could do, he was angry, furious; a full force category ten storm raged inside and threatened to

229

explode out. Three of the most important people in his life had been taken compared with Charlie's one. How was that fair? It wasn't even his problem to begin with!

"This is all your fault. Look at the fucking mess you've created. Ry-Man was here just now while my boss was visiting and he's taken him as collateral until this is done."

"What? Shit!"

"Yeah shit. So not only are my wife and child in jeopardy, but also my life and my career as well. That's the whole fucking thing, my entire world up in smoke thanks to you. You've right royally screwed me over."

"Tom...I'm so..."

Tom hung up.

He had to think, to still his mind and let rational thought regain control over the primitive beast that was straining at the bars to break free. He wouldn't do anything in this state that would help the ones he loved. He checked his mirrors and made a swift U-turn to head back home.

As he pulled up, he saw that he had left the front door open in his eagerness to get out. He closed it now as he walked in and up the stairs. He went into his room and opened up his wardrobe, grabbing armfuls of clothes and tossing them onto the bed and floor, sweeping out the shoes on the bottom. When it was empty, he climbed in and sat down, pulling the door closed with his fingertips, wanting to close the world out.

The darkness was almost complete except for a thin strip of light that filtered through, piercing the gloom. Tom opened the door and pulled it closed again, harder. This time it fell pitch black. The space around him enclosed, coffin-like, as he sat there and tried to recreate this environment in his mind, making it dark and empty, no room for large unwanted thoughts or emotions.

It took a while for this to happen, but once it did, once he was able to filter out all unnecessary activity, he was able to breathe; allowing his lungs to push against the bars of his chest, expand them, but all within the safe confines of his body. Only then did he begin to allow parts of the problem to enter, one at a time.

Like pieces of a jigsaw, he brought them in and manipulated each one until he got the measure of them; their shape adjusting with each new piece added. Some were harder to work with than others and some had sides that could not be defined; these he could place on the edges or, if need be, force them into place. A picture was starting to form as more and more elements were brought together into some kind of understanding, but it wasn't perfect, and the pressure of more and more unknowns placed together made it explode apart.

He banged the back of the wardrobe in frustration and tried again. There must be a way to work this out.

He closed his eyes again and began with a different piece, the trickiest, and really examined it before he brought in anything else. He needed to get to know every angle, every nuance that could affect its position and outcome. Once done, he allowed others in; building the picture once again until clear lines and gaps could be seen. When it was complete it was still fragile, delicate, but at least it could be used as a start.

He let his internal eyes wander over each problem and how each piece related to each other. He could add different home-made pieces of a solution into the gaps to see how they would fit, what impact they would have and if they produced the outcome he wanted. They each brought some sense of an answer, but he knew it would be the things you never think of that were the ones that could sideswipe you.

Some of them required more of himself than others, to let more of his demons out than he wanted. He had to get Stan to talk. He also had a burning hatred that had a need to be satisfied.

After an hour he had something that looked positive, well, it was the most positive out of the options he had and at least gave him a clear direction to take. *'Whenever you are stuck you have to keep making decisions'* he told himself; when those decisions are based on something more than a hunch then it tended to work out better. Tom's solution pieces were less than a hunch but more than a wish; it was better than nothing.

# 23. ALTERNATIVE EDUCATION

## 1988 – AGE 15

The year that followed had been unlike anything Tom had ever known. He and his mother had moved to St George on the other side of town while the divorce and arrangements over the house and money were sorted. This meant that Tom was now six miles from his school and anyone or anything he knew. His mother would give him a lift to school in the mornings and expect him to make his own way home afterwards. He quickly got used to the distance and would run the six miles home, get changed and either run or cycle back to his friends in Totterdown to play. He came home when his friends had to go in and would often find himself coming through the door gone midnight. His mother wasn't usually there so it didn't matter. She was out having fun with men or work colleagues which left Tom pretty much to his own devices; and that's how he liked it.

She would put food and cans of beer in the fridge and Tom would often came back from school in the summer, open the back door, put on Paul Simon's Graceland and crack open a cold one. He didn't have anyone telling him what to do, what rules to follow or what time he had to be back. He could do as he pleased. He saw his father every other Sunday at the house as he attempted to cook a Sunday roast. Actually, it wasn't bad, and his demeanour had changed dramatically to one that was softer and more appreciative. It was a new era in their relationship which meant they actually started to have one!

All of this freedom inevitably led Tom away from school and into other avenues of fun; from the 'cooped up and controlled' regimen of pre-break-up, to the 'you're on your own kid' mentality of post. A friend of his had moved to Keynsham recently and when Tom rode out to see him one Saturday he fell in love with the place. It was a quaint little town with its own character and an open feeling to it that was as far removed from Knowle West or even St George as it was possible to be.

His friend, Benny, lived in one half of King James's hunting lodge, the other half had been turned into bedsits. The house was old and creaky but had the best open plan living room and kitchen you could imagine that was great for house parties. These happened every month or so with kids from his local rugby club and friends from his new school showing up. There was music, dancing and alcohol. Tom was also the new kid so loved the attention he received, especially from the girls.

Benny had told him how amazing it was to be in a school with girls and Tom could easily believe it. What he couldn't understand though was how you could possibly concentrate with them all around you every day? Benny just laughed at him.

Tom's first experience with a girl happened at one of these parties. Benny told him that a girl fancied him and that he should go upstairs and let her suck him off. Tom couldn't believe his ears and was only too happy to do as instructed. The thin bespectacled girl led him upstairs to the bathroom where they began kissing. Their lips searching for each other's, and their tongues wrestling made Tom hard without effort. The girl started unfastening his belt and as she pulled his trousers and pants down, her head followed. The lock on the door was broken so he had to stretch one arm out to hold it closed while the other pushed against the shower cubicle.

The girl took him in her mouth and began sucking. Tom had no idea what to expect but was surprised when it actually started to hurt. It felt like he had placed the end of a vacuum cleaner on his knob and turned it on. He tried to focus on what was actually happening, but the sharp pain kept drawing him away from any pleasure. Suddenly the bathroom door was pushed open, and Tom had to fight to push it back. The girl stood and straightened herself out. Tom pulled up his trousers and followed her out as another girl barged in to throw up in the toilet. They lost each other in the crowd, but Tom wasn't bothered.

There were older people at these parties too, with jobs and cars that Tom got on well with. Occasionally, some of the people who lived in the bedsits next door would be invited in to share the fun. He would go out of his way to talk to them and had even managed to grab a ride home after the party a few times. His friendship with them began to extend beyond the nights at Benny's and Tom started to skip school and catch a bus into Keynsham to hang around with them at the park or the Fast-Food Shack by the clock tower.

His mother was barely around, and school didn't hold the power over him anymore, so his days became filled with alternative means of education. Whole days were spent driving around, getting alcohol and drinking in the park. He would find himself making bets with the drivers that he could do this stunt or that trick in order to win lifts home or get another can of cider. He would somersault over fences, climb onto roofs and throw himself off all in the name of good fun and a favour.

He had hung out around the Fast-Food Shack so much that he knew the manager and workers well and was even offered a job! He was pretty sure they didn't know how old he was; his height and the fact that he wasn't in school must have added several years to his actual age. The thought of having cash in his pocket from working in the place he loved to hang out at was too good to turn down.

The manager, Tina, brought him in one day and started showing him the ropes; how the griddle worked, the deep fryer, the menu and how to put it all together. It was fairly basic stuff, burgers, chips, chicken. Tom got to grips with it easily having had to fend for himself the past year.

He picked up shifts in the day and at night and would spend his time at the shack even when he wasn't working. Tom's first wage came in the form of a small brown envelope handed to him by Tina after a couple of weeks there.

"This is for you, you've earned it!"

Tom had almost forgotten that he was being paid for the work and when he opened it up and counted almost two hundred pounds, he couldn't believe it. He hugged Tina and ran over the road to the jewellery shop he had often stood outside of looking at the watches in the window. He knew the one he wanted to get. It was large, with a complicated pattern of dials and numbers around the edge that looked like it was used in the military. With the envelope grasped in his hand he walked in and pointed to the one he wanted.

He walked out a few minutes later with a much thinner envelope, but an amazing feeling that ran through his body, emanating from his wrist. He walked back over to show Tina what he had bought. She cooed over it and told him how smart and handsome it was; he was. He felt amazing. When his friends came by later that night he was in his element, sleeves rolled up to show them all what he had and who he was.

The next few envelopes seemed to go on drink and food which he didn't mind at all. He was able to bring bags of alcohol to the parties and into the park, pay for fuel and even get some new clothes.

One night he was on a late shift, closing up around two in the morning with Tina, her kids and husband all safe at home. They had become much friendlier over the past few months, but tonight was the first time she had offered to drive him home. He was only too happy to accept but felt that something else might be behind the offer. At least he hoped it was. Although he was scared about having actual sex, especially after the pain he felt doing the other stuff, he was also curious to know exactly what all the fuss was about.

They pulled up to the flat, no lights were on inside and his mother's car was nowhere in sight. He invited her in for a cup of tea and she accepted. Tom's heart raced as he opened the door and led the way into the kitchen. He turned on the light in the hallway, but kept it dim everywhere else; he thought that it was more romantic that way. Tina was talking behind him as he made the drinks, she was telling him how great he was at work and how everyone loved him. When he turned around, she had moved closer.

They looked at each other and moved closer still, until, without knowing how, their lips met. It felt soft to Tom, gentle, the smell of her hair that fell around his face was intoxicating. Their lips moved over each other, parting so their tongues could play; each touch sent shivers through his body.

Their hands began to wander and explore the bodies before them. Over clothes at first and then finding their way beneath, to the skin and the electric sensations that happen when fingers caress parts that had never been touched before. Clothes seemed to fall away without effort and before they knew it, they were both naked on Tom's bed. The lights were off, but from the moon filtering in through the curtains he could see the outline of her body, the curves, the hair. He moved instinctively between her legs and slid inside. The gasp he heard in the darkness told him that he was doing it right. His penis felt like it was enveloped in warm silk as he moved in and out. Tina's hands were clasped to his butt cheeks as she encouraged him to go faster and deeper. He obliged as best as he could, the moans and grip increased with his speed until she suddenly arched her back and let out a groan of pleasure louder than any other. Tom's body responded with little choice, and he ejaculated inside her, that made him gasp for air as a severe tingling sensation erupted throughout his body. They both held still in this position, riding out the waves of pleasure that flowed between them until her back gave way and she collapsed flat on the bed.

Tom's head was buried in her neck, a face full of hair, trying to breathe through this thick filter, feeling his heart thumping against her chest like a sledgehammer. His mind was in a daze, unable to make any comprehensible thoughts from the wash of ecstasy it was floating in. He barely registered Tina kissing him, rolling over and skipping out of the door towards the bathroom. He simply lay there, no longer a virgin, no longer a boy.

# 24. THURSDAY

Hate can do terrible things to a person. It can twist them up inside and make them forsake all other thoughts and emotions for the pursuit of satisfaction. Tom had sat in his chair all night, brooding over thoughts of what he could do to these people who had come into his life and destroyed it. The pains he would gladly take to eradicate them. Even the sun refused to come out from behind the dark clouds that were circling above Tom's head.

His fingers had been playing with the knife in his pocket continuously, it was egging him on, encouraging him to open up the deep dark wounds that had been buried for so long. He tried desperately not to fall into the black hole of what he knew he was capable of, trying to remain the person in control, but that was becoming almost impossible. He wondered what he would be when this was all over, what he would have to become to get it done. Would he be able to claw his way back he wondered? He knew that it was all a matter of perception, that the mind can be influenced to see and feel different things, even if those things are not real, but that didn't change the realness of how they felt.

He had made the phone call to Ry-Man with the details of the plan and had arranged to meet him at Hengrove Park on what was left of the old airfield. He said that the Professor was okay and as long as he didn't fuck things up, he would stay that way. The thought of the old man being kept hostage churned his stomach.

He stood, walked to the door and out to the car. He was late enough for the university to be open, but early enough for it to be empty. The medical building was only a few minutes from his own department, and they all worked on the same card entry system. He had been there several times before to visit with a colleague who worked between both of their departments, researching amputations and phantom limb syndrome.

As he walked in through the doors he knew where to go and what he needed. His footfalls echoed around the clean and sterile corridors. The building was larger than Tom's, but it had the same institutional smell that came from old books and deep thinking. He made his way down to the basement level where the storerooms were kept and worked his way along tall cupboards filled with old equipment until he found what he was looking for. He had brought with him his wife's tote shopping bag and as he dropped the equipment in, he was reminded of a time when he and Ali went shopping together and played a game of putting something naughty, like a packet of condoms, into someone else's trolley.

He pushed that from his mind as he headed for the coolers at the far end. He opened them up and grabbed a couple of bags of liquid as well as all the accompanying peripherals, feeling the weight of the bag grow as it became fuller.

He walked out of the building just as the first wave of lecturers and students were arriving. He saw his colleague friend getting out of his car and heard him calling over, but he pretended not to notice and continued on his way.

Despite the bag now being full he was not finished with his shopping expedition. He headed for Cribbs Causeway next, an out-of-town shopping complex that had all the large retailers centred around one large mall. He walked into Halford's just as they were opening and bought a power converter that allowed the battery of a car to be used with a household plug and a box of one hundred black latex gloves, the kind mechanics wore. Then he went over to Boots and bought a large first aid kit and several bottles of water, all the while feeling like he was there, but not there. He was in a fog of his own world, like a ghost or a spirit, only present enough to have the slightest impact on his interactions with the real world.

239

When he returned to his car and opened the boot, he noticed just how full it was becoming. He had placed in it already the backpack from his house and a change of clothes, the tote bag full and now two bags from these shops were stuffed inside.

As he sat behind the wheel his stomach rumbled. He had not eaten at all yesterday and the feeling was only now starting to return enough for this to become apparent. He knew he needed to eat as much as he could before his appetite failed him completely. He drove into the town centre and parked in the underground car park, close to the docks on Millennium Square. He walked to the surface and headed for ZaZa Bazaar, an all you can eat restaurant that had cuisines from all around the world. You could mix an Indian curry with an Italian bolognese if you so wished. He and Ali had gone there for someone's birthday once and found it both strangely weird and oddly compelling. *'What weird combination would seem the most unusual yet turn out to be delicious'* was the game they played with mostly disastrous results.

When he got to the doors they were locked, the sign said that they would be open at noon. Tom didn't have the energy to go anywhere else, so he decided to sit by the water and wait. Bristol docks was beautiful with boats moored up for fun and for living on that were spread all along the banks. Some were large metal-hulled vessels with huge engines and larger sails; others were more modest with maybe only a single berth inside. As he sat on a bench overlooking the scene, he felt envious at these people's ability to just haul up anchor and go. The freedom to just leave whenever the mood took them; to spend a week sailing to Italy, to moor off the coast and dive into the Mediterranean Sea at a moment's notice.

He looked right towards the famous S.S. Great Britain housed along the opposite bank and wondered what that would have been like to sail in. It was a mandatory part of school history lessons that you learned about the historic luxury passenger liner and of Bristol's links with slavery. Indeed, how Bristol was grown on the profit of slavery. The image of all those people being shoe-horned into the hulls of ships, into every nook and cranny to make as much profit as possible per journey was horrifying. He wondered how those people coped with such a change in life, such a traumatic event that they were left as altered people in a foreign land.

He knew that they kept as much of their traditions and stories alive as possible, but what he didn't know was how they remained true to themselves when the entire world they knew had been torn away from them; what kept them breathing? How did they keep from giving up?

He recalled the day in the park with Ali and William, the song they sang, the laughter and love that flowed between them. His eyes teared as he stared down at his feet. These were the things that he needed to hold onto; these were the things that would bring him back after he had done what he needed to do, the things that would keep him breathing.

At eleven fifty-five he headed back to the restaurant and stepped inside as the door was unlocked. He piled his plate with food that he knew would give him enough energy whilst also being able to stay down. He didn't want to play the food game, not without her. He sat by the windows overlooking the harbour and dreamed of sailing away.

*** 

The hours dragged like an anchor scraping the bottom of the seabed, slowing the ship of time to almost a standstill. Tom wandered around after eating; looking in shop windows, pretending to be a normal person going about their day when in fact he knew that he was far from it. He knew that if he stopped and told people about his day to come they would run away in horror. He was an illusion of a normal person wrapped in the skin of a lie. He watched these people from a distance scurrying around like ants while his timeclock moved him in slow motion. He stepped out in front of a group passing by to prove to himself that he was actually there and not some figment of his imagination. They flowed around him like a river around a rock and showed that he was real, or at least real enough.

The more he watched these people, the more he noticed that they all moved around like leaves on a stream, taking the paths of least resistance, moving around slower objects, following and reacting to the positions of others around them. The clothes they wore, the style of their hair, the words they used; all these things were understandable, predictable and showed so much of their internal view of themselves and the world they saw. They were the external representations of how they thought the world saw them; they were a mirror behind which they could hide, invisible yet projecting the version of themselves they thought would be the most acceptable. Even those who passed in the most deferential outfits still belonged to their own group, their own tribe.

He wondered what reasons they had, what choices they took to make them who they were. What experiences had shaped them into wearing that, or saying that, or thinking that. If you looked back you could trace all of these things, he was sure, but it still left you blind to the choices ahead of you and of their consequences. We are all walking towards the future with our eyes fixed into the darkness hoping that the light of the past will illuminate our next step ahead.

He sat there and wondered if he was the only person alive to know this, the only one awake to this knowledge. As he looked around, he thought he just might be. They were all walking and talking, shopping and consuming in ignorance and joy. He looked on in jealousy, wishing to be as unknowing as they were. Could you ever return to peaceful unknowns after revelations had been uncovered? He was reminded of an old science fiction book, *Flowers for Algernon.*

He floated back to the car park, underground and sat there for a while, trying to will his spirit back into his body and be whole again. He was going to need every part of him for what was to come.

He drove out and headed towards Hengrove Park, the traffic was pretty bad, so it took him a while to get there. For once, he was thankful for that. He parked up between the huge cinema and enormous bingo hall that looked empty. The Beach Hut Cafe was just closing up and the type of kids were transferring from those who played in the park to those who hung around the skate ramps. He walked past both and onto what was left of the old runway. It was amazing that an airfield could be co-opted in such a way that it became a local park yet still held onto its features. There was even a road for taxiing still there at one end.

When he was younger, he came here occasionally. Just the other side of the ring road was Filwood, yet it seemed a million miles away. How could areas in such close proximity be so different? Sure, there were fights and wars between the schools of Knowle, Hengrove and Hartcliffe that made the borders distinct, but could that really change the way they felt?

He walked onto the field and found a nice place to sit in the middle. He was reminded of sitting in a similar position across the way many years ago and thought about then and now, at what had happened that night that led him to be sat here once again, watching the cars and people go by.

From a distance he noticed a familiar shape and recognised the gait and slight limp as it drew closer. He stood up and waved over to Charlie who was scanning around to find him. He slowly walked over and sat down with Tom.

"So, how's it going?"

Tom just gave him a look.

Charlie looked down, "So everything is set up over the way. I've told Suzie to be at home later; that Emily was coming back tonight. What time did Stan say?"

"He messaged and said any time after eight."

Charlie nodded. "And what about Ry-Man?"

"He'll be here around seven thirty."

"You think he's gonna show up?"

"He'd better. He has the Professor and wouldn't have taken him unless he was going to be here. The look in his eyes when I

ANTONY CURTIS

told him the figures of Stan's business was enough to fuel the
fire."

"What about Ali and William?"

"I just have to get that information from Stan. She's a tough
cookie you know, I'm sure she's giving them hell wherever they
are, but she can only do so much."

Charlie smiled and nodded, a silence fell between them as he
picked up clumps of grass and began tearing them into long
strips until he finally spoke again.

"I'm sorry. I'm sorry for the shit that I've caused you and
would never have done it if I'd have known where it would lead."

Tom remained silent.

"I know I've not been the golden child or did things the right
way, but I've tried to. I've tried to do what was right; to look after
Suzie and Emily, to put a roof over their heads and food on the
table. It's not easy out there when you've got nothing to hope
for."

Tom sighed, "I know, but that's no excuse for making
ridiculous choices, that with just a little bit of reasoning would
have told you they were wrong. It doesn't take much effort to
stop for a second and think about the consequences instead of
pushing them aside in favour of wishing for the best."

Charlie continued to destroy the green stalks around him.
"So...does that mean that you still don't want anything to do with
me after this?"

Tom looked over at the people walking by. "Charlie, I'm
going away after this. Ali, William and I are going far away where
the past no longer influences our futures."

"Is there any place that far away?"

Tom thought for a moment, "Perhaps not, but when they're
not on your doorstep it makes their influence that much less."

The wind blew a cold chill around them as the sun began to
make its descent for another night. Headlights started to be
switched on as dusk settled in.

"You know, that night, back then. I didn't do much really, just
what any brother would do. You know I've never asked you

244

about that night. I know what happened of course, but I've never asked you."

Tom looked at him, "Are you asking now?"

Charlie thought about it for a moment. "No."

They sat there in silence for a while until Tom lifted his wrist, lighting up the dial on his watch and stood up.

"It's time."

Charlie got to his feet and nodded. Both brothers made their way back to the park and waited. Before long, two men walked along the path towards them.

"Mr Hook and Mr Hook! Here we are!"

"Is it just the two of you?" Tom asked.

"There are more in the van, but I was assured that it would be as easy as taking candy from a baby. Is that not correct?"

"Yes, it should be."

"And if it's not?"

"When I go in, I'll know. If I come out and I think it will be more difficult then I'll let you know."

"I see!"

"Here is the location of where he is to be taken. It's not far from here," said Charlie, holding out a slip of paper.

Ry-Man took it and passed it to the man beside him, "and what of the business information?"

"That you will get once it's been done," assured Tom. "Is the Professor with you?"

"He's close by, didn't think you'd want him in the back of the van for this!"

Tom nodded.

"We'll drop him off after we've dealt with Stan, once we have the information."

"And I need another favour from you afterwards."

"A favour? I'm assuming you have something to offer for this favour?"

"I do."

"Then we shall discuss that later."

They all walked to the car park and got in their vehicles. Tom led the way followed by Charlie and Ry-Man. It was only a short distance away and in no time, they were parked just off Filwood Broadway, waiting.

\*\*\*

At five to eight, one of the men from Ry-Man's van got out and walked over to the side of the community centre. Here he would have a good view of the shop front as well as the van. As the second hand swept across the twelve at eight o'clock Tom took a deep breath and stepped out of the car.

As he approached the door his heart rate and breathing increased, every footstep turning up the dial until suddenly, when his hand fell on the handle, it all dropped. He pushed open the door, the tinkle of the bell above announced his arrival. The place was as empty as before, the light spilling out from the back brighter now in the dark. He crossed the floor and headed down the familiar corridor once more to the door that waited.

He knocked.

"Enter!"

Tom pushed open the door and was relieved to see Emily sitting on the edge of the shredder like a scared little schoolgirl in the headmaster's office. She looked up, glanced to her right and then ran to him, throwing her arms around his neck.

"Uncle Tom", she sobbed as she held him tight.

"It's okay Emily, I've got you now. Shhh, it's alright."

He finally managed to release her grip, "Just wait outside the door for me honey, okay?"

She nodded and stepped outside; the door closed behind her.

Tom turned and saw Stan and another man behind the desk.

"Please, take a seat," proffered Stan.

Tom walked over and sat down, his eyes glancing between them both.

"This is Marcus, he's the one who graciously brought Emily back to us."

Tom nodded his thanks that was returned. *Was he the man that also had Ali and William?* He felt his anger start to bubble up inside.

"I've told Marcus a little of our conversations and he's very excited about it! I think you two would do well together."

He didn't look like he was excited; in fact, he would be surprised if any emotions found their way onto his face. *Was he the person who took my family?*

Tom struggled against these thoughts as he spoke, "I'm looking forward to Monday where I can meet the rest of your people."

Stan stared across the desk at him, a greasy grin on his face like he knew, he just knew that Tom must be aware by now that his family had been taken; knew that he wanted to say something about it, curious to see if he did.

The anger reached Tom's throat and he had to cough to shake it loose.

"I've made the arrangements with the University for the gathering on Monday, it's all set."

Stan paused a second before answering, "That's great, I'm looking forward to it."

He continued to stare, "So I'll see you Monday then?"

Tom nodded and stood up to leave. The grin on Stan's face grew as he did so, stirring the volcano that was straining to burst free. He had to relieve some of the pressure. He turned and leaned on the back of his chair, "I know you've got them."

"Got them? What do you mean?"

"My family, don't play games with me."

Stan gave a little chuckle that turned up the heat inside Tom.

"It took you long enough to know they were missing! What was it, a domestic? Or did you tell her what you're going to be doing for me and she left you?"

The guy to Stan's side broke into a disjointed smile that looked as if it had been painted on by a four year old. Tom gripped the chair back, his fingers turning white.

"Oh don't be so melodramatic. I had to be sure that you would do as you said, do as you were told; this isn't a game. You're no different from your brother. Once your niece was returned, I had to maintain some leverage and seeing them leave with bags packed seemed like an opportunity not to be missed. You'll see them again after the meeting on Monday. In fact, I may just bring them along so they can hear all the amazing things you'll be doing for me!"

"That's not very nice now, is it?" he said through gritted teeth.

"Maybe not, but you have to learn that although you will be helping to run the circus, it's still my show, and I call the shots."

*'Not for long'* thought Tom as he released the chair and stood up.

"Monday then."

"Monday."

Tom turned and walked out. Emily was still breathing in sobs as he put his arm around her waist and led her out the front. The night had started to get a hold of the sky as he guided her through the shop door and along the pavement. Tom's other hand was by his side, his index and middle finger pointing wide spaced pointing to the ground: two.

The man waiting by the community centre mirrored Tom's fingers to the van; there were two people inside.

He handed Emily over to Charlie, who was crying more than she was and heard the side doors of the van behind them slide open. Six large and well-armed men leapt out, one after the other, and flanked the shop door. These were professionals, ex-military for sure; not like the two goons he met at the docks. No wonder Stan needed to up his game.

As he stared across at the doorway, he remembered something. *'Shit, I've forgotten to tell them about the bell on the door'!*

There was no time now as a short countdown started and the door burst in; the clang of the bell rang out with force. The men entered smoothly, checking angles and corners. He stared at the scene as the last man entered and the door closed; his imagination was alive with images of what was going on inside.

He recalled the movements they would be making, leaning forward, eyes down the barrel, sweeping blind spots, adrenaline pumping, overlapping each other to push forward. His body was unconsciously making the moves like a spectator watching a boxing match. Two muffled shots rang out as their flashes filled the darkened windows. Seconds passed, maybe minutes. Tom had to do all he could to stop his body from running inside to find out if they had him, had them both.

Then suddenly the door was flung open, and a fat Stan was jostled across the road, a black bag over his head, his hands zip-tied together out front. He was followed by another hooded man who was crouching to one side, blood running down his arm. They had them both.

Once they were bundled into the back of the van Tom walked over to the passenger side to speak to Ry-Man.

"I need both of them at the location."

"Do you now? And what do you have for me?"

"Inside the back office on the wall are all the files and documents you need. All the suppliers and contacts, all the prices and invoices, all the delivery schedules and buildings. All of the information you need to step straight into his shoes and continue running everything as if nothing ever happened."

Ry-Man nodded. "And what of his people?"

"I didn't promise you the people, just the business."

Ry-Man stared at him unamused.

"The people I can give you, for the price of the favour."

This was met with a smile. "It's a shame you don't want to be part of the business, you'd do well."

"Thanks, but it's not for me."

"Okay, I'll go in and look at the files and secure what's needed. Once I'm happy then I'll bring them both to you. Shouldn't be more than a few hours."

"And the Professor?"

"He can be taken home."

Tom nodded and walked back to Charlie whose body was still shaking. He looked up.

"There's two of them and it'll take a few of hours for them to get to us. Take Emily home and meet me there in a couple of hours."

Charlie nodded and placed Emily in his van.

Tom walked to his car and sat in. His hands reached out for the steering wheel, but they were shaking too much to take a grip. *'Okay, that's easy part. Now it gets hard'.*

# 25. THE BLACK PATH

## 1989 – AGE 16

The divorce didn't take long to go through. Tom's parents had agreed not to contest anything if certain 'facts' were left out. His mother had kept the house due to her custody of Tom and his father had moved away. He wrote him a note with an address somewhere in Cornwall and encouraged him to look him up whenever he came down.

Charlie had moved back in, now that the coast was clear, and he and his mother had become as thick as thieves. She had gone through a series of boyfriends, none of whom were suitable or stayed for very long. Tom would often come home and find Charlie and his mother drunk in the living room, laughing hysterically at something on the television. He felt like the outsider, perhaps his resemblance to his father simply made him a painful memory best ignored.

Being back over this side of town made getting to Keynsham harder. He no longer worked at The Fast-Food Shack once his age had become known; he wasn't sure if it was a legal issue or embarrassment that made Tina let him go, but he didn't much care. Life had become a kind of floating circus with little meaning.

Living back here meant that school was only down the road again so he would often pop in to see how things had progressed without him. He was going to fail his exams without doubt, but it was nice to see familiar faces.

He had made a new friend that helped him hold onto some kind of normality. Johnny lived in the top floor bedsit next to Benny's house. They had met at one of his parties and got on like a house on fire, drinking, laughing, and enjoying life. Tom had crashed at his that night and continued to do so several nights a week. Johnny had a girlfriend that he saw now and again, but mostly it was just the two of them.

Johnny was several years older than Tom, but that didn't seem to matter. He was getting himself straight before joining the Royal Marines and they would spend hours talking about the military and watching war movies on the Special Forces. Johnny had a knife of his own as well that he would throw into a dart board to practice; Tom still had his and they used to play a game of getting closest to the bullseye for the next can of lager. Tom invariably won.

There were some interesting characters living in the bedsits below. One of them, Si, rode a huge trike that he had built himself from bits of other motorcycles. He had taken Tom and Johnny on the back several times, the rush of it thrilled Tom more than anything; the life and death of going so fast with no seatbelt or crash helmet, just holding on for dear life.

At Si's place one night he was telling them about the ghostly experiences he'd had in there; the building was old with a sweeping staircase that ended right outside his door. It was late and they had had a few drinks, so the atmosphere seemed ripe for spooky tales. He told them about the lights and TV flickering on and off in sequence even though they were plugged into the same socket and the prickles he got up his neck at the same time each night, as if he was being watched.

Tom had noticed a baseball bat with nails sticking out of the end leant up against the door, and knowing what a character Si was, imagined it was for the police, but when Tom mentioned it, he just laughed. "No, that's not for them. That's for something else. Maybe you'll find out later!"

They continued to drink, and Johnny and Si had smoked a couple of joints when all of a sudden, the lights started flashing.

Si had been right; they flashed in a haphazard sequence which didn't make much sense to Tom. Even the lamp in the far corner joined in the dance that was plugged into a different socket altogether.

"This is it!" shouted Si, jumping to his feet.

Tom and Johnny stood up, unsure what to expect. Si walked over to the door and picked up the bat, twisting it in his hands for a better grip.

Tom's heart had suddenly raced into top gear and his stomach had a sense of dread that knotted up like a fist.

From somewhere upstairs there came the sound of knocking on the walls that seemed to move, as if someone were walking down the stairs tapping as they went. When they reached the corner, the knocking began tracing its path along Si's wall. Whoever they were, they were about halfway down the final flight and would land on the bottom step, outside Si's door, within a few steps.

"Right, ready?" Whispered Si, one hand on the bat, the other on the door handle.

Tom wondered what the hell they were doing, scaring this poor person to death by jumping out brandishing a nail-studded bat!

The steps and knocking moved lower; the last three, two, one, "Now!"

Si flung the door open, and they all pounced out only to be met by a completely empty staircase and lobby. Wild thoughts of ghosts and ghouls flew around Tom's mind as he tried to make sense of what had just happened, the prickles on the back of his neck pointing up like needles. They looked around and only when they were satisfied that all was clear did they go back inside, full of conversation and excitement. Tom's mind was grasping for the logical, holding on to the notion of pipes creaking and stairs settling in the cold of the night, but nothing made sense.

The pair of them had talked about it for days afterwards, trying to figure it out without success. It made the nights at Johnny's feel that much creepier, as if something or someone was with them, watching. It made the journey over to Johnny's a lot scarier too, especially when the darker nights came in. The walk from the bus stop to the house took him past a graveyard, down a narrow, deserted lane and under a train track where supposedly a man had jumped from a moving train and splattered across; if you stood underneath when a train went over you could hear him scream, so they said. Tom was careful not to be in the tunnel if there was even a hint of a train coming. He would wait a few yards back and listen, then quick march through without looking back. He would never run; if you run, that's when they chase you.

When he'd get there, he'd open the large front door and walk up the ghost stairs, all the way up to Johnny's at the top. As he did this today the door was unusually locked. He knocked.

It took a few seconds for Johnny to open the door, red bloodshot eyes staring out.

"What's wrong?" asked Tom walking in.

"It's Vicky," he replied, holding back a sob. "She's left me."

He slumped onto the mattress on the floor surrounded by empty cans and began crying again. Tom had forgotten that he even had a girlfriend and wasn't surprised that she had gone and done her own thing, that's what they were doing after all.

He sat down next to him and rubbed his back, not knowing what to say. He searched his memory to find comforting words.

"It's okay, it'll be alright," was the best he could manage.

"It's not alright! I know we've not been close for a while, but I thought that would change, but she's met some prick called Nigel and now he's gone and ruined it."

Tom felt the anger flow out of Johnny and pour into himself. How dare this guy ruin his friend's life and make him cry like that.

"You're my friend, aren't you?" asked Johnny.

"Of course I am."

"My best friend right?"

"I'll always be here for you."

"Then you'll do something for me?"

"Of course, what do you need?"

"I need you to take care of Nigel."

Those words echoed around the bare walls of the room, trying to find a meaningful way that they could enter Tom's ears and make sense.

"What do you mean?"

"He lives over your way and works at Wills's. He works late every other week and takes a shortcut home round the back of some houses. You'll know the place; it's called The Black Path."

Tom knew the place. It was a lane that ran behind the top estate of white houses. The pale slabs that lined the walkways stopped here and would venture no further. Instead, a path of tarmac had spewed forth to create this cut-through that was wild and overgrown. The bushes and branches of trees grew tall like menacing giants and leaned over to create a tunnel that rejected any light from entering. It was a dark, foreboding place.

He had stepped inside but once to peer down its winding route, but never ventured any further. Homeless people, drug dealers and murderers lived and operated in there. He had discovered over the years that there were areas in every city that you don't go; that Knowle West was considered one of them. But there were also places within them that even the locals just don't venture, that no one dared go; the Black Path was that place.

"Do you know it?" Johnny asked, nudging Tom out of his thoughts.

"Yeah, I know it."

"He gets off around two in the morning and walks through on his way home."

*'He walks through there at night. is he crazy?'* thought Tom.

"So, he'll be easy to jump."

"Wait, what?" It was just dawning on him now what he was being asked to do. "You want me to beat him up? On The Black Path?"

"No, I want you to kill him."

They stared at each other, a well of sick forced its way up Tom's throat.

"I can't do that!"

255

"Sure you can, you're going to be a soldier right? That's what soldiers do. They take out the bad guys, and he's a bad guy. Look at what he's done to me and Vicky!"

Tom could only stare at his friend as tears began streaming down his face again. He was going to be a soldier, but this was different.

"Why can't you do it yourself?"

"Because I'm too close. I'm the first person they'd suspect if anything happened to him. No, I need to be with other people that night to give myself an alibi. No one knows you or knows that we're friends."

Tom thought about this. Apart from Si downstairs he was probably right. They had always kept themselves to themselves, staying in the bedsit, never venturing far. Had that been on purpose?

"Look, I'll help you plan everything and get you ready. He's back on nights this Wednesday so that's when we'll do it."

Tom sat there, numb. He couldn't quite comprehend what was being asked of him. He tried to imagine what that would look like, how it would be, but kept coming up blank; all he could see was the dark entrance to The Black Path, his mind wouldn't allow him to enter even in his own imagination.

"You'll do it, right? After everything I've done for you, as my best friend, you'll do it?"

Tom remembered the vow he had made to himself a long time ago; that he would do anything for his best friend, no matter what. But not this, surely not this.

"Tom, you'll do it won't you?"

Tom just sat there and nodded.

\*\*\*

They spent the next two days practicing what and how it would be done. They used the narrow lane up to Johnny's place for Tom to hide in and jump out of when Johnny walked past, getting used to the movements and where the knife would go.

The more they did it the more it felt like a game; they were only messing about, having a laugh, they weren't really going to do it. They got closer as they spent every hour of the day and night together, talking about it, going through the moves, dreaming about it.

On Wednesday Tom had stayed at home. They'd agreed that Johnny should spend the day with other people and crash at their house to give him the best alibi. Tom spent most of the morning in bed, listening to his mother bang around the house before leaving for work. When the door closed behind her, he was alone. The sense of loneliness and isolation swallowed him whole as he lay in his bed, a bed he had laid in most of his life. He thought back to the flat in St George he had lived in practically on his own just months before. He looked around this room that was so familiar yet so alien to him now. He had been a different person when this had been his bedroom for real. He tried to recall that scared and naive boy, but all he got were flashes from his past, not the whole story. He tried to piece them together, to make sense of how they had led him to be here, but he couldn't grasp them; they were scattered puzzle pieces as ethereal as the knocking spectre on the staircase.

After a while an old familiar sound began to echo across the street. He sat up and went to his window. Across the way, behind the houses opposite, he could see the playground of his old junior school. Kids were running around and screaming without a care in the world. How he wished he was back there with them, no cares, no worries; just free to run and enjoy life, but he wasn't convinced that he had ever ran and enjoyed life back then anyway. He knew that if he could go back, he wouldn't actually be able to make a difference to where he now stood. He could have been looking back in time right now at himself in that playground, but he would be just as powerless to change his course as he would be to change that of any of those kids in front of him now.

He got dressed and went downstairs for lunch, a bacon sandwich and a cup of tea. As he took it over and sat down at the table, he noticed the chip that had been taken out of the edge and formed a dent underneath. He recalled his mother being slammed against the wall; thrown back out of her seat, her legs hitting the table as they whipped up. He thought back to how he had almost taken another life that day, his own, and how things would have been so very different if he had. He wouldn't still be here; they would never have found him in time. He would have just slipped away and missed all the commotion that would have followed. He wondered if you ever got to see any of that or could visit your funeral after you die. That might be quite nice, to do it just to hear the good things people say about you when you're gone. Why didn't they say them when you were alive? What a waste.

He washed his plate and cup and went into the living room. He thought that perhaps if he watched a movie or two, he would be able to borrow the courage and bravery from the people on the screen, but after a few minutes he switched it off. These people were brave and courageous it's true, but they were also the good guys, saving lives and rescuing the weak and needy. It made Tom feel sick.

He went back up to his room and lay on his bed. He wrapped himself up in his duvet and tried to find sleep again, but the sleep that found him was not the restful kind that he had hoped for.

His dreams became nightmares around him as he went under; a mixture of old horror movies; werewolves, ghosts and chainsaw wielding maniacs with disfigured faces. The last one he remembered was clearer, it was one that kept returning to him. He was standing in a large junkyard, a dirt track beneath his feet. All around him towered flattened cars piled on top of each other that simultaneously created a sense of space and claustrophobia. Behind him appeared a witch dressed in a black cloak, her wrinkled and mangled face poked out from a dark hood that looked like an opening of overgrown trees and bushes; her gnarled fingers reached out for him. He began to run away as she slowly advanced toward him. His efforts became laboured after several steps, his feet slipped in the dust, and it felt as if a giant rubber band had been pulled across his waist; the more he ran forward, the more it wanted to throw him back. He dropped down on all fours to scramble and drag himself forward, but the pressure just kept on increasing until he could no longer hold on. The ground beneath him was torn away as the band threw him back, straight into the witch's waiting grasp.

He woke up with a start, the bedclothes around him wet. He struggled to remove the duvet that had wound itself around him and get to his feet. The light outside had started to fade early. His mother would be back soon, he wanted to get out before she did. He didn't want any questions.

He grabbed his school backpack and checked inside. There was a dark hat, a pair of black woollen gloves and Johnny's knife. It was considerably larger than Tom's and much better for the job. Tom felt in his pocket for his; it was still there.

He took the bag downstairs and put in some food and a bottle of Coke and zipped it up. He took one last look around the room and left.

He had no real place to go yet, so just wandered the streets. He walked through Inns of Court and past his old den. He considered jumping over and killing time there, but it didn't feel right. He walked up towards Filwood fields and hoped the dark expanse of grass, with the lights of the cars passing in the distance, would be peaceful somehow. He walked across the dark field to roughly the centre and sat down.

Behind him he could see Filwood Broadway, the lights of the shops being thrown across the wide road. The swimming pool was illuminated, rippled shadows danced on the walls and ceiling inside as a familiar smell of chlorine and warmth flowed from his memory. The library opposite was in darkness, all readers safe inside the neat folds of paper at home. He turned back towards the distant road and the old airport beyond and watched as these people went about their business, oblivious to having an observer track them for the few seconds it took to cross his path. Who were these people and where were they going? Tom tried to imagine the lives they had, the houses they lived in, the families waiting for them to walk through the door, the love they shared, and without knowing why, he began to weep. Not sobs that shook his bones, just quiet streams of tears that had found their way out of his body, they no longer wanted to be part of this person. He felt their loss deeply as he sat there and waited.

\*\*\*

He lifted his wrist and illuminated the face on his watch. Both the hands and the digital display agreed that it was one thirty. He grabbed his bag and put on the hat and gloves as he stood; the coldness of the floor had seeped inside to his bones and made his muscles creak and moan. He walked back along the field and branched out to the left as he approached the houses, their windows black, unseeing. As he got closer to the entrance of the path he slowed down, his senses becoming heightened with every step. Each crack of twig, each scurry of animal drew a breath and cranked the tension up inside so much that he felt like a clockwork mechanism ready to snap.

As he reached the overhanging canopy of the path, the tarmac floor seemed to pulsate with energy or maybe it was just his eyes trying to adjust to the pitch blackness within. He leaned forward, creeping along like a cartoon character, each step taken with silent care. The more he moved into this place the more he was able to see the crumpled-up pages of magazines and the splintered plastic cups that littered the floor. A rustle came from his side, and he froze in terror. He slowly turned his head sideways and saw two or three sleeping bags stretched out in the bush beyond. He felt like Jack having climbed the beanstalk, creeping around so that the giant wouldn't wake up and find him stealing across his land.

He crept another few metres in before he found a spot that was suitable to hide in and wasn't already occupied. He slipped off his backpack and took out the knife, replacing the bag as he backed into the gap and crouched on the balls of his feet. He covered his watch with his hands as he lit the screen again. One forty-five.

He tried to go over in his mind the practice that he and Johnny had been doing, but it was difficult to relate it to this place, to the darkness that surrounded him. He wanted to close his eyes to better picture those scenes, but he dared not. Although his vision was down to barely five percent, he had no intention of taking that to zero.

Suddenly there was a crack and the sound of approaching feet, several of them, coming from where Tom had entered moments before. He wondered at how hidden he truly was from the path and shuffled back a little more. Voices became attached to the steps as they drew nearer; Tom grasped the knife handle in a sweaty woollen grip. The noises grew louder as they reached his crouched position. Then the volume began to lower as they moved along and down the path.

His muscles loosened their spasm as he began to breathe again. He couldn't be in that state when Nigel came along, so he tried to draw his mind to something calming, something peaceful. An image of a fish's tail swam across his eyes, its graceful movements relaxing as it glides through the water; the slow deliberate strokes that propelled it forward.

This helped, and his pulse lowered considerably. He could do this. It was nothing, just a game. It wasn't really happening. As his sense of ability and courage increased so too did his capacity to reason. He could quite easily leap out and stab this man, but there was no honour in that. His heroes would scorn him for such a cowardly act. Perhaps it would be better to confront the villain head on, to tell him why he was evil and then to dispatch him. He ran through the two scenarios to see which one felt better. Neither felt great, but the latter felt more in keeping with his intentions of being someone good. But was he good if he was doing something like this?

As the decision was reached, he heard footsteps again, quieter this time, just a single set. He braced himself, tensed his legs, turned his stomach to iron and held his breath. His head was thumping with blood, and he had to strain to hear the footsteps over it. He almost missed it as the sound went past him. He leapt out.

The footsteps stopped and turned.

"Nigel..."

"Who the fuck?"

"Nigel..." No other words could find their way out of the blackness within; he didn't know exactly what he should say, he hadn't prepared for this speech.

All of a sudden there was a loud knock like two claves being banged together and Tom's vision blurred as he saw the world turning sideways before him. A thought crossed his mind as he fell, *'Did he just hit me?'*

He could hear voices shouting and the noise of people and boots running, getting louder as his vision wavered. There was swearing, pushing, someone tripping over his legs as he lay there. He rolled over slowly and forced his eyes to focus on what was happening. Before him stood four men with shaved heads and large boots, boots that were being used to kick something on the floor. One of them stopped kicking and began stomping, as if trying to squash a large bug that was scurrying across the floor. A sudden crack brought the boots to a standstill. There was a moment's pause before the boots and the shaved heads they belonged to ran off.

Tom pushed himself up to his knees. His hands felt warm and wet, an unusual sticky sensation on top of the hard tarmac. He brought them up to his face and saw the dark outline of his gloves, dripping with viscous liquid, seeping inside to his fingers. He parted his hands to see the source of this river that flowed around him now. He gasped and stumbled backwards to his feet; the fog of his mind clearing a little. He turned and ran, swaying between bush and tree as he found his way out. He didn't know how he made it back to his front door and came around at the sight of his key scraping the metal around the lock, unable to find the slot. Then suddenly it was gone, the door along with it and there in its place stood Charlie.

He stared at him for a minute before grabbing hold of his collar and dragging him around the back of the house.

"What the fuck happened?" He asked in a loud whisper, the look on his face Tom had only ever seen once before, but he couldn't answer; he was flipping between consciousness and the horror or what he had seen, not knowing which he preferred.

Charlie started stripping Tom's clothes off, everything, gloves, jumper, pants and socks, leaving Tom shivering there naked on the back doorstep. He used the clothes to wipe off as much blood as he could before leading him back inside. He took him upstairs, placed him in the bath and turned on the taps.

He then ran to his room and grabbed a handful of books and went back outside. He picked up the bundle of clothes and took them to the top of the garden where he began to dig a hole, a pit with his bare hands, tossing stones, leaves and roots out of the way. When it was big enough, he tore out the pages of his books and scrunched them up to make a bed at the bottom, the beautiful pictures printed on them lost in the darkness. When it had a good layer, he took out his tin of tobacco and retrieved his lighter from inside. The paper went up quickly. He began feeding the clothes into the flames, adding more and more paper as he went. It took a long time for it all to go, or mostly go. Some bits were too wet to catch light so these he buried along with the ashes, vowing to come back the next night and finish them off with the books that remained.

He ran back up to the bathroom to see Tom laying there in the pink water staring up at him. He bent down and pulled out the plug, the water that swirled away the colour of candyfloss. When it had drained, he replaced the plug and began filling it up again.

The cold water on one foot and boiling hot on the other brought Tom around for a moment. He looked at his mother's bedroom door just outside.

"It's okay; she's had a bottle of wine tonight so she's dead to the world."

Dead to the world. Those words ran around his mind like a dizzying whirlwind.

"Don't worry Tommy boy," Charlie comforted. "I've taken care of the clothes, there's nothing to worry about."

Tom looked at Charlie questioningly.

"I burned them with my books, I won't be needing them anymore. I'm moving out."

"Where are you moving to?" Tom's voice cracked.

"Suzie's up the duff so I've got to get a place of our own. What happened here Tommy?"

Tom couldn't answer. As the water filled up around him, all he could think about was how nice it would be to see fish with their long, beautiful tails swimming around his legs now.

## 26. FRIDAY

Charlie drove through the iron gates into what used to be the playground of their old infant school, a stone's throw from their family home. He parked the van where the ship shaped climbing frame used to be and walked over to where Tom was sitting. He had changed his clothes already; had begun the transformation. He sat there dark, emotionless.

"You know, I crushed my finger in a toilet door, right here," Tom said absently.

"Ouch, I bet that hurt."

"I could hear the crunching of the muscle and was sure the bone had snapped. It turned out to be nothing in the end but a bruise, but I've never forgotten that sound."

A chill blew in from the clear sky. Light from the fat moon glinted off the many tiny shards of glass that littered the remains of the floor. The stars that were strong enough to pierce through the layer of light pollution shone as best they could. Charlie sat down where the next cubicle would have been and looked out over the black fields behind. Sweeping down the hill to the left was the junior school, still going after all these years. He remembered the hill being great for rolling down as a kid and the line of trees near the base where you were forbidden to pass for fear of mixing with the bigger kids on the other side. Straight on you could see the lights of the bijou apartment block that used to be Wills's tobacco factory; Charlie felt a twinge in his big toe at the thought. Directly in front, at the bottom of the hill on the other side of the road was The Cage.

"How's Emily doing?" asked Tom.

265

ANTONY CURTIS

"She'll be alright. Suzie was there and took her over to her parents for a bit. She's shaken up, but she's a tough kid."

"Just like her parents."

"I'm not so sure about that. I've felt pretty useless this past week."

Tom nodded. "Do you ever wonder if things could have been different somehow? If things could have been better?"

"All the fucking time! I wonder what it would have been like if Suzie hadn't lost the first baby. I wonder what it would have been like to go to college. I wonder what it would have been like if our parents had actually liked each other. I wonder about all these things constantly. That's why I try to do things to improve the situation. I know that means taking chances, but what else can I do? I have no education, no money, no skills that could get me in the door to a job and I can't exactly put Stan down as a reference now, can I?"

"True."

"So, I'm stuck. And now my biggest source of income is about to be wiped out too."

Tom looked at Charlie with pursed lips.

"Well, you know what I mean. I need someone to give me a hand, give me a chance, then I'd show them what I could do."

"Nobody gives you anything, Charlie. You have to go and get it. There's no point in smoking and drinking all your extra money away and then complaining that you have nothing. You have the same number of hours we all have. If you want it badly enough, you'd use that money to learn a trade, get the skills and then build from there. No one's going to do that for you."

Charlie looked down and sighed.

"I used to love this school," he said, changing the subject.

"I can't really remember much of it," Tom replied.

"You can't? You don't remember Mrs Williams who used to teach us sewing and read us stories and would play books on that enormous tape machine?"

Tom searched his memories and came up blank. He shrugged his shoulders.

266

"She played one one day and scared the shit out of me. It was something about a black castle or a black knight. Gave me the willies for weeks." He laughed at the thought before it went quiet again.

"They'll be here soon; you'd better pull your van over to the overgrowth and trees over there. I've got something I need you need to rig up for power."

Charlie looked at him questioningly, but simply got up and did as he was told.

Tom had already put the bags over there and now followed as Charlie drove over and parked up again. He took out the converter and handed it over for Charlie to plug in. He opened his rucksack and took out his pistol in the holster and fed his tactical belt through the opening and clipped the bottom around his thigh. Next, he removed the knife holsters and fed them around the other side of the belt so that both knives were located behind his hips, a knife each side for easy access. Then he reached into his pocket and pulled out his small, blackened penknife and opened the blade. It held together well enough. He closed it up and returned it to his pocket and as he did so, he began to open up the locked chest in his mind, purposely lifting the lid that had been shut for so long; allowing the memories of actions and events gone by to show themselves, to be revealed. He let the light shine in the deep dark places within, the places where his mind wouldn't allow him to go for fear of what was inside; fear of being wrenched in by the gravity of it all and then unable to return. There was nothing that would stop him from doing what was needed for the people he loved. Visions of red soaked fingers flashed before his eyes, explosions and gunfire echoed around his head. His stomach became steel and his pulse became robotic. He exhaled long and slow. He recalled a particular moment when he was out on patrol with his team looking for a man who was being paid to help track down insurgents, but instead had been feeding them misinformation and ambush coordinates. When they got to the man's house he wasn't there, but his family were. They wouldn't talk, at first, but they did, eventually. He brought the sounds, the smells back with him as if he were standing in the evening chill of that desert land.

He stood there now as a soldier, as a man who had a mission to conclude and nothing more. All the years since that night evaporated. The change was complete.

"Okay, should all be good for power. What do you need it for?" Charlie asked, looking at Tom, noticing that there was something different about him.

Tom took out a small piece of equipment from the tote bag and handed it over.

"What the hell is that?"

Tom didn't answer; instead, he arranged the bags along the side of the van for easy access.

"The drum?" asked Tom, his voice low and firm.

"It's in the back. I'll need a hand, this sucker's not light!"

They walked around to the rear of the van and opened it up. Inside was a large metal drum that had once been blue but was now more of a rusted orange. There was a metal clasp that ran around the entire circumference of the top and allowed the whole lid to come away.

They shuffled it to the lip of the van, the contents slopping around inside. It wasn't full but was still difficult to manoeuvre. At the edge they got a good grip and managed to slow the rate of descent to a casual fall; a deep rumble reverberated as it hit the ground.

"Shit, I hope it doesn't leak!" Said Charlie.

They both checked the floor around it to make sure, then lent it back and rolled it over to the tree line.

"Where is the opening?" asked Tom.

"It's just over there," Charlie gestured with his head.

"And you've checked that it'll fit?"

"Of course, what do you take me for?"

Tom could only look his response that was lost in the darkness of the undergrowth.

"The gap is actually much bigger, but this is the largest drum I could get. Five hundred and seventy-one millimetres wide; two hundred and fifty litre capacity. It's a quarter full as you asked."

"Good."

They returned to the van and brought out two sturdy looking folding metallic garden chairs and placed them either side of the van that acted like a screen.

"You sure that will take his weight?"

Charlie shrugged. They closed the doors and waited.

\*\*\*

It didn't feel long before a van pulled into the gate at the top. Charlie flashed his headlights, and it made its way down to them. When it stopped Ry-Man stepped out and came over.

"This is an interesting setup you have here!"

Tom ignored the statement. "So, the information was all good?"

"Yeah, but it would be a lot easier with the staff on board as well!"

"You'll have them. How's the Professor?"

"That's one interesting old man you have there. I think he kind of enjoyed his experience once he got his head around where he was. He started asking questions about the work and even began telling the boys about Nietzsche and Jung!"

Tom smiled at the thought.

"He's been taken home and said he looks forward to seeing you on Monday morning."

Some relief came at those words although Monday would now start off with a very interesting conversation indeed.

"So, what's this favour you want done?"

"Stan has my wife and son somewhere. I'm going to find out where and I need you to get them for me."

Ry-Man raised his eyebrows. Tom couldn't tell if it was from the job or the things that he was going to do to get the location.

"So, another raid is it?"

"No, it should just be a simple pick-up and delivery."

Ry-Man nodded. "So how are you going to give me the people in the business for this simple pick up?"

"I have arranged a large meeting of all of Stan's senior and middle leaders. They're all coming together to learn about the new way forward for the business. Stan actually arranged it. It's a rare occasion so I'm told. It would be your opportunity to set them up with the change you want. You can tell them anything you want about Stan, he won't be around to argue."

"You're a sly fucking fox."

"So, is that a yes?"

"That's a yes. I'll have a couple of guys waiting for your call."

"Thanks."

With that, Ry-Man banged the side of the van and the doors slid open. Stan and his friend were dragged to each of the chairs and double strapped in with zip-ties. The men jumped back in the van and the doors closed.

"It was nice doing business with you," offered Ry-Man. "If you ever change your mind about a job, you have my number."

Tom nodded and they left. Silence settled. Both men remained fairly still in their seats; he wondered what must be going through their heads right now. He walked over to Stan first and removed his hood.

Despite it being relatively dark, Stan blinked hard. When he saw Tom standing there, he began to get animated, trying to speak, no shout through the gag that was around his head. It looked like a leather S&M piece, but instead of a shiny red ball in his mouth, there was a thick cylindrical wad of material, like a cotton towel that had been rolled up.

Tom let the initial anger and profanities clear before he leaned forward and slightly loosened the neck strap, just enough to allow a gap in the corner of his mouth.

His breathing laboured, Stan started up again. "You fucking prick, you're dead, you and your family are all fucking dead. I'm gonna make sure you never see them again except in pieces mailed to you every month."

"And how are you going to do that?"

Stan's eyes began searching for an answer to the seemingly simple question.

"Stan, you are going to tell me where my family are and you're going to be more than happy to do so."

Stan looked at him with a grin, "Not on your life."

"No Stan, on something much worse."

Tom walked over to the bags and took out the first aid kit to retrieve a pair of surgical scissors. He walked over and stood beside Stan who tried to lean sideways away from the blades.

"Oh, don't worry, scissors are useful tools, but not for that."

Tom proceeded to cut off Stan's shirt, leaving his bare rolls of fat exposed to the air.

"Now, there are many ways to do this. Ethically, it should start with the least intrusive method and work its way up, but you see, I'm in a bit of a hurry and it's been a long night so I'm just going to cut straight to the chase."

Tom tightened the gag back and returned the scissors to the box. He then picked up the small electrical tool he had taken from the university and brought it close to Stan's face; his eyes widening.

"This is an interesting piece of equipment that most people never get to see. It's a little old now of course and the blades are a bit dull, but it will still do the job."

Tom turned it on for a few seconds; the sound of whirring that spooled up was a mixture of a dentist's drill and a hairdryer. Stan's eyes were fixated on it, trying to figure out what the hell it was and what it did.

"There are various settings, but the two main ones are for split-thickness and full-thickness. I've never really used one before, but I've seen them in action; fascinating."

Beads of sweat began to emanate from Stan's pores as his imagination ran riot.

Tom started pacing in front of Stan as if he were back in the lecture hall. "Now, there are several ways of causing pain, most are pretty straightforward, you could stab, crush or even burn, but in most cases, the pain is pretty much contained to a small area, and no matter what you do, it usually comes from a single organ. Do you know what organ that is?"

He waited for an answer but was only met with wide eyes. He had Stan's full attention, good.

"The skin of course. The skin is the largest organ of the body, and it just so happens to contain the most nerve endings that register pain. This beauty..." Tom raised the machine up. "...will slice and dice your skin in almost endless strips; simply tear it from your body."

Charlie stood behind Tom and was getting just as nervous as Stan.

"Of course, it's used in medical procedures, skin grafts and such, but for you Stan, I'm willing to throw away the manufacturers guidelines and be a little more...creative."

Tom crouched down between Stan's feet so he could see the settings printed on the side.

"Now, personally, I don't think the light touch of split-thickness would do the job do you? We need something more than a thin layer of skin for what we're doing. What we want is the full dermis, hair follicles, sweat glands, nerve endings and roots, the whole lot. We want them to be yanked up and torn away. That would do the trick. So, for that, I think I'll just go ahead and set it to the deepest setting it has."

Tom turned the dial all the way around, Stan's eyes extending on stalks with each number clicked through.

"Now, before I get started on the huge expanse of skin before me, is there anything you would like to tell me?"

Stan struggled to get enough air through his flat nose which made his chest pulsate in a fast, shallow rhythm. He blinked the sweat from his eyes a couple of times and found some resolve. He shook his head.

"You know what, I'm kinda glad it wasn't that easy."

Tom started the machine and the whirring sounded up again. He placed the machine on the shoulder blade; Stan tried to pull away as best he could. It rattled as it took hold of the skin and with a single sweeping motion, a wide rectangular patch of skin was torn away.

Stan began yelling and screaming through the gag, his body shaking. The chair was barely holding together. The red section the machine had left was glistening and oozing; ragged pieces of torn muscle and nerve fibres dangled.

"Ooh, that looks like it hurts," said Tom and he poked the site with his latex gloved finger.

A muffled scream continued for a while as Tom moved in front of him. He unwound a beautifully neat portion of skin from the machine. It came out with frayed ends still clinging to the underside of the skin. Tom held it between his thumb and forefinger like a wet tissue and examined it.

"Fascinating, isn't it?"

Stan began to calm again as the severed nerves started to register that their ends no longer existed.

Tom walked over to the bag and dropped the skin in. He took out the scissors again.

"I've been told that the pain experienced from a shoulder graft is probably about a three on the pain scale. So, consider that a tester. Now the place that gets a whopping ten is your inner thigh. That's a pretty sensitive area, I know!"

Tom moved forward and began cutting away Stan's trousers. Starting from the cuff at his feet, working around the cable ties, all the way up, unfolding the material as he went, exposing the leg underneath.

Stan's eyes moved from the machine to his leg in rapid succession, his breathing began to rise again.

"Are you sure there's nothing you want to tell me Stan?"

Stan closed his eyes and shook his head, bracing himself for what was to come.

"Okay!"

The machine started up and Tom drew it close enough to Stan's leg so that he could feel the breeze of the whirring blade. Stan tensed himself, moving his thigh as far to the side as he could manage.

Tom let the machine make contact, the motor's noise deepening as it bit in. He moved the machine much slower this time, not wanting to waste the effort with a quick swipe. When he reached the groin, he pulled away.

Stan was writhing in his seat, his head flinging back and forth as if he was on a roller coaster, the noises that made it past the wading in his mouth was a mixture of screams and yells. Tom went ahead and dropped the skin in the bag and returned as Stan opened his eyes, blinking through the sweat that was pouring down his face.

Tom reached into his pocket and pulled out his tiny pocketknife. He unfurled the blade and crouched down between Stan's legs.

"You know in every square inch of skin there are about twenty feet of blood vessels, a hundred oil glands, six hundred and fifty sweat glands and more than a thousand nerve endings!"

Tom took the tip of his charred knife and plucked at one of the remaining nerves that dangled loosely. Pain shot through Stan's body like electricity, jolting him back in his seat, starting the screaming again.

"Now, with the size of that, I think I've got around nine thousand, nine hundred and ninety-nine more to play with before I start on the other leg."

As Tom reached the blade forward again, Stan's muffled voice began yelling stifled words in objection. He looked up into his eyes and saw them pleading with him to stop, that he had something to say.

He stood up and loosened the strap a little once more. Huge gasps of air flowed past as Stan wheezed and panted. "You fucking...bastard...cock sucker..."

Tom reached for the strap again which instantly changed his tone. "Okay, okay, stop, I'll tell you."

He paused and drew back to wait for the answer to his question.

"They're...they're in a building near Birmingham airport. Elmdon Trading Estate."

"Thank you," Tom replied. "Was that so bad? Now, I'm just going over there to speak to your friend and ask the same question. If he gives me a different location, I'm going to come back and pluck out every single nerve ending one at a time and I won't stop until they're all done before asking again."

He walked over to the bags leaning against the van and pulled out a pouch of plasma fluid and an IV line to show Stan. "And I've got enough stuff here to make sure you won't pass out or die before I get every last one."

He replaced them in the bag and went to walk around the other side of the van.

"Wait, wait."

Tom stopped and looked behind to see all of Stan's power and strength drain away along with the colour in his face. He walked back over to him and placed his ear close by.

"They're ... in a farm ... at the end of St Peter's Lane ... Birmingham".

Tom smiled and replaced the gag, pointing to the van. "I'm just going to check. I'll be back in a moment."

This time Stan's eyes just fell into his lap, staring at the bloody patch, red and yellow that was oozing there; he had nothing left to give.

Tom picked up the machine and pulled the extension cord around the other side of the van. The guy was sat there, frozen to the spot. The dents in the ground where the chair had sunk in were intact; he hadn't moved a muscle since being placed there; not a muscle. There was a small pool of blood beneath his right elbow, but nothing serious, just a flesh wound.

Tom turned the machine on to test it still worked which made the man jump. He placed it on the floor and walked closer to him. When the bag was removed from his head, his eyes were wide and round. Tom moved close and loosened the gag a little. It felt as though this guy wasn't breathing at all, that he dared not. That was a good sign.

"Did you hear what this thing does?" Tom asked, pointing to the machine on the floor.

The guy nodded energetically.

"Good, that will save some time. Now do I show you how it works, or will you tell me where my family are straight away?"

"Chestnut Farm," he gasped before Tom had even finished the question.

"And where is that?"

"Birmingham, St Peter's Lane."

"Good, thank you. Do you know what's going on here?"

The guy thought about it for a few seconds before answering, "A takeover?"

"Yes, a takeover. But how useful do you think you would be in the new organisation if you squeal so easily?"

The guy frantically searched for an answer that would keep him alive. His forehead creased as he dug deep inside.

Tom leaned forward and placed a hand on his shoulder, "I'm kidding."

They guy stared at him and then relaxed, tears welling up in his eyes. Tom tightened the gag and went back around the other side.

Charlie stood there with an almost identical look on his face to the guy, staring at Tom as if he saw him for the first time. Not him, but a monster. Their eyes met for an instance, but Tom looked away as he passed.

"Good news, you both seem to agree with each other."

Stan didn't reply; he didn't even look up. Tom looked over at Charlie. He was still staring at him, staring at someone who resembled his brother. Tom nodded at him that brought him back around. He jolted forward and moved behind Stan to the barrel. He pulled open the clasp and dropped it on the ground; then he pulled off the entire top lid. With the release of pressure, a light layer of smoke flowed over the lip like a witch's cauldron.

"Now Stan, this is not going to be pleasant, but it will be a damn site less painful in the long run than the alternative."

Stan perked up and began twitching around to see what was behind him, at what his fate was going to be, but he could see nothing. He was in the unique position of being able to see everything that was before him, everything that now led up to the end of his days, but he no longer had the ability to look behind.

Tom replaced his hood and pulled the cord tight. He unplugged the machine, picked up the bag of skin and dropped them both in the barrel. Steam hissed with a clunk and a slap as they hit the liquid.

Tom moved around and looked at Stan, bleeding and helpless, just sat there squirming. He looked up at Charlie who was waiting for what may come next in dread anticipation. He looked petrified at what Tom had done, worried about what he might do now. Tom made a decision and opened up the van to remove a taser from the bag inside. There was a look of relief on Charlie's face.

"Stan." His head twitched. "Before I do this there's something I've been wanting to get off my chest for a long time and seeing as we are being honest with each other now, I think it's time I told you. Can you remember, way back in the early eighties, you used to drive around in that ridiculous car? Do you remember one time it got scratched up, a long deep line down one side? Well, I'm sorry to say that it was me. I don't know what came over me. It was there and well, after the way you treated my brother, I sort of thought you had it coming."

The hood over Stan's head slowly looked up towards Tom's face and he could only imagine the look on his face; he heard a mumble coming from inside.

"Now that's out of the way, I'm afraid in the circumstances, this is the best I can offer you."

His head began twitching from side to side as if he was trying to find the answer by reading the inside of the bag. Tom stepped forward and zapped his bare chest sending thousands of volts through an already weakened heart. Stan's body straightened and strained against the ties, breaking the ones on his legs, forcing his body back and the chair's rear legs to finally give way. He fell backward and lay there motionless.

They both stood staring at him, unsure if he was unconscious or dead. Charlie stepped forward, "Umm, how the fuck are we going to get him in the barrel now?"

Tom looked up, "Ummm."

"We need another pair of hands," Charlie said, looking through the van, to the guy on the other side.

Tom shrugged and walked around. The guy snapped his head up and looked at him as he came around the van.

"So ... we have a proposition for you. We were going to get rid of the both of you, but you have proven to be useful and very cooperative so we're going to cut you a break."

The guy's eyes lit up with hope.

"But, in order for us to trust you, you need to help us with something."

The guy nodded furiously.

"And don't even think about running," Tom said as he removed his pistol, checking there was still a round in the chamber.

To this the man looked serious and shook his head.

Tom replaced the pistol and removed one of the knives from behind his waist and cut the ties that bound him. The guy stood up to attention, waiting for his orders. Tom beckoned him around the van and pointed to the body.

"We need to get him...in that," he said, pointing to the barrel.

A look of concern washed over the guy's face as they stepped forward and took a limb each.

It took several attempts to raise his body high enough so that it folded into the opening; the guy's wounded right arm wasn't helping matters. When they finally managed it, the rest was as easy as lifting his legs and allowing the fat to scrap the sides of the barrel as he slowly slid down, letting gravity overcome the air pressure created as he reached the bottom. They pushed him down and had to awkwardly fold his legs in to be able to fit the lid back on and reseal it with the clasp, careful of the liquid that was spilling out around the edges. *Poor Archimedes'* thought Tom *'no eureka moment for you'*. He dropped his gloves into the little space remaining before it was sealed.

They took a second to recover their breaths before Charlie walked over to a double access point in the floor that fed into the drainage system underneath. The pipe that went down led to a cavern below that could easily fit the barrel. It was part of the flood overflow system that all met at The Cage. Tom thought about the legend and how it just might become a reality now. They all rolled it to the edge and over the lip, letting it go as it fell like a cylinder being placed in a child's shape sorting toy.

Charlie replaced the covers as Tom led the guy back to the van. "I need you to call the farm," he said, handing him his phone. "Tell them that the woman and child are going to be picked up in a little while."

The guy took it and dialled a number from memory.

"And tell them that you want to speak to her."

He nodded. After a few seconds he spoke, "Hey, it's me. Just a head's up that the woman and boy are going to be picked up in a bit, so get ready. Wake her up and put her on the line."

He handed the phone back to Tom who took it with sweaty palms and his heart in his mouth.

A minute passed before he could hear the phone being picked up and Ali's voice come through, tired and crackly.

"Hello."

Tom turned away, tears filling his eyes. "Hey baby."

"Hey...is it done?"

Tom stifled a sob, "Yeah, it's done. You'll be out of there in a couple of hours."

"How are you doing?"

"How am I doing? How the hell are you?"

"Ah, we're okay, I guess; it's not been the best of weeks. We're on a farm so I managed to get them to let us out to feed the animals and collect eggs for a bit. I told them there's no way we are being kept in a room for a week!"

"And they listened?"

"I can be pretty persuasive when I want to."

"I know that!" Tom smiled. "How's William?"

"He's fine, missing you and school, but other than that I've made sure he's okay."

"You're an amazing woman you know."

"I know, and I won't let you forget it."

"I'm so sorry for what's happened, I didn't know you were gone until Wednesday when your folks called."

"That's okay. I knew you'd figure it out."

"Not quite what we planned for, eh?"

"No, but that's the way it goes. How are you doing, really?"

"I'm holding it together."

"Keep holding it, I'll be there soon, and we can hold it together."

Tom's heart was about to burst with the love he felt for this woman.

"Okay, I'm going to go now and sort out your ride. I'll see you in a few hours."

"Okay, I love you."

"I love you more."

He hung up and felt all his energy drain from him. Charlie came over and took the guy away who seemed to be wavering between fear and shock and put him in the van. Then he came back over and hesitated before placing a hand on his brother's back.

"You okay?

"No, not really."

"How are Ali and William?"

"They're alright."

"That's good. So, it all ends well?"

Tom turned and faced his brother.

"No Charlie, it doesn't all end well."

Charlie nodded and looked away. "I'll take this guy away then and lay it on thick about keeping his mouth shut."

"Make sure he does, his DNA is all over the body just as much as ours."

"For now, the battery acid will take care of that."

"Still, err on the side of caution."

"I know."

An awkward silence fell around them, neither one knowing if they should shake hands or hug; like the ends of a magnet, the events that had happened repelled rather than attracted.

"So, I'll be seeing you then?" Charlie said, turning to go.

"Maybe"

Charlie walked away.

Then Tom was alone. The intensity of the night, of the day, of the last couple of weeks abruptly made its presence known; bursting through the dam he had built up, draining the last drops of him. He slumped to the ground, a broken bag of bones and wept. The tears were a mixture of relief and anger; awareness of all that he had done and of what he had let out in order to do so. He felt as if he was waking from a dream, a nightmare that had overtaken his soul and smothered his spirit so much that he had to fight to regain consciousness, to come back around, and when he did, he brought all the horrors and emotion with him, to either deal with or to allow it to consume him. He could feel the strain of trying to place them back inside the box again; sense their anger and unwillingness to go back inside without a fight; wanting to stay out and cause havoc. He felt dirty, tainted; the stains coming from the inside to show on the linen on his skin for all to see. They were the stigma that wouldn't wash off; they were stains on his soul. He didn't know what he was going to do with the emotions this time; he had to find another way of coping, of dealing with these things to feel worthy of what he had. He knew that she would be there for him; that they were there for each other and that would make the difference.

He tried to allow his intellectual mind to take charge, to remember all that he taught about reality and to not trust the things your senses showed, but it didn't stop the images flashing before his eyes like an old film projector. The mathematical state of reality had no bearing on the visceral, tactile emotions that were flooding his system.

His eyes looked around at where he lay, at where he had begun, back at the start. He felt a finality about it like the completion of a loop, the circle of life coming back around on itself. Maybe life wasn't a path you follow after all, but rather a series of spirals that take you around and around; not leading you forward but turning you back on yourself to repeat or relive the past in one form or another. How are you supposed to break free of this ring, this circuit of life? Perhaps it's not about breaching the curve or jumping the track; perhaps it was more about finding those people you want to go around that track with, those who made each turn bearable, enjoyable even. He looked down at his own ring on his finger and knew who that would be for him; he just hoped that he...that they, had the strength to return to where they had been, to the life they both wanted.

# AFTERWORD

Although the characters in this novel are fictitious, there is one name that appears in the book who was a legend in the Knowle West community when I was younger. Stan-the-man was the name we used for him although that wasn't his real name. He was a tall, thin man with wild blond hair that wouldn't have been out of place on the California boardwalk. You would often see him roller skating along the road in tiny shorts or some outrageous outfit or other raising money and collecting for charity. The character in the book is probably the antithesis of who Stan-the-man was, but the name and the link to the area was too good not to use.

I also have a favour to ask of you, the reader. It would be a real privilege if you could write a review on Amazon so that others may enjoy my work too. I read every review and comment and although it may only take you a few minutes, it would mean a great deal to me. Thank you.

# ABOUT THE AUTHOR

Antony was born in 1973 and raised in Knowle-West, a suburb of Bristol in the UK.

He has had many experiences in life including the Royal Marines, as a Behaviour Specialist, a Managing Director, an Assistant Principal, a photographer, a Hypnotherapist and more. Each area he moves into is influenced by the ones that came before. He has written non-fiction books based on research and work carried out in schools and has extensive experience with children and behaviour.

He wrote The Black Path based on real memories from childhood and a desire to show how the events of childhood shape and restrict the choices we make as an adult.

He is also a former Taekwondo Champion and coach of the British team and a gold and silver medallist for Team GB in the pentathlon series of Laser-Run. He has been featured in many books and publications and has also won The Prince's Trust Inspiring Leader's award for his work.

Find out more – www.antony-curtis.com

Find out more and sign up for lots of exclusive content – www.antony-curtis.com

Follow me on:
Intstagram @Antony_Curtis_Author
TikTok @antonycurtisauthor

#theblackpath

Printed in Great Britain
by Amazon